Praise for
LINDSAY McKENNA

"A treasure of a book…highly recommended reading that everyone will enjoy and learn from."
—Chief Michael Jaco, US Navy SEAL, retired, on
Breaking Point

"Heartbreakingly tender…readers will fall in love with the upstanding hero and his fierce determination to save the woman he loves."
—*Publishers Weekly* on *Never Surrender* (starred review)

"McKenna skillfully takes readers on an emotional journey into modern warfare and two people's hearts."
—*Publishers Weekly* on *Down Range*

"Packed full of danger and adventure. Fans of military romance will appreciate the strong female characters, steamy sex scenes, and details of military life."
—*Booklist* on *Taking Fire*

"This was a beautiful and heartwarming story. Grayson and Skylar are an awesome alpha pair."
—*Night Owl Reviews* on *Wolf Haven*

"Readers will find this addition to the Shadow Warriors series full of intensity and action-packed romance. There is great chemistry between the characters and tremendous realism, making *Breaking Point* a great read."
—*RT Book Reviews*

LINDSAY McKENNA

THE LONER

HQN™

Recycling programs
for this product may
not exist in your area.

ISBN-13: 978-0-373-60320-6

The Loner

Copyright © 2013 by Nauman Living Trust

www.Harlequin.com

Printed in U.S.A.

To all the servicemen and -women
who have suffered PTSD during combat.
You are not alone. Nor are you forgotten.
There is help out there. Please know we honor your
courage. And thank you from the bottom of our
hearts for your service and sacrifice to our country.

And to the wonderful, warm and caring staff at
Hotel Opera Roma in Rome, Italy. This dedication was
well earned. Thank you. www.hoteloperaroma.com.

Dear Reader,

Having been in the US Navy and having had Marine Corps friends in combat, I've seen what war does to a person. Post-traumatic stress disorder was first named in the 1980s. Before, it was simply "battle fatigue" or the "thousand-yard stare." Whatever it is/was called, the wounds our men and women in the military get from combat are real. Dysfunctional families, where parents dole out anger and abuse, create PTSD in their children. War isn't always in a foreign country. Police, firefighters and EMT/paramedics can suffer from it. PTSD is a global phenomenon and can take decades, even a lifetime, to heal from, if ever.

In *The Loner*, I wanted to bring PTSD to the surface and show how it affects the hero, Dakota Carson. A person who has PTSD may well feel like a "loner." This can be overcome with help, love and understanding. When sheriff's deputy Shelby Kincaid meets Dakota, she is drawn powerfully to the angry loner. Shelby feels strongly that everyone should help Dakota instead of throw him away. They soon realize they share a horribly tragic link, and this creates a meaningful connection between them—and unexpected danger. Can Dakota engage his SEAL experience in order to save her?

Strap in for one helluva ride.

Lindsay McKenna

CHAPTER ONE

DAKOTA CARSON SENSED DANGER. A fragile pink dawn lay like a silent ribbon along the eastern horizon. As he exhaled, white clouds congealed for a moment in front of him, telling him it was below freezing on this June first morning. Standing on a small rise at the edge of an oval meadow, he studied a football-field-long swath of willows that ran through the center.

His left arm ached in the cold, reminding him why he'd been discharged from the U.S. Navy and his SEAL team. He'd suffered permanent nerve damage during a firefight. Never mind the post-traumatic stress disorder he coped with 24/7. Now his hyperalertness was telling him something wasn't right. But what was wrong? Eyes narrowing, he scanned the quiet, early morning area. To his right rose the majestic Teton Mountains, their white peaks taking on a pinkish alpine glow.

It was quiet. Too quiet. He'd been a SEAL for ten years and at twenty-eight, he was no stranger to threatening situations. He knew one when he felt it. To his left, he saw a gray movement. It was Storm, a female wolf he'd rescued a year earlier. Thus far, she treated him like her alpha mate, but he was sure she wouldn't hang around as she matured. There was every possibility she'd leave him and join the Snake River wolf pack that ruled this valley in Wyoming. Storm was loping at the edge of the forest, ears twitching back and forth, nose in the air, picking up scents.

Yesterday Dakota had laid five rabbit traps out in these willows. It was one of many places he trapped in order to live outside society and the town of Jackson Hole. Since being released from the hospital and months of painful physical therapy to get his shoulder working, Dakota wanted to hide. He didn't look too closely at why, only that he had to heal up. Ten years spent in the SEALs had been the happiest time of his life, but deployment into Iraq and Afghanistan had taken their toll on his body and emotions.

Sniffing the air, he tried to locate the source of the threat. Grizzlies had their own odor. So did elk. No stranger to studying the land and vegetation, Dakota could spot things few others could. His sniper SEAL training had taught him stealth and tracking.

Storm had disappeared into the tree line again. The months of May and June were prime elk birthing season. It was also the same time when hungry grizzlies came out of hibernation, starving for anything to eat. Elk babies were the number-one food source on their menu. Storm always hunted her own meals. She was looking for smaller prey. One wolf could not take down a baby elk. A pack was needed, instead.

Dakota studied the willows, his hearing keyed, but he heard nothing. Had an elk mother calved a baby in there? What was he sensing? Just because he could sometimes feel a threat didn't mean he knew what the threat was. If a new elk calf was in there, a grizzly could be skulking around, out of his sight, trying to locate it. The bear could have picked up on the scent of the afterbirth before the mother could eat it and destroy the odor. The thick, naked willows reminded Dakota of a porcupine with its back up, the crochetedlike needles raised skyward. The problem was they grew so high and thick, he couldn't see through the grove. There was no movement. No sound.

The air was still. Nothing seemed to move, which was odd because dawn was the busiest time of the day for nocturnal and diurnal animals. The pink along the horizon deepened and the sky above lightened. Dakota could no longer see the myriad stars above his head; they were diluted, having disappeared in the dawn light. It would be a long time before the sun would rise, however. He heard a raven cawing somewhere off in the distance. Other than that, it was as if the earth herself were holding her breath.

For what? He rubbed the back of his neck with his gloved hand, but his old shoulder injury protested with the movement. After allowing his hand to drop to his side, Dakota shouldered a .300 Win Mag Winchester magnum rifle with a sling across his right shoulder. He'd been a sniper in the SEALs and had used this rifle to hunt down the bad guys. Out here in the wilds of Wyoming, where grizzly were the predator, Dakota never tracked or hunted anywhere without a big rifle. Grizzlies, especially this time of year, were hungry, irritable and mean. All they wanted was food and they'd kill anything and anyone to protect their carcass or find.

Dakota wasn't foolhardy. Patience was his best protection. A bear would move eventually, and the willows would tremble and wave back and forth. But if it was an elk calf?

Dakota waited on the rise. He was downwind, something he made sure of because he knew the grizzlies were hunting in earnest. Dakota didn't want his scent to inspire one of those bears to hunt him, thinking he was a posthibernation meal on two legs. His mouth pulled at one corner over that thought. He'd seen enough mayhem and killing.

After his discharge from the navy, his medical issues as fixed as they were going to be, he'd located a cabin high in the Tetons on the Wyoming side of the mountains. He'd cleaned it up and started living in the ramshackle, abandoned structure. Never mind that it didn't have electricity or running water. He'd spent the past year in hiding and needed the solitude. There was so much grief and loss in him, he didn't know what to do with it or how to discharge it. Sleep was a luxury. He rarely got two or three broken hours of sleep at night. His heart sank as he considered all that he'd lost since he was seventeen years old and then more losses in the navy. Wounded in a field of fire deep in the Hindu Kush Mountains of Afghanistan, he found his life repeating the nightmare cycle of his teen years.

It's too much pain... Too damned much. Purposefully, Dakota lasered his attention on the willow stand. This was the present. When his mind wandered into the past, it was nothing but a mire of serrating grief, rage and helplessness. He didn't like feeling those turgid emotions. His stomach growled. It had been one day since he'd last eaten. The winter had leaned him down considerably, but he wasn't starving. Dakota set out enough traps to keep meat on his table, but a sudden, unexpected snowstorm yesterday had stopped him from walking his traplines and gathering up the rabbits he'd caught. A cutting, one-cornered smile creased his face. In Afghanistan, his SEAL team endured days without food, water or resupply. So twenty-four hours without food wasn't a tragedy.

He had the traps set up in those willows. Rabbits were plentiful in the wide valley through which the Snake River wound lazily. Had a starving grizzly already found his traps and gobbled up the rabbits? Was that the reason for the sense of danger he felt?

He had to take a chance. Shifting the Win Mag to his left shoulder, he looked down at the P226 SIG Sauer pistol strapped low on his right thigh. The two black Velcro straps around his thick leg held the pistol at just the right angle in case he needed to quickly reach for it. All SEALs were given this particular pistol after they graduated from BUD/S. The .40-caliber pistol was specially made in Germany for them. And it had stopping power. One slug would take a human's life.

The wind had piled up the blizzard snow. Patches of long yellow grass peeked out here and there. As he walked, the grass in the meadow crunched beneath his boots. Each yellowed blade of grass was coated with thick frost. With each step, Dakota tried to stay as silent as possible. The sound could possibly alert the elk mother hidden in the willows. He moved down the gentle slope toward the center of the meadow. Dakota knew from experience an elk mother would defend her calf with her life. And an elk weighed a good thousand pounds, its hooves sharp and dangerous.

Dakota brushed the butt of his SIG Sauer with the palm of his gloved hand. It was an unconscious habit honed in the badlands of the Middle East. He'd unsnapped the retention strap across the pistol so that if he had to reach for it, his palm could fit swiftly around the butt and his fingers could wrap around the trigger. He could draw it up in a single, fluid motion in order to protect himself. He had no wish to shoot an elk. His meat needs were far less than that.

Slowing, the light increasing, Dakota inhaled the scents on the frosty air, his nostrils flaring. He halted and searched for tracks. Some of the grass was clean, shaken free of the frost and snow, about twenty feet south of where he stood. It had to have happened earlier this morning. Craning his neck, Dakota evaluated them. Big print? Little print? Something in between? He had keen eyesight, honed by years of hunting as a teen and, later, as a SEAL. The tracks appeared to be that of an elk.

Dakota stood, debating whether to enter the willows or not. He was used to being afraid but didn't let that rule him or blot out his logical thinking processes. As Dakota turned his head, he could see Storm was trotting the other way along the tree line above him. Her long pink tongue lolled out of the side of her mouth, her gray body blending into to the surrounding shadows. He stared back hard at the willows in front of him. He'd placed the rabbit traps deep within them. Rabbits weren't stupid; they were not going to hop around on the outer perimeter of the willows. Something would quickly spot them from air or ground and they'd be dead in a heartbeat. No, they lived deep within the willows and could thrive.

Just as Dakota took a step forward, the willows exploded in front of him. A cinnamon-colored male grizzly bear roared and crashed through them and launched himself at him. The roaring vibration ripped through him. Dakota took half a step back, seeing the bear's small dark eyes filled with rage. In an instant, Dakota knew the grizzly had been in the willows all along. He'd probably eaten all the rabbits he'd trapped and was snoozing until he heard Dakota approach the stand. Startled and provoked, the bear charged him. The attack was so swift, all Dakota saw was the grizzly's thick rust-colored body hurtling toward him at the speed of a bullet.

Dakota's shock collided with his survival training. It would take too long to pull the rifle off his shoulder and fire off a shot. Without hesitation, as the bear flew toward him like a flying tank, his hand moved smoothly in an unbroken motion for the SIG Sauer on his right thigh.

The bear's spittle, his roar, surrounded Dakota. As he lifted the pistol, he shifted his weight to the right to try to stop the grizzly from fully striking him. If he hadn't moved in a feintlike maneuver, the bear would have slammed him flat on his back, leaned down and ripped his throat out with those bared yellow fangs. At the same moment, Dakota saw the female wolf come out of nowhere. Storm snarled and flung herself directly at the grizzly, her jaws opened, aiming for his sensitive nose. In her own way, Storm was trying to protect him. The valiant wolf was a mere forty pounds against a thousand pounds of angry bruin.

Everything slowed in his line of vision. Whenever Dakota was in danger of losing his life, the frames of reality intensified and then crawled by with excruciating slowness. The grizzly saw him shift, but Storm latched onto the bear's nose. The grizzly roared, swiping at her. The wolf yelped and was flung high into the air. The grizzly tried to make a midcourse correction. As he raised his massive paw, the five curved claws flexed outward, the blow struck Dakota full force.

The SIG Sauer bucked in his hand. Dakota held his intense focus, aiming for the bear's thick, massive skull. The grizzly roared with fury as the first two bullets struck his skull. They ricocheted off! Dakota felt the grizzly's paw strike his left arm. Pain reared up his arm and jammed into his already torn-up shoulder. He grunted as he was struck and tossed up in the air like a puppet. The massive power of a pissed-off thousand-pound grizzly was stunning.

As Dakota tumbled end over end, all of his SEAL training came back by reflex. He landed and rolled, the cold glittering frost exploding around him on impact. He leaped to his feet. The bear roared, landed on all fours, whipped around with amazing agility and charged him again. Only ten feet separated them.

Dakota cooly stood, legs slightly apart for best balance, hands wrapped solidly around the butt of the SIG Sauer. This was not a bear gun, but if he aimed well, he'd strike the charging grizzly in one of his eyes and kill him before he was killed himself. His breath exploded from him as the bear leaped upward, its jaws open, lips peeled away from his dark pink gums to reveal the massive, murderous fangs. Dakota fired three more shots and saw the third one strike into the right eye of the bear.

Too late!

As he threw up his left arm and spun to avoid the grizzly pouncing on him, the bear's massive teeth sank violently into his forearm. There was instant, red-hot pain. The bear grunted, fell downward. Dakota was flipped over and dragged down with the bear, his arm still locked in the animal's massive mouth.

The grizzly landed with a thud, groaning heavily as it sank into the yellow grass. Dakota wrested his forearm out of the bear's teeth. Breathing hard, he staggered to his feet. There were fifteen cartridges in a SIG Sauer.

He held it ready and stumbled backward, stunned

by the ferocity of the attack. He watched the bear breathe once, twice and then slump with a growl, dead.

Dakota gasped for breath, felt the warmth of his own blood trickling down into his left glove. Would the bear move? No, he could see the eye socket blown away by his pistol, the bullet in the animal's brain. The grizzly was dead. Wiping his mouth, Dakota looked around, his breath exploding in ragged gasps into the freezing air. His heart hammered wildly in his chest. The adrenaline kept him tense and he was feeling no pain.

Once he was finally convinced the grizzly wasn't going to get back up and come after him a third time, he created distance between him and the beast. He saw Storm come trotting up to him. She whined, her yellow eyes probing his. She was panting heavily. Dakota looked her over to make sure the grizzly hadn't hurt his wolf. There were some mild scratch marks across her left flank, but that was all.

"We're okay," he rasped to the wolf.

Dakota holstered the pistol and drew up his left arm. He always wore thick cammies. The bear's fangs had easily punctured the heavy canvas material, sunk through the thick green sweater he wore beneath it and chewed up his flesh. There was no pain—yet. But there sure as hell was gonna be.

He sat down and jerked off his gloves. There was

a lot of blood and, chances were, the grizzly had sliced into a major artery in his left arm. He went into combat medic mode, one of his SEAL specialties. This meant he never left on a hunt without his H-gear, a harness he wore around his waist that had fifteen canvas pockets. Dakota jerked open his camo jacket. His hand shook as he dug into one pocket, which contained a tourniquet. Quickly, he slipped the tourniquet just below his elbow and jerked it tight. Pain reared up his upper arm, but the bleeding slowed a lot at the bite site. Tying it off, Dakota dug in another pocket, which contained a roll of duct tape. From another, he pulled out a pair of surgical scissors, sharper than hell. He straightened out his right leg out in front of him, then dug into the deep cargo pocket above his knee. In there, he grabbed a battle dressing.

He had to get to the hospital in Jackson Hole. *Sooner. Not later.* Dakota hated going into town. Hated being around people, but this grizzly had chewed up a helluva lot of his arm in one bite. He quickly placed the battle dressing across the wound, then wrapped it firmly with duct tape. Not exactly medically sound, but duct tape saved many a SEAL from more injury or bleeding to death over the years. After cutting the duct tape with the scissors, Dakota jammed all of the items back into his H-gear.

He was in shock. Familiar with these symptoms, Dakota picked up his rifle and signaled Storm to follow. She instantly leaped to her feet and loped to his side. Looking up, the sky lightening even more, Dakota knew he had a one-mile trek back to where his pickup was parked. Mouth thinning, he shouldered the rifle and moved swiftly through the thick grass. When the adrenaline wore off, he'd be in terrible pain. The shock would make him drive poorly and he could make some very bad decisions behind the wheel. It was a race of ten miles between here and the hospital to get emergency room help.

Cursing softly, he began to trot. It was a labored stride, the grass slick with frost, but he pushed himself. His breath came out in explosive jets, and he drew in as much air as he could into his lungs. Anchoring his wounded arm against his torso, he moved quickly up the slope and onto a flat plain.

Dakota could feel the continued loss of blood. Arteries, when sliced, usually closed up on their own within two minutes of being severed. However, the only time they wouldn't was when they weren't sliced at an angle. Then he knew he was in deep shit. A major artery could bleed out in two to three minutes. His heart would cavitate, like the pump it was, and then he'd die of cardiac arrest. Fortunately, the tourniquet was doing its job. It bought him time, but not much.

As he lumbered steadily toward the parking lot at the end of a dirt road in the Tetons, he thought it would be a fitting end if he did bleed out and

die here. Some poor tourist hiker would find what
was left of his body days or even weeks from now.
The grizzlies in the area or the Snake River wolf
pack might find him first. The shocked hiker would
find only bones, no skin or flesh left on his sorry-
assed carcass.

Mind spinning, Dakota continued to slip and
slide through grass and drifts of knee-deep snow.
Soon, the sun would bridge the horizon. It was a
beautiful day, the sky a pale blue and cloudless,
unlike yesterday. The snow from the blizzard was
knee-deep in places. Several times, Dakota stumbled, fell, rolled and forced himself back up to
his feet. As he ran, he discovered something: he
wanted to *live.*

Why now? his soggy brain screamed. *All you
wanted to do before was crawl away like a hurt
animal into the mountains, disappear from civili-
zation and live out the rest of your life. Why now?*

Dakota had no answer. He'd hidden for a year.
And he'd healed up to a point. He wanted nothing
to do with people because they couldn't understand
what he'd been through. No one would get that that
was a life sentence—to spend the rest of his days
on the fringes of society.

His heart pumped hard in his chest. Ahead, he
could see his beat-up green-and-white rusted Ford
truck. *Only a little bit farther to go.* Gasps tore
out of his mouth, his eyes narrowing on the truck.
With no idea where this sudden, surprising will to

live came from, Dakota reached his truck. Storm halted, ready to jump in. He staggered, caught himself and then jerked the driver's door open. The wolf was used to riding with him since he'd found her as a pup.

Dizziness assailed Dakota as Storm jumped in. He shook off the need to collapse, and glanced down at his arm. The battle dressing was a bright red, blood dripping down his hand and off his curved fingers. The cold was numbing, so he felt nothing, not even the warmth of his own blood. Struggling, he climbed into the truck. Dakota knew it would be a race to reach the hospital in time. The tourniquet stood between him and death right now. That gave him relief as he put the truck into gear and drove slowly down the wet, muddy road.

Storm whined. She thumped her tail once, catching Dakota's darkened eyes.

"It will be all right," he growled, wrestling the truck around, pain now pulsing rhythmically through his bite site.

But would it? Wasn't that what he always told his SEAL friends who were shot and bleeding out? Sure to die, no matter what he did to try to stop the bleeding? *It will be all right. Sure.* Dakota jammed all those terrifying moments from the past out of his thoughts. He had to concentrate. He had to reach the emergency room of the hospital or die trying....

CHAPTER TWO

SHERIFF'S DEPUTY SHELBY KINCAID was walking toward the emergency room entrance to the Jackson Hole Hospital. She had paperwork on a prisoner that had to be updated by Dr. Jordana McPherson. The cool morning air made her glad she had her brown nylon jacket, although her blond hair lay abandoned around her shoulders. Something unusual caught her eye. Slowing, Shelby hesitated near the E.R. entrance. Was the guy pulling into the parking lot drunk? It was only 6:00 a.m., but she knew from plenty of experience that drunk drivers didn't care what time it was.

The rusted-out Ford pickup crawled to a stop across two empty parking lanes. Shelby frowned and watched as the driver's-side door creaked open with protest. She was less than a hundred feet away from the truck. The driver soon emerged. She didn't recognize him as a local. He wore a two-day beard on his face. Something was wrong. Maybe it was her sixth sense, but Shelby stuffed the papers into the pocket of her jacket and quickly walked toward the man.

She spotted a gray dog in the front seat but kept her focus on the man in camo gear. He was tall, broad-shouldered and reminded her of a hunter she'd see in the fall around Jackson Hole. But this was spring and no hunting was allowed. This man was clearly in pain. His hair was black and military short, face square with high cheekbones. She'd never seen this dude before and she felt a sudden urgency that he was in trouble. The stride of her walk accelerated.

As he lurched drunkenly out of the seat, his large hand caught the edge of the door or he'd have fallen out. It was then Shelby noticed the strapped pistol on his right thigh. She tensed inwardly. Her blue eyes widened for a moment as he spun around, losing his grip on the door, barely able to keep his feet beneath him. That was when she saw his bloody arm pressed against his torso.

As she approached the truck, the dog whined. It was a sound of worry.

"Can I help you?" she called out. "I'm Deputy Kincaid."

The man bent over, as if willing himself not to fall down. A dark red trail of blood ran down his left pant leg. He'd obviously lost a lot of blood. Automatically, she pressed the radio on the epaulet of her jacket located on her left shoulder.

"Annie, this is Shelby Kincaid. I'm out here I the parking lot of your E.R. Kindly get me a gurney and two orderlies? I've got a man out here a hundred feet from your door with an arm wound. He's lost a lot of blood." She clicked off the radio just as he raised his head toward her.

For a moment, Shelby felt her heart plunge. His face was drawn in pain, his lips thinned, the corners of his mouth drawn in, his pain evident. There was nothing tame about this guy. He was well built, powerful, yet the look in his light gold-brown eyes was marred with vulnerability. As he tried to straighten his left arm, he managed to rasp through gritted teeth, "Get me to the E.R."

THE WOMAN REACHED OUT, her hand wrapping quickly around his right arm. "Lean on me," she told him. "I've called for help and they're on the way. I won't let you fall."

The world began to gray out around Dakota as the tall, statuesque blonde in a sheriff's deputy uniform firmly gripped his upper arm. He was surprised at the cool authority in her unruffled voice, the strength of her hand around his arm. She looked like a Barbie doll, one who easily brought him into a standing position and guided his arm across her shoulders. For a Barbie doll, she was in damn good shape.

"Bullet wound?" she asked, taking his full weight.

"Bear bite," he managed to rasp out, closing his eyes. "I'm going to faint. Too much blood loss…"

Instantly, Shelby placed her feet apart for better balance. She felt him go limp. *Damn!* She might be five foot eleven, but this guy was taller and bigger than she was. Glancing upward, she saw the gurney flying toward them with two men in green scrubs pushing it as fast as it would go.

Within moments, the two young men arrived. Together, the three of them wrestled the unconscious hunter up and on the gurney.

"Get him inside," Shelby ordered, her voice tight with tension. She trotted at his side as the orderlies pushed the gurney full speed toward the doors. Gripping his good shoulder, Shelby didn't want him to be knocked off while the gurney slipped and slid on the ice and snow across the asphalt. She glanced down at him. In that moment, the hunter looked vulnerable. But just barely. The duct tape around his bleeding left arm made her frown. *Duct tape?* Helluva way to stop a wound from bleeding out. Who was this guy?

Inside, Shelby spotted Dr. Jordana McPherson, head of E.R., running to meet them as they came inside the warm entrance.

"Shelby?" Jordana called, running up.

"Hunter, I guess. Said he was attacked by a bear

and had lost a lot of blood," she told the doctor.
She stepped aside as they pushed the gurney into a
blue-curtained cubicle. Shelby watched as Jordana
quickly took a pair of scissors and cut through the
silver duct tape on the hunter's bloodied left arm.

"Okay, good to know. Who is he? Do we have
any identification on him?"

Instantly, two other nurses appeared in the cubicle to help the doctor. They locked the wheels
on the gurney.

Shelby moved next to the hunter. His face looked
like chalk beneath his dark stubble. She sensed danger around this man for no specific reason. Quickly
patting down his camo pants, she felt something in
the right pocket on his thigh. She slid her fingers
down into the deep pocket.

"God, he has everything in here but the kitchen
sink," she muttered, pulling articles out and laying
them beside him. Finally, she discovered a wallet
and stepped back as the nurses covered him with
a blanket and started an IV.

She opened up the wallet. "His name is Dakota
Carson." Shelby looked over at Jordana. "Ring any
bells, Doc?"

"Yes," Jordana said, pulling the entire duct tape
assembly away from his arm. Wrinkling her nose,
she said, "I thought I recognized him. He's an ex-
SEAL, just got a medical discharge from the U.S.
Navy. I saw him once, a month ago. He was sup-

posed to come here for follow-up physical therapy on his left shoulder."

Nodding, Shelby placed the wallet on a tray where the nurse had placed all the other items. "Never seen him before."

"Mr. Carson is a loner." Jordana's mouth tightened as she surveyed his chewed-up lower arm. "This bear has done some major damage to him…." Jordana looked to her red-haired nurse. "Alanna, get me an O.R. ready. And call in the ortho surgeon, Dr. Jamison. Get me his blood type." Taking out her stethoscope, she pulled back the camo jacket and placed it over his heart.

Shelby felt the urgency and saw it in Jordana's face. She'd come to like the E.R. doctor who was good at what she did. "How bad?"

"Bad," she muttered, throwing the stethoscope around her neck. "He's right, he's lost a lot of blood."

Just then, Dakota's eyes slowly opened. "He's coming around," Shelby warned the E.R. doc.

"Amazing."

Shelby placed her hand gently on his right shoulder. "Mr. Carson? You're here in the E.R. at the hospital. You're in good hands." She looked into his murky-looking brown eyes, which were full of confusion. He opened his mouth to speak, but only a groan issued forth. Shelby tightened her hand on his shoulder. The man was in incredible shape. *A former Navy SEAL.* She knew enough about SEALs to understand he was a warrior, the toughest of the tough. His eyes wandered for a moment, but then they stopped and focused on Shelby.

Sucking in a breath, Shelby felt the full measure of his intense gaze. Those eyes were hunter's eyes. Huge black pupils on a field of golden-brown color. Surprise flared in his expression, and then, something else she couldn't interpret.

She gave him a slight smile. "You're in good hands. Dr. McPherson is here. You're going to be all right."

Jordana came around and Shelby released him and stood aside.

"Mr. Carson, I'm Dr. McPherson. Can you hear me?"

Dakota managed a sloppy grin, only half his mouth working because of the surging pain. "Yeah, Doc. I remember you. I missed a bunch of appointments. I'm blood type A. I'm gonna need transfusions. Bear cut an artery in my left arm...."

"That's what I needed to hear," Jordana said quietly, patting his shoulder in a motherly way. "I'm leaving the tourniquet in place until we can get you into surgery and stabilized." She lifted her head, called to the second nurse, "Joy, get me two pints of type A ready in the O.R."

"Right away, Doctor."

"You're gonna need one and a half pints to put in

what I've lost," he grunted. His gaze moved from the worried-looking doctor to the woman standing behind her. *Barbie Doll.* Damn, but she was beautiful with her sandy-blond hair falling around her shoulders. Her blue eyes were wide and curious. What didn't make any sense was her sheriff's uniform, all dark brown slacks that hid her long legs and a nylon jacket showing her name and badge on it. Shelby Kincaid. Funny, for a moment, he thought he recognized her. But from where? His mind wouldn't work. He memorized her name.

"We'll see," Jordana said. "You're going to need more than stitches on that bear bite, Dakota."

He smiled a little as the nurse came and stuck a syringe of morphine into the IV tube to drip into his vein. "I figured as much. Just wanted to make it here so you could work your magic, Doc."

Patting his arm, Jordana said, "I'll see you in a few minutes, Dakota. I've got to go scrub up."

Dakota felt the pressure of the nurse putting a clean dressing on his wound. At first, it hurt like hell, but then, as the morphine began to flow through his veins, the pain eased considerably. All the time, he held the gaze of the beautiful deputy sheriff standing nearby. Who was she? Looking at her oval face, those blue eyes that reminded him of the turquoise beaches of Costa Rica, that set of full lips, he just didn't think she fit the image of a deputy sheriff. There was concern in her eyes—for him.

"Mr. Carson," Shelby said, keeping her voice low as she approached him, "who do you want me to notify? Your wife? Parents? Someone needs to be contacted. I can let them know." Automatically, Shelby reached out, her fingers resting gently on his broad shoulder. This time, the muscles beneath her fingertips responded. An unexpected heat surged through her. Shocked, Shelby tried to ignore her reaction. This man was half dead from loss of blood, yet the warrior energy around him beckoned to some primal part of herself.

Dakota tried to focus. The Barbie doll sheriff's deputy had a nice, husky voice. It felt like warm honey drizzled across him, easing his pain even more. Her face was inches from his. Her blond hair had darker strands mingled with lighter ones. Some reminded him of gold sunlight, others, of dark honey. His gaze drifted back to her eyes. God, what beautiful eyes she had. He could dive into them and feel her heart beating. Wildly aware of her long fingers against his shoulder, he muttered, "I've got a wolf out in my truck. Her name is Storm. She's bonded to me. Don't take her to a dog pound. Keep her…keep her with you… I'll get out of surgery and take her home with me, please…."

He wasn't making sense, but Shelby knew the nurse had given him a dose of morphine to stop the pain. People said funny things when drifting in a morphine cloud. His focus began to fade. "Mr. Carson, who can I call? I need to tell your family where you are."

The husky urgency in her voice felt like a warm, sensual blanket. Dakota was feeling no pain now, thank God. Instead, he could focus on this incredibly arresting woman, her face so close he could rise, capture that sinner's mouth of hers and make it his own. She looked familiar. But from where? A broken laugh rumbled out of his chest. "I have no one, Barbie. Just me and my wolf. And she doesn't answer my cell phone."

"Where do you live? I can take your wolf back to your home," Shelby asked, trying to remain cool and professional. Again, she saw that devil-may-care grin cut across his tense, chiseled face. He was darkly tanned for this time of year, which told her this ex-SEAL was outside a helluva lot. She didn't want to admit how much she liked touching this man. And she saw something else in his lion-gold eyes—desire. It was the morphine, she was sure.

"You'll never find it. No address. Just a shack in the woods. Just keep my wolf with you." He struggled to sit up. "This repair on my arm isn't gonna take long. If you can take care of her until I get released, I'll appreciate it."

Hearing the sudden, emotional urgency in his gruff tone, Shelby straightened. She gently pushed him back down on the gurney. The pleading expression on his face startled her. In that moment, Dakota Carson looked like a scared little boy watching his world self-destruct. There was something magical, a heated connection, burning between them. "Yes, I'll take care of her for you, Mr. Carson."

Instantly, the man seemed to relax, a ragged sigh escaping from his tightened lips. He closed his eyes. What she didn't expect was his right hand to reach out and grab hers. She felt the strength of his fingers as they wrapped around her wrist.

"Th-thank you...." he rasped.

His fingers loosened and fell open. The nurse had put another syringe into the IV, the drug rendering him unconscious in preparation for surgery. Shelby gently picked up his arm hanging over the gurney and placed it at his side.

"He's out," Alanna told her.

"Good. How long will the surgery be, you think?"

Shrugging, Alanna motioned for the two orderlies to come in and transport the patient to the E.R. "I don't know, Shelby. Maybe an hour if all goes well. Could be nerve damage. We'll see...."

"Okay, I'll drop back in an hour. I've got some paperwork for the heard nurse to fill out at the nurses' station before I leave."

"Great. Want me to call you on the radio when Mr. Carson comes out of E.R?"

"Yes, could you?"

Alanna nodded and smiled. "Can do."

Shelby watched the two orderlies wheel the unconscious ex-SEAL off to surgery. Standing there for a moment, she digested all the unsettled emotions the stranger had stirred up in her. He was dangerous, risky to her heart. Frowning, Shelby shook her head. She looked down at the blood smeared across her jacket. *His blood.*

This was the first time she'd seen a bear-attack victim, and it wasn't pretty. Her fingers still tingled when he'd suddenly reached out and gripped her. Strong fingers, but he monitored the strength of his grip around her wrist, she realized, even in a morphine state. Definitely a special kind of soldier.

She knew little about SEALs. They were black ops. Secret. Defenders of this country. And heroes in her opinion. The look in his eyes guaranteed all of that. The man had shaken her, but not in a bad way, just an unexpected way. He'd somehow gotten to her womanly core. She'd been responding to him man-to-woman. Blowing out a breath of air in frustration, Shelby turned on her booted heel and forced herself to get the paperwork finished. First things first. She'd leave the papers with the nurses' desk and then go out and make sure the gray wolf was all right.

As Shelby approached the desk, an older nurse

with steel-gray hair beckoned to her. Shelby recognized nurse Patty Fielding.

"Hey, Shelby, do you know about that guy?" Patty whispered, coming up to her at the desk.

"No. Why?" Shelby handed her the papers that needed to be filled out.

"He's known as The Loner around here. He got here a year ago and was supposed to see Dr. McPherson about his shoulder injury once a week. He never came back for subsequent appointments after the first one."

Shelby's heart went out to Dakota Carson. "He's a military vet," she whispered, feeling sorry for him.

"Oh, honey," Patty said, taking the papers, "he's also a SEAL. Those guys rock in my world. They're on the front lines around the world fighting for us. They're in harm's way every time they take a mission." Patty shook her head. "Such a shame. He's an incredibly valiant vet. He's got a lot of problems, physical and mental."

"And was he seeing Dr. McPherson for his arm injury?"

"Technically, yes, for nerve damage. But she's our PTSD expert here at the hospital, too."

Standing there, Shelby asked, "Is that why he lives alone? Out in the middle of nowhere?" She recalled the Vietnam vets who had PTSD. At that time, it wasn't diagnosed except to call it "battle fatigue."

Patty filled out the forms and signed them with a flourish. "Yes, and those guys got no help at all. It broke my heart. Oh, and no address on Mr. Carson."

"What about family?"

Patty sighed and said, "His parents died in a crash when he was eighteen. Froze to death during the blizzard. They found their car two days later and it was too late."

Shelby's heart plummeted. "That's so sad."

"Yeah, this guy has had a very rough life. You don't know the half of it." Patty smiled and handed her the papers. "Gotta go!"

"I'll be back in an hour."

"Take care of that wolf of his," she said, lifting her hand in farewell. "She's a sweet girl."

Shelby smiled a little and thanked the nurse for the information. As she headed out the doors of the E.R., the sun just crested the eastern horizon. What was it about this ex-SEAL that grabbed her heart? Grabbed all of her attention? Somehow the name Carson was one she knew. Stymied, Shelby walked carefully over the slick areas of black ice and circumvented the patches of snow. Out in the parking lot, she could see Carson's beat-up truck. It looked a lot like him, Shelby thought sadly. There was something in his eyes that shouted incredible loss. Loss of what?

CHAPTER THREE

SHELBY HAD THE FEMALE gray wolf and she rode quietly in the backseat of her Tahoe cruiser. She just dropped off the papers to the courthouse when she received a call from Alanna.

Picking up the radio, Shelby continued to drive slowly through Jackson Hole traffic, on her way out to the hospital. The hour was almost up. "Go ahead, Alanna," she said.

"Shelby, Dr. McPherson said for you to drop by at 9:00 a.m. Can you do it?"

"Sure," she said, glancing at the clock on the dashboard. "I thought I was supposed to come back in about twenty minutes."

"No, Dr. McPherson said the surgery on Mr. Carson's arm is going to be longer than she anticipated."

"Roger that."

"Thanks, out."

Placing the radio back in the bracket, Shelby grimaced. If the surgery was taking longer, it meant Dakota Carson's bear bite was a lot worse than anyone had thought. Her shift ended shortly, but she'd told the commander at the sheriff's office what had happened. Steve McCall was humored to see a gray wolf in the backseat of her cruiser. Lucky for her, Steve, who had been her father's replacement as Tetons County sheriff, accepted her sometimes quirky days. But all deputies had unusual days every once in a while.

As she drove, Shelby couldn't shake the intense look in Dakota Carson's eyes. What was his story? She had more questions than answers. Maybe, if she got lucky, she'd intersect with Jordana and find out. As the head of E.R. for the hospital, Jordana McPherson knew just about everything and everyone. Another good source was Gwen Garner, who owned the quilt shop on the plaza.

A call came in, an accident on a side street, and Shelby figured she had time to take the call before showing up at the hospital. Even though she was focused on the accident, her heart was centered on the mystery of Dakota Carson. What the hell was he doing out at dawn killing a grizzly bear? That was against the law. And the Tetons National Park ranger supervisor, Charley, wasn't going to be happy about it, either. The ex-SEAL was in deep trouble whether he knew it or not.

DAKOTA CARSON WAS IN recovery when he slowly came out from beneath the anesthesia. As he opened his eyes, he saw two women standing side by side. Dr. McPherson smiled a silent hello. But his gaze lingered on the sheriff's deputy. In his hazy in-between state, Dakota was mesmerized by the strands of bright color in her hair.

"Dakota? Good news," Jordana said. "We were able to fix your arm." Her lips twitched. "And it's got a nice, new dressing on it without the duct tape."

Dakota liked and trusted the woman doctor. One corner of his mouth hitched upward. "Good to hear, Doc. Thanks for patching me up."

"Do me a favor? Move your fingers on your left hand for me. One at a time."

He moved them. "All five work," he said, feeling woozy and slightly nauseated. Carson knew it was the anesthesia. The nausea would pass.

Jordana slid her hand beneath his. She gently turned his heavily bandaged arm over so that his palm faced up. "Do you feel this?" She pricked each of his fingers with a slender instrument, including his thumb.

"Yeah, it hurts like hell. They're all responding," he assured her.

"Good," Jordana said, moving his arm so that it rested naturally at his side.

Dakota looked around. "When can I leave?"

"You need to spend the night here, Dakota."

"No way," he grunted, trying to sit up. Head spinning, he flopped back down on the pillow. The deputy was frowning, but even then she looked beautiful. She no longer wore her big, puffy brown nylon jacket. It hung over her left arm. Shelby was tall, maybe a few inches shorter than he was. Her shoulders were drawn back with natural pride. The look in her blue eyes, however, was one of somber seriousness. He had a feeling she wanted to question him about the dead grizzly. There would be hell to pay for killing a bear out of season.

"Way," Jordana said, placing her hand on his white-gowned shoulder. "You're still in shock, Dakota. You know what that does to a person? You're no stranger to it."

He scowled. Dr. McPherson was a PTSD expert. When he'd come back to Jackson Hole, the navy had ordered him to see her once a week for his symptoms. Of course, he saw her only once. He looked up at the physician. "Doc, I just want the hell out of here. You know why. Just sign me out, okay? I'll be fine."

Jordana patted his shoulder. "I can't do it, Dakota. You're a combat medic. Would you let your wounded SEAL buddy who had your injury and experience walk out of here?"

Dakota grunted. "SEALs suffer a lot worse out in the field, Doc. We're used to pain. Suffering is optional. You know that." He pinned her with a challenging glare.

Shelby was startled by the acerbic exchange.

Carson didn't seem to like anyone. But he was in pain and coming out from beneath anesthesia. Both could make a person feisty.

Jordana glanced over at Shelby. "You have a spare bedroom?"

Shelby blinked. "Why…yes." What was the doctor up to? She felt suddenly uneasy.

"You have Dakota's wolf with you?"

"She's out in my cruiser and doing fine." Shelby frowned and dug into Jordana's gaze, confused.

"I've got a deal for you, Dakota," Jordana said, her voice suddenly firm and brooking no argument. "If Deputy Kincaid will consent to drive you to her house, which isn't far from the hospital, and let you stay overnight, I'll release you. I know how you hate hospitals and closed-in spaces. Deal?"

The look of shock on Barbie doll's face told Dakota she wasn't prepared to have him as a visitor. "No way, Doc. As soon as I'm able to wear off this damned anesthesia, I'm outta here and you know it whether you sign a release on me or not."

Jordana's beeper went off. She pulled it out of her white coat pocket. Frowning, she said, "I've got to go." Looking over at Shelby, she said, "Talk some sense into him, will you? Because I refuse to sign him out of here unless he goes home with you."

Surprised, Shelby found herself alone with a man who exuded danger to her heart. His face was washed out, but now there was a flush in his cheeks, at least. "Mr. Carson, are you staying in this hospital?"

Dakota studied her beneath his spiky lashes. He felt and heard the authority in her tone. She wore no makeup, but God, she didn't have to. He liked what he saw way too much. He'd been without a woman for too long. And she had a great body beneath that uniform.

"How's my wolf?" he demanded, ignoring her question.

"Storm is fine. I gave her a bowl of water just before I came in here." Shelby met his belligerent glare. "Are you in pain?"

"No more than usual."

"I see."

"You don't, but that's all right."

Testy bastard, she thought. "Look, I need some answers on why you killed that grizzly this morning."

Okay, she was going to play tough. "Because it charged me," he growled. "I know it's illegal to shoot a bear in a national park, Deputy Barbie Doll." He really didn't dislike her, but his mood was blacker than hell. The drugs were loosening his normally reined-in irritability.

"My name is Shelby Kincaid."

He smiled a little. It was a tight, one-cornered smile. Did Dakota dare tell her she was a feast for his hungry gaze? The anesthesia was wearing off fast now, and he felt some returning strength. "Okay, Deputy Kincaid. I was out to pick up my trapline in a stand of willows when the bear came out of nowhere and charged me." He stared up at her. "What was I supposed to do? Let the bastard kill me because it was out of season?"

Her mouth twitched. "No," she said. Pulling a small notebook from her pocket, she wrote down his explanation. "Why are you out trapping animals?"

"Because I choose to. That's not against the law."

"No, it's not. Where do you live? I need an address."

"Third mountain to the north in the Tetons. Where I live, there is no address."

"Try me. I was raised here. I think I know just about every dirt road in this county."

"Do you know how beautiful you are when you're pissed?"

Shelby leaked a grin. This ex-SEAL took no prisoners. Neither did she. "Thanks, but let's stick to the investigation?"

Shrugging, Dakota actually found himself enjoying her spirited conversation. In some ways, Shelby reminded him of his late sister, Ellie. Both had a lot of spunk and spirit. A sudden sadness descended upon him and he scowled. "The bear charged me. I shot the bear. End of story." Her blue eyes narrowed. Still, he savored her husky voice. It reminded him of honey, sweet and dark. He looked at her left hand. No wedding ring. He assumed she was in a relationship. A woman this damned good-looking would have men hanging around her.

"Tell me where you live."

Dakota sighed. "I'll give you GPS coordinates if you know how to use them. It's on a no-name dirt road. It doesn't even have a forest service designation number to it."

"Which mountain?"

"Mount Owen," he growled. "Now do you know where it's at?"

Shelby stood her ground with the ex-SEAL. She reminded herself that he was still coming out of shock and surgery. "I do. When I was a teen, I was up tracking in that area many times with my dad."

"Tracking?" Dakota certainly didn't expect that answer. He was a damned good SEAL tracker. He'd spent years tracking Taliban and al Qaeda in the Hindu Kush Mountains.

"Why so surprised?" Shelby grinned at him. If Dakota wasn't so testy and sour, she'd like his company. If he didn't have that two-day growth of beard, he'd be a cover model for *GQ*. He was in top, athletic shape and she liked the way his thickly corded neck and shoulders moved.

"Tracking isn't exactly what I expected to hear coming out of your mouth."

"Surprises abound, Mr. Carson. There's an old

miner's shack up at eight thousand feet on a narrow dirt road. It was pretty well in ruin the last time I was in that area. There's an old sluice box next to the creek. That shack sits about fifteen feet from the creek. At one time, gold was found in the Tetons, but the miners exhausted it." She studied him. "Now, is that the cabin where you live?"

Amazed, he simply uttered, "Yeah, that's it." How the hell did Deputy Barbie Doll figure out his hiding place? Dakota found himself readjusting his attitude. There was more to her than he thought. And it triggered a curiosity in him he rarely felt. Most women he'd been with in the far past were interested in getting married, having kids and settling down. As a SEAL, he was in a two-year cycle, with six months of it being deployed into the badlands of Afghanistan. It didn't leave much time to cultivate an honest-to-God relationship with a woman, which was why all of his entanglements crashed and burned.

"So, you were heading for your trapline when the bear charged you?"

"Yes, it's that simple."

"Do you have a phone?"

He managed a sour laugh. "Up there? You know there's no phone or electric lines up to that shack." Dakota saw her face go dark for a moment. She obviously didn't like being reminded about the obvious.

"Cell phone," Shelby amended in a firm tone. What was it about this guy? He was positively bristling and his hackles rose in a heartbeat. It was like flipping a switch off and on with him. Yet when his mouth relaxed and his eyes lost that glitter of defensiveness, she saw another man beneath that grouchy exterior. She liked that man and found herself wanting to know him better. Much better.

"Yeah," he muttered. "I got one." He gave her the number and added, "Of course, I get, maybe, one or two bars, depending on the storms up there at that elevation."

"I know," she said, writing the info down on her pad.

"How would you know?"

She felt the gauntlet thrown at her feet once more. His eyes were dark with distrust. "Because," she answered in an unruffled tone, "I was tracking a lost child up in that same area a year ago. I found the lost boy I'd been tracking. When I tried to call in on my cell, I couldn't get a signal."

Surprise flowed through Dakota. "You tracked a lost boy?" This blew his mind. Women did not know how to track.

"Yes." Shelby kind of resented his genuine surprise. He wasn't the only one with skills. Then the sudden relaxation came to his face. Interest glimmered in those gold-brown eyes of his. She felt a shiver of yearning move through her as the look he gave her was primal, sexual. What was happening here? Stunned by her own reaction toward this snarly ex-SEAL, Shelby said, "Let's stick to the facts, Mr. Carson."

Dakota opened his mouth and then closed it. He regarded her with a little more deference. "The only thing women can track is a sale price of clothing at a department store."

Shelby couldn't contain her laughter. "What are you? A Neanderthal? I can track as well as any man. Better."

"Who are you?"

Her entire body reacted to his growling question. Now the wolf was circling the prey—her. "We don't have time for that, Mr. Carson. I need to get the location of where you shot the bear in order to notify the Tetons Forest supervisor. They'll want to find the bear, get it out of there and bring it back to their headquarters for autopsy."

All business. Still, Dakota's mind reeled over the fact that she was a tracker, of all things. And he knew this area like the back of his hand. It was serious, rugged, backcountry mountainous area. Even a skilled hunter could get lost and disoriented. And she hadn't. As he gazed up into her sparkling blue eyes, he saw banked humor in them. He gave her the directions to the meadow where he had killed the bear.

"Great, thanks," Shelby said. She walked away, pressed the button on the radio on her left epaulet.

Watching her, Dakota liked what he saw. She was definitely a throwback to the Victorian age with the proverbial hourglass figure. Her breasts were hidden by the Kevlar vest, but he could tell they were full. Her hips were flared and she had long, long legs. Damn, she was a good-looking woman. He warned himself that she was in a relationship, lay back and closed his eyes. He had to get out of this place. There was no friggin' way he was staying overnight.

"How are you feeling?" Shelby asked when she came back over to his gurney. "Better?"

Opening his eyes, he said, "Yeah. Better."

"We have two forest rangers going out to find your bear."

"Am I going to be charged?"

"I doubt it. I'll talk to Charley over at Tetons HQ tomorrow. It sounds like self-defense to me."

His mouth curled into a slight grin. "Oh, it was, Deputy. It was. You should have been there."

"No, thanks. I've had enough grizzly interruptus too many times when I'm tracking. I like to stay away from them. They're big and they're fast."

He held up his bandaged arm. "Tell me about it."

She liked his black humor. "You were lucky."

"No luck at all. I had the situation under control." Well, almost. If not for Storm charging the grizzly and biting the bear's nose, he wouldn't have gotten the second shots to kill the charging beast.

"Yeah, right." Her mouth twitched. "I'll see you tomorrow."

"No, you won't."

Shelby frowned. "You have to stay here for the night, Mr. Carson. Or go home with me."

He sat up, his head clear. The nausea was ebbing. "Bull. I'm leaving...." He threw off the blankets and gave her a look that warned her not to stop him.

CHAPTER FOUR

SHELBY WATCHED DAKOTA CARSON get up, unsteadily at first. His calves were knotted, which told her what good a shape he was in. He calmly removed the IV because he knew how to do it and dropped the needle and tube back on the gurney.

"Your clothes are kept in that locker room," she said, pointing to a door on the left. "Probably got your last name on one of the lockers so you can find them."

He stopped and studied her. Something about Shelby intrigued him. "You're smart."

"I'm field smart, Mr. Carson."

His mouth twitched. Yeah, she was damned smart for not getting in his way. "If you were a man, you'd rear up on your balls and try to stop me."

"I have a titanium set, but I choose my battles very carefully."

His mouth drew into a sour smile. "You ever been in the military?"

"No."

"Shoulda been." He turned and walked slowly but surely toward the door.

Shelby wasn't sure if it was a compliment or an insult. She waited until he was gone and called Jordana McPherson. By the time she arrived, looking upset, Dakota Carson was coming out the door, fully clothed. When he saw Jordana, he glanced over at Shelby.

"I called her," Shelby said.

"Yeah, I remember. You pick your battles."

Smiling, Shelby nodded.

"Dakota?" Jordana called.

"No sense in trying to talk me out of leaving this place, Doc. You know I can't handle closed-in spaces. I'll just be on my way."

Jordana shoved her hands in the pockets of her white lab coat, giving him a pleading look. "There's a high probability of infection after a bite like this, Dakota. I've written you a prescription for antibiotics, but I'm worried. Usually, if there is infection, it's going to hit you in the first twenty-four hours after the operation. That's why I wanted you to stay overnight for observation. If you could agree to stay at Shelby's, her house is only a block from this hospital, I wouldn't worry so much. Please…"

Halting, Dakota studied the deputy. Oh, he'd like to go home with her, all right. For all the wrong damn reasons. "No."

Jordana reached out, her fingers wrapping around

his right arm. "Dakota, you have to! That's a bad wound. You're a combat medic and you know the drill. If you could just stay overnight and let me give you an antibiotic IV drip? One night, and drop by and see me tomorrow morning to check it. I'll feel better."

"Sorry, Doc, but I gotta go...." He shook off her hand. Glancing at the deputy, he growled, "Now?" Dakota expected the deputy to try to stop him.

Shelby stepped aside. "Timing's everything."

Walking slowly by her, Dakota got his bearings and moved toward the elevator. Neither woman made an attempt to stop him.

The elevator doors whooshed closed. Jordana gave Shelby a desperate look. "He shouldn't leave."

"I know," she muttered. "Give me his prescription and I'll get it filled and make sure he has it before he drives off. I'll follow him at a safe distance."

"Can't you talk some sense into him?" Jordana handed her the prescription.

With a sour laugh, Shelby said, "He calls me Deputy Barbie Doll. Do you really think I have any sway over him?"

"Hardly." Scratching her head, Jordana groused, "Unbelievable."

"Is that SEAL behavior?" Shelby asked, walking with her to the elevator.

"No. It's his PTSD, Shelby. He's got a very bad case of it. Closed-in places throw him into deep anxiety. He prowls around like a caged lion if he can't escape." Jordana added, "I feel so bad for him. He's a decorated vet, with the silver star and two purple hearts. But he just won't come in for weekly therapy."

The elevator doors opened and they stepped in. "I'll see what I can do," Shelby said. "But no promises."

"He's been out on that mountain for a year, Shelby," Jordana said in a softer voice. "Alone. And he's unable to socialize, to fit back into society. It's as if he's still in combat mode and he can't do anything about it."

"I saw him struggling earlier," Shelby murmured. The doors opened to the main floor of the hospital. Walking out, she turned to the right. "There he is."

"Get those antibiotics for him and follow him," Jordana said, touching her shoulder. "He's a vet. He's earned our help even if he doesn't want it."

Mouth quirking, Shelby shrugged into her coat. "He fights everyone. All the time, whether he should or not."

"Good luck."

She'd need it. Shelby watched him walk gingerly down the hall toward the main exit sliding glass doors. He didn't look over his shoulder, although she watched him operating like a predator on the hunt. Dakota Carson missed nothing, his gaze swiveling one way and then the other. He might have just come out of anesthesia, but the man was alert. Jordana was right: he was operating in combat mode. He might be in the U.S., but his mind and emotions were still in Afghanistan.

Dakota made it to his truck. He fished the keys out of his pocket. Two parking spaces down was the Tetons sheriff's cruiser. Storm was looking out the window at him, wagging her big, fluffy gray tail. He smiled and felt a sense of safety. When he looked up, he saw the blond deputy crossing the street to where he was. She stopped and handed him an orange prescription bottle.

"The doctor wanted you to take this antibiotic," she said. Their fingers touched momentarily. An unexpected warmth moved up his arm, which aggravated him. He stuffed the bottle into his pocket.

"I need my wolf," he told her, getting into the cab. He shoved the key into the ignition and turned it.

Nothing. Just a clicking sound.

Cursing to himself, Dakota turned the key again.

"Battery's dead," Shelby said matter-of-factly. "Cold weather can suck the life out of one real fast."

Dakota sat back and glared at her. "Sure you didn't do something to my truck so I couldn't get home?"

Shelby shrugged. "No, but if you don't believe me, lift the hood and check it out yourself."

He did just that. In cold weather, batteries

drained quickly. He saw some rust corrosion around the terminals, but that wouldn't stop the battery from turning over the engine. *Son of a bitch.* Dropping the hood, Dakota straightened. The woman stood right where she was the last time he saw her, a concerned look on her oval face. He met her shadowed blue eyes and felt as if he could fall into them. What was it about this woman that gave him that sense of safety? Dakota pushed the feeling away.

"I imagine you're feeling pretty good about this?"

"Not at all, Mr. Carson. I want to help you, not make your life any more miserable than it already is." Shelby didn't like their sparring exchanges, but he was terse and defensive. Given his PTSD, she could forgive him and just try to make life a little easier on him.

Dakota studied her in the tense silence. Her husky voice riffled across his flesh. He felt her genuine care. He'd been without a woman for so damn long, it scared him. But a lot of things scared the hell out of him. The morning sky was clear after the blizzard from the day before. The strong sunlight warmed him. "Can I get you to drive me and my wolf back to my cabin?"

Her heart contracted with pain for him. The anger in his eyes died as he must have realized the hopelessness of his situation. He swallowed his considerable pride and asked her for help. She ached for him. "Yes, I can do that. When I get back, I'll take your battery over to the service station and get it charged. You need to come back here tomorrow morning to see Dr. McPherson, anyway. We can pick it up then and you'll have your truck again."

"You do choose your battles."

"I don't see you as a battle, Mr. Carson. I see you as someone who needs a helping hand right now."

Shaking his head, he slid out of the truck. "Okay. Wheels up. Let's rock it out."

Shelby didn't expect a thank you. She wasn't familiar with the military slang he used, either. His face was pale, and she knew he was fighting to appear confident. He didn't fool her at all, but she said nothing, walking over to her cruiser and unlocking the system.

When Dakota climbed in, his wolf whined and wagged her tail in welcome. He grinned and stuck his fingers through the wire wall between the front and backseats. The look in Shelby's eyes startled him as she climbed in. For a moment, he thought he saw tears in them. Her blue eyes were wide with happiness. An unexpected heat surged through him. He turned around, pulled on the seat belt and closed the door. Shelby didn't behave like most women he knew. She was different. Very different.

On the way out of the town, Shelby asked, "Do

you have enough food and water up there? We can always stop at a grocery store."

"I'm fine," he managed. As he leaned his head back against the seat rest, exhaustion finally caught up with him. In moments, he was asleep.

Shelby headed out of town, up the long hill that would put them on the road toward Grand Tetons National Park. She knew exactly where Dakota Carson was holed up. The radio chatter broke the silence, but her mind and heart focused on the injured vet sleeping in her cruiser. Once, she looked at his profile. His nose reminded her that he might have some Native American heritage in his blood. And his skin, although washed out, looked more tan than white. In that moment, he seemed vulnerable. It twisted her heart to think of the terror he must have undergone and survived. She quirked her mouth. She had a few symptoms of PTSD herself, but so did everyone who worked in law enforcement. It just wasn't as bad as for a military person.

When the cruiser stopped, Dakota snapped awake. Wide awake. Looking to the left, he saw his cabin. "You found it."

Shelby grinned. "I told you I knew where it was." She turned and studied him. "How do you feel?"

He lifted his bandaged arm. "Better."

"Good. You needed the sleep." He needed some care. And she found herself wanting to do just that for this gruff, injured vet. Why? Something tugged at her heart. And triggered her needs as a woman for him as a man. She had no idea why. Shelby opened the door and climbed out.

Dakota couldn't figure this woman out. No one knew where this road was. But she did. After getting out, he opened the back door and Storm leaped out.

The first thing Shelby did was go to the shack. Carson had done a lot of work over time to fix it up. Once, it had been a log cabin with white plaster between the thick logs. Over the years, all of the plaster had cracked and fallen out, leaving huge gaps between the logs. Now mud and moss stuck in between them, to ward off the cold. Up here, snow was still about three feet deep in shaded spots. Trees were thick, and only the happy gurgle of a nearby creek broke the muted silence. Turning, she saw Dakota making his way toward his home.

"You've fixed it up," she noted, gesturing toward it. "New roof. It needed one. And you've repaired the spaces between the logs." At least he wasn't lazy. Shelby noted the entire area was picked up, clean and organized. He cared, she realized. In his own way, the man was trying to make life a little better for himself, even if it was in the middle of nowhere.

"I've had a year to make it less windy inside."

Shelby watched the wolf bound happily up to the

door. The animal sat, panting and wagging her tail, as she waited for Carson to walk up. He pushed the grayish wood door open with his foot.

"Not locked?"

"No need. I have a wolf alarm."

Grinning, Shelby said, "Point taken. You're good to go?"

Dakota hesitated at the door. "Yeah."

Shelby stepped forward, pulling a business card from her shirt pocket. "Here's my business card." She took a pen and circled her number. "This is my private cell phone. If you need anything, call me. Day or night, it doesn't matter." His eyes narrowed as he took the crisp white business card. Her fingers tingled briefly when they met his. "Dr. McPherson is really worried about infection. I want you to have a lifeline, all right?"

The silence fell between them. Dakota regarded her from beneath his straight black brows. "You do this for everyone?" he demanded, his voice suddenly gruff. He tried to stop the warm feelings flowing through his chest because she cared.

"Anyone," she assured him quietly. Just the raw, anguished look in his eyes hit her in the chest like a fist. There was such need in Carson, but he was so broken that it brought tears. She turned so he wouldn't see them. Shelby's voice was roughened. "Meet you here at 0700 tomorrow?"

He nodded, watching her turn away from him.

She seemed so out of place. Her blond hair was like sunlight in the dark, muted shadows of the woods surrounding the area. She was like a ray of sunshine in his own darkness. "Yeah."

Nodding, Shelby headed back toward the cruiser.

"Hey…thanks…" he called.

Turning on her boot, she flashed him a tender smile. "Anytime. Take care…."

"Are you sure you weren't in the military?"

Shelby forced tears away and met his confused gaze. "No. My dad, though, was in the Marine Corps. He served in the military police for ten years before getting out." She gestured toward Jackson Hole. "We ended up here and he became a sheriff's deputy. Later, he became commander. He just retired two years ago to fish the trout streams."

Mouth compressed, Dakota said, "That's good to know."

"Why?"

"Because you're behaving like a SEAL. You take care of your teammates."

Shelby didn't know what that meant, but it was important to him. "I'm just glad to be of help, Mr. Carson."

"Call me Dakota."

"Will do…"

For a moment, all Shelby wanted to do was turn around, walk straight up to him and throw her arms around his shoulders. That was what he needed: a little TLC. Yet the exhaustion in his eyes and face, that gruff exterior, warned her off. She'd been a deputy for years and could read body language and facial expressions pretty well. That ability had saved her life in the past, but Shelby didn't feel threatened by this ex-SEAL. If anything, her heart reached out for him, wanted to help him even though he pushed all her efforts away.

She watched him disappear into the claptrap cabin. Frowning, Shelby walked back to her cruiser. She was sure that Cade Garner, who was now second in command at the sheriff's department, and her boss, would be happy to hear she was off duty. She climbed into the cruiser. Cade would understand because of the unusual circumstances. So often, even as law enforcement officers, they dealt in humanitarian ways with the citizens of their county. It wasn't always about handing out a speeding ticket. She was raised in the giant shadow of her father, who had taught her that she should always look to help others who needed it. Shelby looked up to him and was inspired to go into law enforcement as a result. It was a good choice, one she had never regretted.

As she turned the cruiser around, worry ate at her. She wasn't a paramedic, although she had advanced first-aid training. Jordana's worry was real. Over the past two years, she'd become friends with the doctor and knew she didn't show her worry often.

Shelby drove slowly down the steep, muddy road, heading back toward Jackson Hole. Something gnawed at her. Taking a deep breath, Shelby tried to shrug it off. Dakota was a man in his element up here in the raw, untamed Tetons. Apparently his SEAL training had given him the ability to survive in the harshest of environments.

As she drove down the narrow, twisting road, she figured out she'd do a Google search of SEALs and educate herself. Her father had been a military police officer in the marines. As a child of a military family, she recalled her moving from one base to another every two years. She lost good friends she made, never to see them again. It had been emotionally hard on Shelby, but her father was good at what he did. And she was proud of him, as was her mother. But she'd never heard him mention SEALs. Once her shift was over, Shelby would drop by for a visit to her parents' home on the other side of town. Maybe her father would know more about this special breed of military men.

CHAPTER FIVE

THE NIGHTMARE BEGAN as it always did. Dakota was following his LT, Lieutenant Sean Vincent, up a slippery scree slope in the Hindu Kush Mountains of Afghanistan. It was black. So black he couldn't see a foot in front of him without his NVGs, night-vision goggles, in place over his eyes. Everything became a grainy green. The only problem was there was no depth of perception when using them, and the four-man SEAL team slipped, fell, got up and kept moving.

They were hunting an HTV, high-value-target, Taliban warlord who was hiding out in the cave systems of the Hindu Kush Mountains. The wind was cold and cutting, the Kevlar vest and winter gear keeping him warm. A terrible feeling crawled through Dakota. They called him "woo-woo man," because he had a sixth sense about danger and coming attacks. After three tours in the Sand Box with his platoon, everyone listened to him.

They were ready to crest a ridge at twelve thousand feet. Their breath was coming in explosive inhales and exhales. The climb of four thousand feet at midnight to catch the warlord by surprise, would be worth it. Or would it?

Dakota was ready to throw up his hand in a fist to signal *stop,* to warn the other SEAL operatives.

Too late! Just as the LT breasted the ridge, all hell broke loose. Enemy AK-47s fired. Red tracer bullets danced around the LT. Dakota saw him struck, once, twice, three times. The impact flung the SEAL officer off his feet, sent him flying backward, the M-4 rifle cartwheeling out of his hands.

Dakota grunted, crouched and leaped upward, catching the two-hundred-pound SEAL before he crashed into the sharp, cutting rocks. Slammed backward, Dakota took the full brunt of his LT's weight. He landed with an "oofff," on his back, the rocks bruising and biting into his Kevlar vest plates. He heard the two other operatives scramble upward, in a diamond pattern, to protect him and the LT as they skidded out of control down the steep grade of the mountain.

A hail of bullets, screams of Taliban charging their position, filled the night air. The SEAL team held their position up above, firing systematically, picking off the men as they launched themselves at them. Head shots, every one.

Dakota came to an abrupt halt, a huge boulder stopping their downward slide. His flesh was torn up beneath both his legs, his elbow raw and bleeding. "LT!" He dragged the unconscious officer around the boulder for protection. Dakota was their combat medic on the team. It was his job to save the lives of his team, his family. Glancing around the boulder, he saw Mac and Gordy on their bellies, firing upward, taking out every Taliban who surged over the mountain at them.

Hands shaking, he carefully turned the officer over. He'd worked with Sean for five years. They'd grown up together in the platoon. He was twenty-eight and had just married Isabel before going out on this rotation, their first child on the way. Blood gleamed dark along the LT's throat. Dakota saw where two of the three bullets had struck the LT in the chest. The Kevlar had stopped them from killing him outright.

A loud RPG explosion occurred. Automatically, Dakota threw himself over his LT, a rain of rocks hailing down all around them. He heard Mac yell. The next moment, a grenade was fired by the SEAL. More explosions lit the night on that cold ridge. Rolling off the officer, Dakota heard the throaty fire of the M-4s. Both his teammates were fighting back with fury. He heard their comms man, Mac, call for air support. They needed it.

As he pulled away Sean's collar in his quick examination, Dakota noticed the terrible wound the third bullet had created as it sped through the side of his neck. Gulping, tears blurring his vision for a second, Dakota forced down his emotions. Rapidly, he applied a battle dressing with pressure to the side of Sean's neck. He could feel the warmth of the SEAL's blood as it leaked quickly out of the white dressing and through his fingers. He was going to bleed out, his carotid artery cut in half by the bullet. *Oh, God, no, no, don't let this be!* Bullets whined around Dakota. He heard a roar of the Taliban to his right. Jerking his head up, he saw at least ten Taliban rush around the slope from another direction, firing at him.

Dakota had to return fire. In doing so, he had to lift his hand and stop the artery from bleeding out. It was a terrible choice....

Groaning, Dakota awakened in a heavy sweat. His chest was rapidly rising and falling, his mouth opened in a silent scream. Flailing around on his bed, the springs creaking, he tried to run from the rest of the nightmare that dogged him. His heart pounded so hard he felt as if it would tear out of his chest. Throwing off the wool blankets, burning up, he pulled himself upright. The moment his bare feet hit the cold surface of the floor, he opened his eyes. Perspiration ran down his temples. He could taste the sweat at the corners of his mouth. Tears were running out of his eyes and no matter what he did, Dakota couldn't stop them.

Oh God, no...no.... Sean died right there. Right behind that friggin' rock in the middle of nowhere.

He jammed his palms against his closed eyes, trembling. His muscles bunched and knotted. If only... if only he'd have died instead of Sean. He left his beautiful, pregnant wife behind. Somehow, they got off that ridge before being decimated. The Night Stalkers sent in an MH-47 Chinook accompanied by two army Apache combat helicopters. Making a heroic landing, one of the four wheels on the mountain, the others in thin air, Dakota carried his dead LT and himself on board. Then the other two SEALs jumped off the ridge, slid down the rocky scree and leaped into the awaiting helo. As the Chinook powered up and left the ridge, the Apaches lit it up like the Fourth of July, cremating every one of those bastards, sending them straight to hell.

The shaking wouldn't stop. Dakota rubbed his eyes savagely, trying to force the tears to stop. Sean was like the brother he'd never had. Sean's platoon was his family. *Burning up.* He was burning up. At this time of year, it was below freezing at night, but barely. Why wouldn't his body cool down? His mind felt spongy. Dakota realized he wasn't thinking clearly. The nightmare still had its claws into him. *Still...*

Forcing himself to his feet, Dakota staggered. Dizziness assailed him and he found himself falling backward onto the bed. He hit it with force, one metal leg bending and snapping. The jolt of the bed falling on one side shocked him. Breathing hard, his heart refusing to stop pounding as if he were in the middle of a heart attack, Dakota forced himself to focus. It was something SEALs did well. He placed two fingers on his pulse. It was leaping and bounding as if it were about to tear out of his skin. By now his body should be calming down, cooling down. But it wasn't. His flesh felt scalded beneath his fingertips. *What the hell?* And then it hit him: he had a fever. *Shit.* Doc McPherson was right: infection had set in after the surgery.

Lifting his head, his eyes narrowed, sweat running and following the course of his hard jaw, Dakota tried to think. As he tried to get up, the dizziness felled him. The bed sagged and tipped to one side where the leg had been broken off. His left arm throbbed like a son of a bitch. He looked at it. The arm had swollen so much that the skin on either end of the tape bulged outward. When he touched it, his arm was hard and hot. Bad news.

Help. I've got to get help or I'm gonna die. I've gone septic...

Moonlight shifted through the small glass windows, which were smudged with dust and dirt. A flash of white on the wood table caught his wandering attention. Dakota knew he'd never get to his truck, much less drive it down the mountain to get help.

Barbie Doll...need to call her... Said she'd help...

The cell phone lay next to her white business

card on the table. Could he reach it? Dakota forced himself up, staggering those five feet to the table. He sat down in the chair before he fell down. With shaking fingers, his mind hallucinating from high fever, he slowly punched in the numbers. Would Barbie Doll answer? Did she really mean what she said? She'd help him if he needed her, or was it just lip service? Dakota had never felt so goddamned useless. He'd been a SEAL. He knew how to survive. And yet a high fever was raging through him, had dismantled him in record time. If that blond-haired angel didn't answer her cell phone, he knew without a doubt she'd find him dead on the floor when she dropped by at 0700.

His senses began to spin. Dakota tried to focus on the phone ringing and ringing and ringing.... Blackness began to assail him. He fought the fever. Fought the darkness encroaching upon him. He couldn't see anymore. Everything was turning black. *Oh God, I'm going to die....* The grizzly bear had gotten its revenge....

Soft, beeping noises slowly brought Dakota out of the darkness. He heard women's voices. Far off. Too far to understand, but he tried to listen anyway. He had that familiar sensation, as if he was drowning and swimming toward the surface. It reminded him of being a SEAL frogman. He'd had his LAR V Draeger rebreathing system malfunction at fifty feet in the warm waters of the Arabian Sea during a night mission. Holding his breath, Dakota swam strongly, pushing his flippers hard toward the surface. It was barely dawn, but he could see the light above him through his mask. His chest swelled, he felt the pressure, felt the reflex to breathe. But he couldn't! If he did, he'd inhale a lungful of water and drown. Struggling, fighting, kicking, he willed himself to hold his breath just as he'd done back in BUD/S in that pool. Was he going to make it?

And then a gentle hand touched his sweaty lower arm. Instantly, it broke the hold darkness had on him. Dakota inhaled audibly, gulping in a huge, deep breath. The fingers tightened a little, as if to steady him, help him to reorient. Yes, the hand was cool, fingers long. He could feel their softness against the dark hair and sweat rolling off his arm.

Dragging his eyes open to slits, Dakota saw nothing but blurred green walls. The hand. That cool, soft hand. He forced himself to close his eyes and concentrate. Between heaven and hell, Dakota fought to move toward the light. Toward that hand that was like an anchor promising him life, not death. His mind churned, hallucinated and then like a tide, flowed out, leaving him lucid for a few moments.

"It's all right, Dakota," a voice whispered near his ear. "You're going to be all right. You're safe…."

Her breath was warm, a hint of cinnamon on it, maybe. Dakota absorbed her husky, breathy tone, the warm moisture caressing his ear and cheek. He felt her fingers tighten just a little, as if to convince him to believe her. Most of all, he was safe. He felt safe even though he swam in a mix of hallucinations and God knew what else. Where was he?

Shelby kept her hand on Dakota's arm. Jordana McPherson stood on the other side of the bed, watching him. Lifting her gaze, she met Jordana's. "He's coming around…."

"Yes," the doctor murmured, checking the IV drip that was slugging his body with antibiotics and fighting the massive infection within him. "Finally. He's past crisis. He's going to make it."

THE AFTERNOON SUN slanted through the window near the hospital bed. "It was a close call," Shelby said in a low tone. She watched Dakota struggling to regain consciousness.

Snorting, Jordana rolled her eyes. She watched the monitors for a moment. "No need to tell you. You're the one who found him at two o'clock this morning." She frowned. "If you hadn't responded to his call, he'd have died. He went septic. I was so afraid of that."

Shelby noticed the red streaks—a sign of sepsis—running up his left arm. His biceps were sculpted and hard. If a streak had reached his heart, it would have killed him. Now the red streaks were receding. Even in his semiconscious state, with a high fever, there was nothing but pure masculinity about Dakota Carson. The man was in top shape. He wasn't heavily muscled, just lean and honed like a fine knife blade.

"Okay, monitors are looking better. His heart rate and pulse are finally lowering." Jordana sighed. "His fever's coming down and now at one hundred three. And his oxygen concentration is okay, considering what he just went through. Stay with him until he gets conscious, okay? I don't want him waking up and being thrown into instant anxiety because he doesn't know where he is. He's going to be woozy for a while."

"I'll stay with him."

"Thanks. Are you off duty?"

"Yeah, for the next three days."

"Don't you love shift work?" Jordana grinned.

"I do." Shelby gazed down at Dakota, who was still struggling. "It came in handy this time."

"Tell me about it. If you need me, buzz." Jordana waved and disappeared out the door of the private room.

Quiet descended on the small room. Shelby shifted a little, keeping her hand on Dakota's good arm. She wanted to touch this man, this warrior. Her talk with her father yesterday had shed a ton of light on SEALs. And truly, Dakota Carson was a genuine hero. A real warrior. As she gazed down at his pale features, the darkness of the beard making his cheeks look even more gaunt from the ravages of the fever, her heart expanded. She moved her fingers gently up and down his arm. She felt even more drawn to this enigmatic man. This loner who held so much pain deep in his heart. How much darkness held him prisoner? Shelby wondered.

His eyes slowly opened. Leaning down, Shelby smiled, catching his wandering gaze. "Dakota? It's Shelby. You're back in the Jackson Hole Hospital."

His eyes moved slowly back to hers. Shelby felt his neediness in that moment. Her breath hitched. There was anxiety and fear in his expression, turning them a muddy brown color. Without thinking, she reached out and threaded her fingers through his damp, sweat-soaked black hair. "It's okay. You're okay. You had a close call with an infection, but you're going to be all right."

Shelby sounded like an angel whispering to him, calling him out of the darkness that still wanted to drag him back down into hell. As her fingers touched his burning scalp, the coolness soothed his agitation, stopped the panic deep in his chest. The look of calm on her face touched him. In seconds, he relaxed. Watching her, Dakota was sure he'd died and gone to heaven.

His voice was raw. In a barely heard, ragged whisper, he managed, "Angel…"

Shelby withdrew her fingers from his hair. "Not me." She laughed softly. "I'm no angel."

A sense of warmth, of coming home, stole through Dakota. That half smile of hers, that humored look dancing impishly in her eyes, gave him a sense of peace he'd never felt before. What was going on? He didn't care. All he could do was absorb her grazing touch across his forearm. It was Shelby, he decided. His mind shorted out, wandered and then came back to sharper focus.

"Wh-what…"

Shelby leaned near, her lips inches from his ear. Quietly, she repeated the information to him, watching to see if his eyes would focus. As she spoke, he seemed to relax. She saw the evidence in the monitors on the other side of his bed. His pulse became normal. His breathing settled. She understood a soft voice could tame a person in shock at an accident site. Knowing this from her own experience, she repeated once again the information slowly.

His gaze followed hers as she slowly straightened, continuing to keep her hand on his arm. His pupils grew larger, as if grappling with comprehension. What kind of anguish was he experiencing right now? What was he seeing?

When she lifted her hand away, he groaned. The monitors chattered. His blood pressure rose, his pulse skyrocketed and his heart started to pound.

Shelby automatically placed her hand back on his right shoulder. The blue cotton gown hid the hard muscles beneath, but she could feel them leap and respond to her touch. Amazed, Shelby watched the monitors stop beeping so loudly. All his functions lowered back to normal. *Touch.* That was it. A thread of joy coursed through her, sweet and unexpected. Tilting her chin, she gazed at Dakota's lashes resting against his pasty cheeks. His mouth, once pursed with pain, was now relaxed.

What would it be like to kiss this man? His mouth was beautifully shaped, the lower lip slightly fuller than the upper. If given the chance, he'd probably be one hell of a kisser. Absently, she moved her hand across his shoulder. His chest rose and fell slowly, no longer swift or moving with anxiety.

She was shaken and emotionally moved by the unexpected experience. Even watching him fall into a deep sleep affected her. He'd been trapped within some unknown nightmare, fueled by the high fever. When she looked once again at the monitor, she was stunned. His temperature had been a hundred and three. Now it had reduced to a hundred and one! How was that possible? Shelby wished she knew more about medicine. She'd asked Jordana later.

Hooking the chair with her foot, she slowly pulled it over to Dakota's bedside. Because her touch was a powerful healing agent, the least she could do was stay. And allow her touch to give him some peace. As Shelby sat down, she slid her hand across his gowned shoulder to his lower right arm and remembered her dad's words of warning.

"He's a man carrying so much grief and pain he doesn't know where to put it all, Shelby. He's seen too much. He's survived things we can't imagine. He's a wounded warrior and the past runs his life."

Shelby felt close to tears. Tears for him, for the horror he still carried within him. Dakota was perilous to her heart. And yet she felt driven to be near him. Most shocking of all, she wanted to care for him. Somehow, Shelby knew love was the key to this man who now slept. Shaking her head, Shelby told herself she was crazy. A man like this would be like a black hole, sucking the life out of everything he ever touched, destroying it.

Or would he?

Shelby heard her dad's warning words. "Be careful, Shelby. You care about this vet too much. You have no experience with his kind. If you get close to him, he'll emotionally destroy you. He's got a severe disorder and he doesn't know how to handle himself, much less a woman who's trying to help him. Stay out of his way, Shelby. Don't get involved."

CHAPTER SIX

DAKOTA AWOKE SLOWLY to the sound of a robin singing nearby. Dragging open his eyes, he was met by brilliant sunlight coming through frilly white lace curtains. The light hit the pale blue wall opposite of where he lay. His brows drew down. Where the hell was he? What had happened?

The door quietly opened. His eyes widened when he recognized Shelby. She was dressed in a simple orange T-shirt, body-hugging jeans and a pair of well-worn moccasins. Her hair gleamed like gold as she walked through the slats of sunlight. When she saw he was awake, she smiled.

"Welcome back to the land of the living. You're at my home."

Dakota pushed himself up into a sitting position. He found himself a helluva lot weaker than he wanted to be. Looking down, he noticed he was wearing a set of blue pajamas. A clean white waterproof bandage covered his left arm. His flesh appeared normal, no longer swollen, bluish or oozing pus. He was no longer feverish, his skin cool and dry to his touch. He looked up as Shelby poured some water from a pitcher.

"Thirsty?"

"Yeah," he managed, his voice hoarse. He took the glass.

"You've been out for two solid days," she said, watching him gulp the water. Jordana had warned her he'd be thirstier than a camel when he came out of his fevered state.

Wiping his mouth with the back of his hand, he handed her the glass. "More?" And then he added, "Please?"

Shelby poured him another glass. "You had us all worried there for a while," she said. His hair was spiky and stiff with sweat. He definitely needed a bath. Still, she thrilled to the fact that his eyes were once more clear and he was fully present.

The water satiated him. "I thought the grizzly was going to get even with me."

Her mouth quirked. "Almost did. Dr. McPherson flooded you with antibiotics through an IV. It was touch-and-go for a while because you had sepsis, blood poisoning."

"Karma's a bitch," he said, his voice stronger. "How did I get here?"

Shelby sat on the edge of the bed, near his feet, facing him. "Dr. McPherson had you brought over here by ambulance a couple hours ago." She saw his brows raise. "She didn't want you waking up in a hospital. She said you didn't like small rooms. I volunteered my place. It's close enough to the hospital in case you relapse."

Looking around, Dakota felt comfortable in the queen-size bed in the large room. He lifted his chin and met her gaze. "Why are you doing this?"

"Because I've seen your cabin and frankly, it sucks. I wouldn't put a sick dog up there to get well." She wanted to add that vets deserved the best, not the worst, when they were injured.

Her lips twitched, merriment gleaming in her blue eyes.

"You should have seen it before I got there. It was a dump," he said.

"Oh," she said as she laughed, "I did. Remember? I've been to it many times before you homesteaded it."

His mind wasn't functioning fully yet. Frowning, Dakota finally remembered. He moved his hand across his jaw. "I need to shave. And I stink."

"Wouldn't disagree."

Smart mouth. Beautiful lips. Dakota appreciated her dry sense of humor. And he was feeling remarkably calm. Almost always, he had anxiety upon awakening. But it was gone. Completely gone, which confused him. "Give me a little while to get my bearings."

"Take as long as you need. By the way, I've checked on Storm daily. She seems happy to stay outside the cabin. I couldn't find any dog food for her."

"She hunts for her food. And she'd rather be outdoors than in." He was grateful for her care of the wolf. It told Dakota she cared a lot more than most people did. "Tell me what happened. The last thing I remember was trying to call you."

"You did."

"I don't remember your answering. I think I blacked out after punching in the numbers."

"My phone rang and I picked it up. There was nothing at the other end, but I could hear Storm whining in the background. I hung up and checked the callback number and I put it together."

"And you drove up there?"

"Yes. When I entered the cabin, you were out cold on the floor. You were burning up, your dressing was oozing pus and smelled foul. Storm was whining and sitting near you. I called the fire station and told them to meet me with an ambulance at the bottom of the mountain. No one would ever know how to get up to your cabin."

Nodding, he studied her beneath his lashes. "You can't be strong enough to haul my ass off that floor by yourself."

Her mouth drew into a wicked grin. "I did." Wasn't easy, but Shelby did it because the other choice was leaving him to die on that cold floor.

"You aren't a Barbie doll after all. I owe you a full apology."

Thrusting out her hand, she said, "Apology accepted. Call me Shelby, will you?" When his hand swallowed hers up, Shelby felt his animal warmth, his strength, and yet he monitored how much pressure he put around her fingers. This was the second time he'd touched her. Really touched her. There was incredible masculinity and power around Dakota. It called her and she felt almost helpless not to respond to it—to him.

"Shelby…yes, I'm sorry I called you Barbie Doll. I guess—" he reluctantly released her long, beautiful hand "—my prejudice about women with blond hair is showing?"

"Dumb blonde prejudice?"

"Yeah."

Shelby didn't want him feeling any worse than he already did. There was a sincere apology in his eyes. "Don't worry about it. Are you hungry, Dakota?" She liked the way his name rolled off her lips. Right now he looked fully relaxed. When would that change? What would cause his anxiety to return? Jason, her older brother, had the same kind of symptoms after three tours in Iraq. And no one had been able to save him. Not even her. Shelby tried to remember her dad's words of warnings when she'd filled him in on Dakota's military background. Yet when she met and drowned in

Dakota's gold-and-brown eyes, she felt her heart opening so wide it made her momentarily breathless. Did he realize the effect he had on her? She didn't think so.

Rubbing his stomach, he said, "Yeah, a little. But look, I don't want you going out of your way—"

"I'll let you know when you're a burden, okay?" Shelby said it half in jest and half with seriousness. Standing up, she asked, "What would you like? I'm a good cook."

He gazed up at her. She was tall, her shoulders thrown back with natural confidence. Without her uniform on and with that orange T-shirt outlining her upper body to show every curve, he lost his train of thought for a moment. "I...uh... Eggs and bacon sound good."

"Toast? Jam?"

He nodded. "If it's not too much trouble?"

"Coffee?"

He groaned. "God, that sounds good. Really good."

"Cream? Sugar?"

"No, black."

"Anything else?"

"You? For dessert?"

Shocked by his response, Shelby was fully aware of the sudden glint in his eyes, that predatory look a man gives to a woman. Heat surged up her neck and into her face. "Let's stick to the eggs and bacon, shall we?" Shelby turned to leave and said teasingly, "I think that's about all you can handle right now."

He had the good grace to give her a sheepish smile. "I think you're right." He watched her leave as soundlessly as she'd arrived. What the hell was wrong with him? Dakota sat up, pushing the covers aside. Shelby was beautiful, playful, intelligent and smart-mouthed. It all conspired to make him brazen.

Looking down, he realized he was aroused. *Damn.* He jerked the covers over the lower half of his body and tried to piece together what had happened to him two days earlier. He couldn't get Shelby's body out of his mind. She had nice, wide hips, the kind a man liked to slide his large hands around to hold and guide her. Her breasts were full and he wondered what it would be like to cup them. Shaking his head, he cursed softly. Horny as hell, Dakota didn't like the fact that his body was acting like some love-starved teen's.

Shelby deserved better. When she came back about twenty minutes later with a tray of food, the first thing he said was, "I'm a lousy houseguest. I'm sorry for what I said earlier. You didn't deserve it."

She set the wooden tray across his lap and noticed the bulge beneath the covers. She tried to keep her face carefully arranged. "Apology accepted. You nearly died a couple of days ago. You're still coming out of it. After almost dying, everyone feels emotionally up and down. In my experience, people say a lot of things in that state."

He took the pink napkin and laid it absently across his broad chest. The eggs looked perfect, several slices of thick bacon and whole-wheat toast on the plate. His stomach growled. "You give a person an amazing amount of rope to hang himself on," he told her wryly, picking up the fork.

Shelby sat down, facing him. "Being a deputy, you find people teach you a lot along the way. I've handled a lot of situations where there's shock and trauma going on." There was something satisfying and even healing to her as she watched him hungrily eat.

He stuffed the eggs into his mouth. Closing his eyes, Dakota simply absorbed their warmth and taste. How long had it been since someone made him a home-cooked meal? For a moment, he felt overwhelmed. He opened his eyes. Shelby sat with one leg tucked beneath her, relaxed, her expression calm. "I imagine you're a pretty cool dude in a gunfight."

"Is that SEAL talk?"

"Being a gunslinger? Yeah, I guess it is."

He ate, starved now. Dakota could tell he'd probably dropped ten pounds, and his stomach was reminding him of that loss in spades. He could feel the food taking hold, reviving his body, replacing his lost strength.

"Do you miss it? I mean, being a SEAL?" Jason seemed to miss his platoon, always wanting to return and go back to Iraq to be with them, not stick around here to visit their parents or her. The military was a powerful draw, but she couldn't grasp why.

Her voice had gone soft and it was as if she had whispered against his skin. Did Shelby know how her husky voice affected him? Dakota shrugged. "Yeah, I miss it." More than she would ever realize.

"Do you have family around here?"

"I did. My parents died in a snowstorm after their truck slid off on a back road and got stuck in a ditch."

"I'm so sorry. When did it happen?" Shelby knew of other people who had died of hypothermia during the long, brutal winter across Wyoming.

Pain filtered through Dakota and he stopped eating. He could tell she wasn't asking to create social conversation. She cared. "I was eighteen." As dark rage and grief stirred deep within him, he quickly tried to shut down all feelings. "It was a long time ago," he said more gruffly than he'd intended.

Shelby sensed a shift in Dakota. She saw devastation in his eyes and then he quickly dipped his head, breaking contact with her. Moistening her lips, she asked softly, "Do you stay in touch with your SEAL teammates?"

"Yes, with a few of the guys."

"They're like your family?" He had none of his own, so she could see Dakota regarding the guys he worked with as family.

"Yes, they are. How'd you get so wise for someone so young?"

Shelby shrugged, a ribbon of sadness flowing wide and slow through her. "Ever since I found out you were a SEAL, I've been trying to understand and learn about them. Because Jason, my brother, was an Army Ranger, never spoke about his life or what he did in the military. When he came home on leave, he never talked about what he did over in Iraq. Not ever." Shelby felt shut out and disconnected from her brother, whom she loved so much. Every time Jason came home on leave, there was a thick wall standing between him, her parents and herself. No matter what she tried to do to reach him, she failed.

"Why?"

"Because you're a big question mark in my world." *Because you remind me of Jason. I couldn't save him. Maybe I can save you?* The words were nearly torn out of Shelby. Stunned by the powerful, invisible connection Dakota had wielded with her, she was unable to deny it or stop it from happening.

A rush of desire coursed through Dakota. There

was such an openness to her, as if she trusted the world. How could she? There were bad guys everywhere. It was a world covered in camouflage as far as he was concerned. A powerful sense of protection toward her welled up within him. Okay, she was a law enforcement officer and knew how to take care of herself. But here, in her home, in this room, there was a terrible vulnerability that suddenly shone in her expression, especially her eyes. Something had happened to her. That much he knew. It was his sixth sense working. It always did when there was danger or threat.

Dakota tried to probe beyond her expression. Shelby was good at hiding, he discovered, but she couldn't stop it from showing in her eyes. If he sensed correctly, something tragic had happened recently to her. But what? He couldn't ask now. *Maybe later.* He managed a one-cornered smile, wanting to lift her out of the darkness only she knew about. "Don't be too curious about me. I'm a dead end."

She sighed and wrapped her arms around her drawn-up knee. Dakota was trying to tease her, but right now her gut was a knot. Her heart was squeezing with fresh grief, which wouldn't stop flowing outward and making her want to cry. "Interested, not curious. There's a difference."

He smiled thinly and picked up the mug of steaming coffee. "Interested why?"

She took his challenge and tried to deflect the real truth. "I like to learn about people. I see them as my teachers." Jason had been a hard teacher, nearly breaking her. She'd loved her brother with a fierceness that couldn't ever be controlled or stopped. They had been so close growing up. So many happy memories until…

"So, I'm a bug under your microscope of life?" he teased, a grin edging his mouth.

"I wouldn't say a bug," Shelby protested. Jason and Dakota were so much alike, it scared her. The PTSD was their shared, dark connection. Struggling, Shelby forced herself out of her own personal mire and focused on the man in her bed. How handsome Dakota was when he was relaxed. It was a remarkable change from meeting him out in the hospital parking lot. And where had his PTSD symptoms gone? She wondered if he was peaceful because she was here with him. Did one person make that big of a difference to someone like Dakota? Did she really have that much influence over him?

Shelby had never had that kind of effect on Jason. He grew irritated and irrational when she tried to talk with him. But Dakota was different, or at least, for the time being. The terrible, unanswered questions ate at her. Had she pushed Jason too far? All she wanted was that closeness they'd shared before he'd joined the military.

"What, then?" Dakota challenged, relishing the fresh coffee.

Shelby fumbled, avoiding his sharpened gaze. There was nothing weak about Dakota, the beard making him all the more male and therefore dangerous to her emotions.

"Out of words for once? Or are you carefully choosing our battles?"

Upon hearing the growl of his teasing, she lifted her chin. Her smile faded. The grief from her past stained the happiness she felt being around him. "I…sensed something about you, Dakota. I couldn't put my finger on it. I felt your desperation, your need." Shelby gave him a helpless look. "I knew someone once, who was a lot like you." She choked back the rest of the admission. It was too painful to say. Too painful and shaming to admit. Finally, her voice husky with emotion, she admitted, "There's just something about you that draws me."

Her softly spoken honesty rattled him as nothing else ever could. Seeing the flush across her cheeks, the sudden, unexpected grief shadowing her expression, Dakota felt like the proverbial bull in a china shop. Before he could think of something to say, Shelby looked as if she was going to cry.

She quickly uncurled from the bed and picked up the tray from his lap. "I brought some of your clothes down from the cabin the other day and washed them. You'll find fresh Levi's, a T-shirt and socks in the bathroom across the hall." She turned and left the room without another word.

Well hell! That went well, didn't it, Carson? Shelby had been generous with him. And he'd acted like a total jerk. Something deeper, more visceral was going on between them. Dakota threw off the covers in frustration. He had to get out of here or he'd do something really stupid. He felt protective toward Shelby. He wanted to hunt her down, pull her into his arms and love her until they both died of pleasure. Snorting to himself, Dakota knew he was no prize. He was a horse's ass, if anything. Looking around, he felt more like his old self before the infection damn near snuffed out his life. He was strong and solid again. He spotted a towel, washcloth and soap on the dresser, and walked over to pick them up.

Opening the door, he padded out into the highly polished oak hall and spotted the bathroom. Dakota heard the pleasant clink of dishes and running water out in the kitchen. The sounds were familiar and soothing to him, reminding him of his happy childhood. It sent a pang through him, reminding him of how much he'd lost. Scowling, he sauntered into the bathroom and shut the door. He had to get the hell out of here.

CHAPTER SEVEN

DAKOTA CAME OUT of the bathroom in bare feet, a pair of gray socks dangling between his fingers. He rubbed his recently shaved jaw. Something was different, but he couldn't name what it was as he ambled up toward the kitchen to find Shelby. Was it the long, hot shower washing off three days of crud? Getting rid of the high-fever sweat? Or was it her? As he'd lathered up with the pine-scented soap, he felt his heart opening. It was the damnedest sensation, one he'd never felt before. The soap bubbles and rivulets of hot water mixed with steam had cleansed him. His old strength flowed quietly back into him.

His focus, his being, centered on Shelby. She didn't have to take him in. Dakota sensed there was a reason behind her doing so. And he had to know. Now. Shelby stood at the sink, hands on the counter, gazing out the window. She didn't hear him coming. He'd been taught how to walk quietly during SEAL training, and that skill was with him to this day.

Shelby was lost in a morass of emotions, mostly grief and guilt, when she realized Dakota was standing a few feet away from her. Looking up, she saw his hair was mussed and damp. His eyes, clear and intense, unsettled her. The dark green T-shirt stretched across his broad shoulders and powerful chest. There was nothing weak about this man. *Nothing.* He was standing in a pair of Levi's, his feet bare. A number of white scars ran across both feet.

"Look at me," Dakota ordered softly, placing his finger beneath her stubborn chin.

A wild tingle fled through her over his unexpected touch. Lifting her lashes, she met and fearlessly held his gaze. Her breath hitched as his finger moved, slowly tracing the line of her jaw.

"There's something you haven't told me, Shel… Why would a woman let a stranger, someone she didn't know, into her house?"

He called her Shel. The endearment came out tender and coaxing from between his lips. His roughened finger lingered at her neck. Heat radiated off his athletic body, male heat. Her entire lower body went soft and hot. He'd barely touched her and she was melting inwardly, starving for his touch. Shelby started to speak, but grief unexpectedly flooded her.

Shifting his hand, he cupped her cheek with his roughened palm. "Shel?"

The callused palm against her cheek shattered a door she'd kept locked for almost nine months. Shelby swore she wouldn't go there. Would never... Oh God, she was crying! Hot tears winded down her cheeks. Dakota's gaze held hers. This wasn't a stare-down. Somehow, he'd sensed her grief. Her loss. And when tears slipped from her eyes, his face went tender with concern.

She whispered brokenly, "I—I lost my older brother, Jason, less than a year ago." She closed her eyes, the shame too much to bear. "H-he was an Army Ranger. He'd come home on leave after his third tour in Afghanistan." Sniffing, Shelby felt her heart being torn in two with all the grief she'd managed to wall up and hide from. She blinked, everything blurring because the tears continued to fall.

"Tell me," he urged, moving closer, their bodies inches from each other. Her pain was driving him crazy. Whatever it was, Shelby was devastated, her mouth contorted, the tears falling faster and faster. Sliding his long fingers around the slender nape of her neck, burying them in the softness of her hair, he angled her chin just enough to catch her tearful gaze. "You helped me. Now let me help you."

A fist of pain and gutting grief raced up through her. She could barely breathe the words. "Oh God, I'm so ashamed, so ashamed, Dakota. Jason committed suicide once he left us and went back to Afghanistan." There, it was out. Unwilling sobs rolled out of her. Blindly, Shelby sought refuge from it and took a step forward—into Dakota's arms.

His gray socks dropped to the tile floor. A groan issued from deep within Dakota as she fearlessly came to him. Her knees began to buckle, and he swept her up hard against him, holding her as she sobbed. The sounds were wild, harsh, and her grief nearly overwhelmed him. Nestling his jaw against her hair, the strands tickling his cheek, he held and gently rocked her. Her brother had been in the army. His mind whirled with the implications and information. Worst of all, he'd killed himself. Without thinking, simply responding, Dakota caressed her mussed hair with his lips. He kissed her fragrant skin where the hairline met near her ear.

Because of how much pain she'd been carrying, she must have seen her brother, Jason, in him. Dakota reined in his sexual hunger for her. God knew, he was aching and he wanted her, but this wasn't the right time or place. Instead, he focused on caring for Shelby the way she'd already cared for him. He moved his hand downward, rubbing her back as he tried to ease her pain. Shelby's weeping grew deeper. *Hold her. Just hold her,* he told himself.

Dakota didn't know how long they stood melded together in the kitchen. Slowly, Shelby's sobs lessened and finally ceased. Her fingers were pressed against his chest and he felt her warmth, her woman's strength even though the storm had passed. Lifting his chin, he leaned down, his lips brushing her ear. "Tears are never wasted, Shel…."

Shelby felt his moist breath, his tenderness. The strength of his arms gave her a sense of safety. As wounded as Dakota was, somehow he had the heart, the soul, to give back to her when she needed it the most. With the slow thud of his heart where her cheek rested against his chest, Shelby felt the backlog of pain dissolving.

Dakota continued to hold her. Right now she felt like a newborn, completely incapable of doing anything on her own. Shelby had never felt weak or unable to do anything she set her mind to. The grief and shame of Jason's suicide had wrecked her in ways she was unprepared for. And Dakota was here, holding her safe, absorbing her pain, her loss. Somewhere in the haze of her sorrow, she could see just how mentally tough Dakota really was. He was a deeply wounded warrior, and yet, in her hour of need, he rose to help her.

Shelby slid her arm beneath his, her fingers moving against his narrow waist. "I—don't know what happened. I didn't mean—"

"Shh," he rasped against her ear, content to feel her smooth, soft skin against his cheek. "No I'm-sorrys. Okay? You loved your brother. I know what it's like to lose…"

She felt him hesitate and then clear his throat. His arms tightened around her for a moment.

"You've been sitting on a lot of grief for a long, long time," Dakota told her. "I think my being here brought it all up. He was a Ranger and he did work similar to what the SEALs do. That's a lot of stress on a man, Shelby. Constant, sometimes nonstop stress for a solid year. It's hell on everyone."

Barely opening her eyes, she hiccuped. "I—I should have known he was in trouble, Dakota. I should have…"

"Why? You aren't trained to see pain a man wants to hide from you. Hell, I fooled a ton of shrinks for years so I could go back and be deployed with my platoon." *My family.*

She felt and heard his dark chuckle. The vibration riffled through her, soothed her torn emotional state. "There was never a sign…never. My poor parents, they're still devastated by it. We're all hurting so much…."

"I know, Shel, it's not easy to get over." Hell, he still hadn't gotten over the loss of his sister, Ellie, but now was not the time to bring that up. Dakota wanted to focus on Shelby's needs. Her warm, soft body molded against his. Her breasts were full, and he swore he could feel the nipples through that orange T-shirt she wore. Her breathing was softening, becoming normal now. The hiccups disappeared. Lifting his hand, he moved his fingers against her flushed cheek, removing the last of her tears.

"Things like this have their own time and way

with us. I'm sure your brother, Jason, was pretty burned out from constant danger, constant threat of dying. He probably lost some of his best friends over there. It all accumulates over time, Shel. It takes a toll on us. Some guys know how to defuse the grief. Some don't. Those are the ones who drown in it. Some turn to drugs. Some to drinking. And—" he lowered his tone "—some kill themselves because the pain is just too much for them to bear."

He gently brushed his fingers against Shelby's skin. How incredibly tender he was compared to his warrior self, moved through her thoughts. Her flesh tingled and Shelby found herself never wanting him to let go of her. "My dad was in the Marine Corps, a military policeman. Jason and I were military brats. Jason so badly wanted Dad to be proud of him."

"The Rangers, like the SEALs, demand a certain kind of mental toughness that damn few men will ever have," Dakota told her in a gruff tone, drying her cheek. Shelby's eyes were closed, a few small beads of tears clinging to her blond lashes. *Fragile.* She was fragile. Desperately, Dakota searched for the right damn words. But what were they? Hell, he was no philosopher. Not a poet. He was a SEAL in his heart and soul. "Shel, you can't blame yourself for what Jason did. You can't control anyone but yourself." Somehow Dakota wanted to ease her pain. But how?

Sighing heavily, Shelby nodded ever so slightly. She soaked up his male warmth, the strength he was feeding her. "I just don't know how to get over it. Neither do my parents. Every time I see them, there's this sorrow in their eyes. They're hurting so much. I want to help them, but I don't know how."

"Time will heal all of you, Shel." Dakota said the words but didn't believe them himself. Ellie's murder was like a hard lump of coal burning out his heart, slowly destroying his soul. His rage toward her rapists and killers was never far away from his memory. If he could get his hands on those two slimy sexual predators who had stolen her life, he'd kill them without remorse.

Slowly, Shelby eased away from Dakota. She didn't want to, but she knew she must—or else. Fully aware of his arousal, she understood he was there to somehow, in his own way, help her. Heal her. Yes, Dakota's touch was many things: healing, sexual, sensual and oh, how badly she ached to take him into her bed and lie with him. Looking up, she saw a golden glitter in the depths of his eyes, that of a man wanting his woman. The grief had subsided and seemed to have dissolved.

Surprised and relieved, Shelby knew she was an emotional mess right now. He released her from his embrace. He wanted her as much as she wanted him, but now was the wrong time.

Shelby leaned her hips against the kitchen counter, moving her fingers through her mussed hair, trying to tame the damp strands that had soaked up some of her tears. As she looked over at Dakota, she saw the dark blotches on his T-shirt where she'd cried so hard. Where she'd sobbed out her pain. Lifting her hand, her long fingers grazed the damp material. "I owe you another T-shirt."

Dakota caught her hand, brought it up to his lips and brushed a kiss on the back of it. The scent of her as a woman intoxicated him, his nostrils flaring as he inhaled her as deeply as he could into his aching body. "You were there for me. Remember?" He managed a lopsided smile as he released her hand. "I still don't know how the hell you got me off that floor and into your cruiser."

Tucking her hands in front of her, Shelby whispered, "Because I couldn't stand to see you die... and I knew you were dying."

"I was another Jason?"

Compressing her lips, she hung her head. "Y-yes, I guess you were."

"Only, I wasn't committing suicide, Shel."

Lifting her head, she managed a weak shrug. "No...no, you weren't. But inside me..." She touched her heart with her fingers. "I didn't want you to die. Jason took his life out in the bush. He had no one, Dakota. And neither did you." Her heart stirred with anguish. "Jason talked to no one about how he felt. The guys in his platoon never knew why he'd taken his life. They were just as shocked by it as we were."

"Your brother was a hero, Shel. I don't care what anyone tells you or what you think you know." He saw her eyes go dark with agony and he stepped up to her, slid his hand beneath her jaw and held her gaze. "Jason was a warrior. And you need to honor him for that, not how his life was taken. He's a hero in my eyes. So many times out there, you see too much. And some guys can't handle the amount of emotional hits they take over time, they can't process it...."

"Jason never talked about the missions. They were top secret. I—I tried to draw him out, because I could see how much he was suffering." Shelby closed her eyes, wanting his closeness. He gently moved his hand across her hair and allowed it to come to rest on her slumped shoulder. "I failed."

"No," Dakota rasped, his voice stronger. "You did not fail him. You felt he was in trouble, but you're no mind reader, Shel. None of us are."

She absorbed the warmth of his roughened hand on her shoulder. Did Dakota realize he was steadying her? "Then how did you realize I was hurting?"

His mouth pulled into a pained line. "At first, I

didn't. But then, as I showered, it all fell into place. I saw I'd somehow upset you in the bedroom."

"I was just thinking about you in that bed… knowing you'd almost died, but we were able to get you to the hospital in time…." Shelby admitted.

He heard the weariness in her voice, the ache of loss. "And no one was able to reach Jason in time?"

Nodding, Shelby lifted her hand and rubbed her face. "Right."

"And that's when you started feeling the grief you've been sitting on. I watched you close down."

"Yes, I was thinking about Jason. It wasn't your fault," she said, searching his hooded gaze. "Please, believe me. It wasn't you, Dakota. I guess these past couple of days have torn off the scab I was keeping over all the emotions I was running from since Jason died."

Moving his fingers in a gentle motion, he followed the line of her shoulder, slid his fingers up across her neck until he cupped her jaw. Moving forward until he could feel the female heat coming off her body, he leaned down. His mouth hovered inches from her own. "Sometimes," he whispered, "when two people are in pain, the best thing they can do is help each other. Shel, I want to kiss you, but I won't unless you tell me it's all right."

Her lashes moved upward and he drowned in the blue of her gaze. Her pupils were huge, black and shining with life once again. In that second,

Dakota knew he'd helped Shelby, even if just a little bit. Their breaths quickened, mingled moisture flowing against each other's faces.

His mouth hovered above hers. His body screamed for release, wanting her in every way possible. Her eyes held a touch of fearlessness, black against that gleaming background of turquoise.

He felt the rush of her breath against his mouth, saw her lashes shutter against her flushed cheeks. He heard her whisper the word, "Yes." In moments, he curved his mouth against hers, and Dakota knew his life was about to change forever.

CHAPTER EIGHT

A SMALL MOAN rose in Shelby as Dakota took her mouth, his arms wrapping around her, drawing her close, into himself. She moved her arms upward, sliding around his broad shoulders, which felt like granite beneath her fingertips. Oh God, this was exactly what she needed! In some distant part of her barely functioning brain, she could feel his mouth cherishing hers, his arms holding her as if she were fragile and might break at a moment's notice. His breath was short, sharp as he slowly tasted her mouth for the first time. Reveling in the sense of safety and protection he automatically gave her, Shelby returned his deep, searching kiss. Nothing had ever felt so right. Nothing...

Her cell phone rang.

At first, it startled Shelby. She clung to his male mouth, tasting him, absorbing him as a man, as a warrior. Yet she felt him tense when the phone went off, too. Sadness mixed with the raging need buried deep in her belly. She wanted Dakota. All of him. In every way imaginable.

The phone continued to ring.

"Damn phone," Shelby muttered against his mouth. "I've got to get it, Dakota... I'm sorry." She reluctantly pulled out of his arms.

Throbbing heat soared through Dakota as he released Shelby so she could walk quickly to the table where her cell was. His mouth tingled wildly. He could taste her on his lips. Her scent teased his nostrils. She was flushed, her eyes drowsy, filled with arousal—for him. Having felt so beaten down by the past year, Dakota felt strong and good once again. Shelby's lips had been sweet, woman-strong, and she was meeting him without reserve. God, how he wanted her in his bed, beneath his hands, wanting to take her...

Grabbing the cell, Shelby opened it. This was the sheriff's cell phone and she knew it would be about business. "Shelby."

"Cade here."

Closing her eyes for a moment, she turned and stared longingly toward Dakota. His face was hard, eyes intent upon her. He wanted her. She wanted him. Damn the phone call. "What's going on?"

Dakota stood relaxed near the kitchen counter listening closely to Shelby's breathy voice. The flush in her cheeks slowly left. His gaze locked on her mouth. He could feel her kissing him eagerly, with abandon, once again. Knowing he could have healed some of her raw pain and loss, he wondered

if there would ever be another time. Seeing her
brow wrinkle, her voice suddenly go low, he sensed
something very bad had just occurred.

Leaning down, he picked up the socks, ambled
over to the table, pulled out a chair and sat down.
He tugged them on each of his feet, and listened to
the conversation. Their moment together was gone.
He grieved over the loss. Shelby straightened, her
body going tense, her voice strained. What the hell
was happening? Did Cade Garner call her at home
like this often? She was supposed to be on her off
day. Disgruntled, Dakota felt his state of arousal
ebb away. Whatever the conversation, it was deeply
affecting Shelby. The soft, drowsy look he'd seen
as he kissed her was replaced with sudden intensity coupled with anxiety. And if he read her right,
it was fear.

Shelby listened closely to Cade.

"Is Dakota there? I'd called over at the hospital and Jordana said she'd had him moved to your
place."

"Yes…he's here. Do you want to talk with him?"
Shelby stared across the table at Dakota. He looked
grim now, the desire doused in his eyes. Regret-
ting losing the heated moment, she said, "Okay,
hold on." She reached across the table and handed
the cell to him. "It's Cade Garner. He needs to
speak to you."

Surprised, Dakota took the phone. Their fingers met and he hungrily absorbed her fleeting touch. Her eyes were anxious-looking and he saw her chew on her lower lip for a moment. "Dakota here," he rumbled, putting the cell to his ear.

Shelby turned, wrapping her arms tightly about herself as she walked to the kitchen counter. God, her world had suddenly been turned inside out. Her mind raced. Yet she kept one ear on Dakota's reaction to what Cade was going to ask of him. Rubbing her brow, she felt a slight headache coming on. Oh God, they escaped! And now her life wouldn't be her own until they were caught—again.

She turned, desperate to hold on to the beautiful, healing moments before with Dakota. His face had gone tense, eyes flashing with what she interpreted as anger. His mouth, those lips that had moved commandingly against hers, had stolen her breath, taken her on a wild, hot ride into near oblivion, were now pursed. Thinned to a single, hard line. Shelby could feel his powerful reaction to what Cade was filling him in on. Wincing internally, Shelby watched as if a bomb had gone off near Dakota. He slowly rose out of the chair, his mouth taut, his fingers curling slowly into a thick fist. What was going on? She didn't understand, feeling the tension suddenly swirl through the room as if a tornado had just struck.

"We'll be there in about thirty minutes," Dakota growled. He flipped the phone closed, set it on the table and lifted his head. His gaze locked onto Shelby's. For a moment, she looked fragile. He recalled that wild, hot kiss that held such promise of things to come. Drenched with rage, with shock, he held her frowning gaze, those beautiful lips compressed.

"We need to talk," he said, gesturing for her to come and sit down at the table. "Cade wants us at the sheriff's office in thirty minutes."

Hearing the low growl in his tone, Shelby nodded. She allowed her arms to drop to her sides and then sat down opposite Dakota. "Two convicts escaped. He wanted to ask you if you would track with me to find them."

Dakota rubbed his recently shaven jaw. "Yeah. Only," he said as he sighed roughly, "there's more to it you don't know, Shel." He reached out, gripping her hands folded in front of her on the table. "Damn, I didn't want to discuss this with you yet."

She tilted her head. "Do you not want to track with me?" She remembered his initial reaction to a woman being able to track. His hand was rough on her soft skin, but it felt comforting to her.

Shaking his head, Dakota released her hand, reared back on two legs of the chair, looking up to the ceiling, fighting his violent emotions. "No… no, it has nothing to do with that, Shel." He took in a ragged breath, looked at the ceiling for a long moment and then back to her. "I was hoping not to have this conversation with you for a long time. You're hurting right now. Damn. I'm sorry. So sorry…"

Shelby could hear the undisguised anguish in his tone. "I don't understand, Dakota. What is it? You look really upset." Her first reaction was to get up, throw her arms around him and hold him. The raw, gritty look in his eyes startled her. Made her afraid. What was he hiding?

"Cade told you that two death row convicts, Vance Welton and Oren Hartley, just escaped. That they're heading for Yellowstone National Park to disappear into the forests so the authorities can't find them." His eyes shuttered closed for a second. His mouth became a hard line, as if he was fighting back a barrage of unknown emotions.

"Dakota? What is going on? Do you know these two criminals?"

His heart twisted hard in his chest. For a moment, Dakota wasn't sure he could handle it. It took every ounce of SEAL control over his feelings to stop it from happening. The wariness on the edge of Shelby's voice helped him. Gulping hard, he shoved everything—everything—back down deep inside himself. Opening his eyes, he stared down at the table for a moment. "This is coming at the wrong damned time," he breathed, his voice sounding like a rasp against metal.

Shelby reached out. She wanted to touch him.

Her fingers slid over his tightly balled hands. "Dakota? What's wrong? Let me help?" She tipped her head to catch his downcast gaze.

How could he feel so goddamned miserable? Dakota couldn't recall any firefight feeling as dangerous and life-threatening as how he felt right now. He opened his hands, needed Shelby's warm, firm touch. Studying her long fingers, he turned them over gently in his palms. He struggled to find the words he needed to speak.

He lifted his head. If it had been anyone but her, Dakota wouldn't have said what he was going to say. The words, each one, tore out of him, a razor slicing into his tightened throat, bleeding him out, bleeding him dry until he thought he was going to die as Ellie had died.

"When I saw you out in the parking lot of the hospital, I thought I knew you, Shelby. I was in too much shock to pursue it. And talking to Cade just now, I realize where I saw you—in the Cody, Wyoming, courthouse nine years ago."

Shelby kept staring at him. Her mind wrenched back to that time and place. It became clearer. She shook her head. "Your last name…Carson…I thought I knew the name, but so much was going on at the E.R., I just couldn't remember."

"I know these two bastards, Shelby. My sister, Ellie Carson, was nineteen when those two jumped her when she was leaving Cody University one evening. She—she was taking classes to become a registered nurse. I was seventeen at the time. They hauled her into an abandoned house nearby and…" His voice dropped. Tears jammed into Dakota's eyes and he was helpless to stop them from forming. Shelby's hands tightened around his and her face suddenly went pale. The rest had to be said, like cutting into a very old, festering wound to release the toxins eating away at his soul. "They tortured her, raped her repeatedly and finally slit her throat and killed her."

Without thinking, Shelby stood up and quietly moved around the table. Dakota had pushed his hands across his face, trying to hide the tears coming down his drawn cheeks. She pulled up a chair, sitting facing him. Slipping her arms around his tense, bunched shoulders, she nestled her head against his clenched jaw. "I'm so sorry, so very sorry, Dakota. My God, I didn't know…." She held him with her woman's strength.

The past struck Shelby full force. She'd had one day in court to testify and she remembered seeing the Carson family, the grief on their collective faces. Vaguely, she recalled the teen boy with the parents. That had been Dakota. Time had changed him markedly from a tall, slender boy into the man he was today.

A new feeling flowed through her as she held him. They were both frozen in time over a horrific event that clearly connected them today. Dakota was still held prisoner by it. A shudder worked through him, and Shelby sensed his internal strength to control the violence of his grief. He was strong in ways she would never be. Kissing his cheek, Shelby inhaled his male scent. She continued to place small, tender kisses against his brow, cheek and jaw. Little by little, she felt him begin to relax, to trust himself to her caring arms.

Gradually, Dakota stuffed all the rage and horror down into a hole he never wanted to open again. Shelby's arms were strong and he greedily absorbed her silent care. Her lips were soft and healing against his flesh, and God, how badly he needed her. An IED going off under him would have thrown him into the same kind of shock he was experiencing right now with the news Cade Garner had just given him.

He eased Shelby away from him and held her hand, a lifeline for him as he stared into her eyes filled with compassion. "Thanks," he managed, voice rough with unshed tears.

She continued to hold his hand. "I remember you in the courtroom now, Dakota. And your parents. I was there for only one day to testify in capturing them. I wasn't there for the whole trial, although I had been briefed on it by the prosecutor's office." She swallowed against a forming lump. "That's why you looked familiar to me and vice versa."

Shaking her head, she muttered, "At times like this, we all need someone. You were there for me. Now I'm here for you. Did you tell Cade you'd track with me?"

Nodding, he studied her soft, long fingers. "Yeah, I did."

"There's more to this story, Dakota."

What else could there be? He frowned. "What are you talking about?"

"I was just coming on the sheriff's force as a deputy, my first week, and my father was still the commander here. I'd graduated from high school at sixteen. I was one of those bright kids who skipped grades." She managed a disconcerted smile. "I went to a law enforcement academy and graduated at eighteen. We got word of the terrible murder of your sister. Law enforcement was able to prove those two escaped into Yellowstone. My father had been teaching me to track since I was five years old. He knew I was good at what I did. He ordered me to go with a multi–law enforcement team of other trackers and dogs to try to find those two."

Looking deep into her eyes, feeling as if he could fall into them, be lost forever and never look back, Dakota nodded. "Cade didn't tell me that."

Shelby moved her fingers across his hand, a hand with so many scars on the front and back of it. Each white slice was pain he'd experienced. Softly, she wanted to give him respite from a life that was obviously filled with nothing but suffering. "I left the team once we were inside the park. I had a hunch, and it played out to be correct. I found the car they'd stolen near Norris Basin. I called it in and followed them on foot into the woods."

His skin crawled as he realized she had been in absolute jeopardy with Welton and Hartley. Eyes widening, Dakota knew if they'd ever found her, they'd have raped and murdered her just as they had Ellie. His throat closed off. "You must have found them first?" He saw a tight grin pull at her lips.

"Better believe it. They were like two bulls. Broken brush, bent limbs they'd stepped on. You know how hard it is to track on a pine needle floor, but they left plenty of other clues for me to follow."

In utter disbelief, he demanded, "Did you corner them?"

"Yes." She rolled her shoulders to relieve the tension of that moment when she'd suddenly come upon the two murderers. "I was fresh out of law enforcement training. The only time I'd ever fired my pistol was at practice targets. I found them resting by a group of boulders, pulled my pistol and told them to freeze. I called on my radio for backup."

Disbelief soared through Dakota. He remembered first seeing Shelby in that courtroom. Even though she wore a sheriff's uniform, to him she didn't look more than a mere slip of a young girl. "What did they do?"

"Cursed at me," she said wryly.

"They didn't think you were going to really shoot them?"

"Oh, they got it," she answered, her voice hardening. "They were sexual predators of the worst sort. I'm prejudiced against that kind of man, anyway."

"Welton was the ringleader. Didn't he challenge you?"

Shaking her head, her eyes taking on a dark look, she said, "I told them to make my day."

Dakota remembered the famous line spoken by Clint Eastwood in *Dirty Harry*. A grin edged his mouth. "They believed you."

"It's a side of me you haven't seen yet, Dakota. I hated them. I'd never felt hate before, but standing there, my pistol in my hands, aimed at them, I hated. I told them to just give me one excuse to blow their heads off their shoulders."

Dakota saw the spark of anger deep in her blue eyes. There was nothing cute or fuzzy about Shelby right now. He was seeing her strength, an internal kind that he was well acquainted with. It was shocking to see she possessed it, too. But why not? Women were strong, he knew. "They sat there?"

"Yes. I had them lie on their bellies, hands behind their necks. The rest of my team arrived and they cuffed them, read them their rights and hauled their asses back to Cody, Wyoming."

"Unbelievable." He gave her an assessing look. "You must be one hell of a tracker, then."

"I am. My dad taught me well."

"Wasn't he worried for your safety? He knew Welton and Hartley had already killed my sister."

"Yes, he was. But he also knew he'd taught me how to track and use a rifle ever since I could remember. I knew Yellowstone like the back of my hand, Dakota. What my dad didn't want me doing was peeling off from the main team, which I did." Her laugher was throaty. "When I got back to the office to write up my report, he chewed my ass royally. He told me never to leave my tracking partner again."

"At least someone had some common sense."

Shrugging, Shelby sighed and released his hand. "I was young and green. I've got nine years in with the sheriff's department and I'm a lot more seasoned now. And smart," she added, seeing the look of respect come to his face. It made her feel good because earlier, Dakota had treated her like a helpless, brainless doll.

"I sat through the entire trial. My parents were shattered by the loss of Ellie. I sat there hating them, wanting to wrap my hands around each one of their throats and slowly killing them, like they'd killed my sister."

She sighed. "You were only seventeen. It must

have been so hard on you," she murmured, "and on your poor parents."

Nodding, Dakota wiped his face harshly with his hand. The past was staring him in the face. Again. "I wanted to even the scales. So many times, I tried to imagine the terror, the pain that Ellie felt. It nearly drove me insane. I finally had to get away and I escaped and went into the navy. I couldn't handle all the feelings ripping through me. My parents were depressed. I couldn't help them."

"I'm sure I'd feel exactly the same way." Shelby watched him struggled with his emotions. "Are you sure you want to track with me? Will you be able to control your emotions, clear your head to track?" Instantly, there came a feral change in his gold-brown eyes, that of powerful focus. She actually felt an energy shift around him. The change was startling. Was this his SEAL training coming out, the warrior side taking over? Because if it was, Shelby had no question that Dakota would not only track with her; he'd find them. And he'd want to kill them.

"You only know a small part of me." He said the words in grate. "I'm a SEAL. I'm no longer in the navy, but the training will always be with me. I have my reflexes. My knowledge gained by six months of deployment every two years into Iraq and Afghanistan. I have the control I need to hunt down these sick bastards."

"Okay," she said, standing up, "then we need to saddle up. Cade is expecting us shortly."

His gut clenched and he stared at her. "You let me do the tracking." He wanted those two bastards so bad he could taste it. Find them and kill them.

Her brows rose. "Excuse me?" She saw his face grow cold.

"You don't need to go along," he grated.

She scowled. "There's no way I'm staying off this case."

Gut churning, Dakota felt a desperation similar to when Ellie was announced as missing. He'd intuitively picked up that she was in trouble. That same feeling washed over him again. Shelby stood there, looking so damned confident. And his heart lurched with new terror. What if they got ahold of Shelby this time? What if he wasn't there to protect her? She'd gotten lucky the first time she'd caught those two. He rubbed his chin, holding her stubborn stare. "You can't go along with me."

Shelby held on to her mounting anger. Instead, she tried to understand what was going on in his mind. Was he worried about her? Shelby considered his reactions carefully, her instincts telling her that Dakota's past was bleeding into the present. He might not even see her right now. He might see Ellie. And if he did, Dakota would want her safe, not on the trail tracking with him. She opened her hands, a plea in her husky tone. "Look, I know a lot's gotten dumped on you, Dakota. I can take care of myself out there."

His heart lurched with other emotions he thought he'd never experience. And just as abruptly, he buried them. The tender expression in Shelby's eyes touched him. All he could do was shake his head. There was no way he could get involved with her on a personal level. His rage was always there, lurking. Dakota was sorry he'd kissed her. Sorry to his soul because she didn't need a wounded, broken man in her life. He wanted to protect her from himself, as well. She deserved something a helluva lot better than him.

"We'll see…" he growled, finally. He would talk to Cade Garner and convince him to keep Shelby safe and he'd do the tracking by himself. Alone, as he had been for so many years already.

"Okay," she murmured, wanting to defuse the tension. "We'll talk about it later."

Rising, the sound of the chair scraping back across the tiled surface, Dakota muttered softly, "Wheels up." He walked over to her, cupping her elbow, looking down into her uplifted gaze. "We're going Down Range."

"What does that mean?"

"Going into combat." He was. She wasn't.

The warrior emerged in him. No longer did she see grief or unbridled emotions in his flat, hard eyes. His entire demeanor had shifted. Dakota was not open or vulnerable anymore. Just the opposite, hard as titanium with a ruthless, calculated expression. He meant business. He was going to extract the revenge he'd always wanted against these two convicts.

The realization left her throat dry. If she hadn't seen and experienced the softer side of him as a man, she would have been deeply shaken by his countenance right now. Was this how Jason was on a mission as a Ranger? Did he change faces? Put on this warrior mask to do his work?

Mouth dry, she whispered, "Yes, we're going Down Range...together."

CHAPTER NINE

VANCE WELTON SMILED. They'd just stolen their third car within Yellowstone Park and were five miles away from the south entrance to the national park. Driving the speed limit, Vance told Oren, "We did some serious planning. The cops have *no* idea where we are."

Oren Hartley, twenty-nine, black hair and blue eyes, stretched out his long legs. "Well, we did this once before. We ought to get it right the second time around, don't you think?" He absently chewed on a toothpick lodged in the corner of his mouth.

Snorting, Oren said, "Dude, you got that right." His short, thick hands moved firmly on the steering wheel of the stolen Toyota Camry. They'd stopped at Grant Village at a gas station and restaurant inside the park. Looking for a nondescript car had been their objective. The dark blue Camry filled the bill. It had been easy to steal it from the corner of the busy parking lot.

Oren pushed his fingers through his short hair.

"They're gonna think we're hiding in Yellowstone again."

Oren's thin brows drew down. "Yeah, well, we aren't making that mistake again."

"Hiding out in the Tetons and goin' after that bitch, Shelby Kincaid, was a good idea," Oren drawled. He shifted the dark sunglasses on his nose. He'd found the pair in the glove box of the car. Not only that, a suitcase in the trunk was full of men's summer hiking clothes they could wear. Best of all, whoever the owner of the Camry was, he was about their height of five feet ten inches. Making sure they changed clothes and cars every few hours had been a major part of their plan in order to evade law enforcement. Even though the dude who owned this car would eventually walk out to find it gone, the reporting on it would take time.

Hands tightening on the wheel, Welton snarled, "She tracked us down and put us in prison." Thin mouth moving into a hard line, he added softly, "First things first. We'll take one of the many dirt roads in the Tetons park, find a cabin somewhere on a slope, hide for a few days and get settled in."

"Goodbye, Yellowstone," Oren sang out, lifting his hand as they drove out of the national park. He chuckled. "Dadgum, but this is easy."

"Don't get too cocky, hillbilly."

Oren sighed. "I figure we'll stop halfway be-

tween here and the Tetons and swap out cars. Colter Bay Village is our next stop."

"Yes." They wore latex gloves to ensure that
their prints would not connect them with the car
theft. Vance knew law enforcement because he'd
had battles with them since he was twelve years
old. He'd shot a dog, and the neighbor had seen
him do it. He liked to see how a bullet would kill
an animal, but he really got pissed when he was
thrown into the juvenile court system. It was just
a stupid dog! That was all right, he got even with
the neighbor who reported him to the police. At
fourteen, he'd sneaked out of the house in the early
morning hours and set fire to the guy's house. And
too bad, the family had died in the fire.

Chuckling to himself, Welton felt proud that no
one ever pinned that house fire on him. At an early
age, he found out he liked sex, too. Never mind his
father liked to play with his genitals since he could
remember. Vance liked hunting down innocent little girls and sticking it to them. Of course, that
came to a roaring halt when a mother discovered
him with her seven-year-old daughter. At fifteen,
he was once again thrown in a juvenile detention
facility. Good thing his records were sealed when
he turned eighteen.

"Hey, I can hardly wait to start tracking the bitch
myself." Oren rubbed his hands together, a grin
coming to his round face. He wore a blue baseball

cap. They knew they had to disguise themselves in order to stay under the radar of cops and the public. "But, man, I got needs, Vance. You sure we can't take some time out, get our rocks off and then go hunt Kincaid down?"

Vance snarled. "Hell no! Keep it in your pants, you dumb hillbilly. I've been planning this for a long time and I'm damn well not diverting from it so you can screw around."

Oren sighed dramatically and pulled the bill of the cap lower over his eyes. "You're no fun, partner."

"Kincaid caught us." His voice lowered to a growl. "We're sticking to my plan. That bitch, once we find her, is gonna be so friggin' sorry she ever tracked us down in the first place." He had nightly dreams about tying her to a bed, torturing her and then raping her. He was going to watch the fear come to her eyes, listen to her scream, watch her bleed. Oh, he'd keep her alive for a couple of weeks, torturing her daily, enjoying her pain, paying her back for what she did to them.

Oren dug into the glove box, looking for something to eat. "I'm with you all the way, good buddy. You sure you have a place that's hidden away so no one will ever find us?"

A chuckle erupted from Vance. The forest was on either side of the two-lane highway, the sky a powdery-blue midafternoon. "I do. Remember? We lived in this area before we got caught? I'm going straight to Curt Downing in Jackson Hole first. We ran drugs for him. Now maybe he can help us out a little. We need a truck that isn't stolen. He owns a trucking company. He'll have plenty of trucks around we can use."

Gleefully, Oren located a couple of protein bars in the glove box and drew them out. He tossed one in Vance's lap and tore off the wrapping on the second one. "I never trusted Downing. He's too full of himself," he murmured, chewing the honey-sweetened grains. "You never know what he's thinking. And my hillbilly instincts tell me he's not gonna be happy to see us show up."

"Too bad. He owes us. He just has to be reminded of it, is all. Downing can supply us with money and a truck."

"He's a slick bastard, Vance. I don't think he's gonna willingly do anything for us."

"Well, we'll have a little chat," he said, smiling smugly. A sheriff's cruiser passed them. They'd seen a number of law enforcement vehicles throughout the park—all looking for them. Although Vance had a bald head, he was going to let the hair and beard grow so that he wouldn't be so easily identified.

"There goes another deputy dawg," Oren drawled, hooking his thumb over his shoulder.

"They all think we're hidden in Yellowstone. The dumb assholes."

"What's first on our list?"

"Get another car, get inside the Tetons National Park and then find us a cabin."

"Then go seek out Downing?"

"In that order," Vance said, looking in his rear-view mirror to make sure that black Tahoe sheriff's cruiser was still heading into Yellowstone. It was. Glee filled him. All the years of careful planning were finally going to pay off.

"THIS IS A FUBAR," Dakota said quietly to Shelby as they stood near the rear of a multi–law enforcement meeting in Yellowstone. His eyes flashed with frustration as he watched the FBI, the U.S. Forest Service rangers and the sheriff's deputies from two other surrounding counties standing around a huge table filled with maps of the park.

Shelby stood next to him remembering their kiss. They had driven up on orders of Commander McCall. Leaning close, an excuse to touch him, she whispered, "Cade Garner is the only one who might be able to break this logjam. He'll be here shortly."

Instinctively, Dakota inhaled her fragrance. After they'd gotten the call, their intimate time with each had come to an abrupt, jarring halt. His gaze dropped to her mouth. Instantly, his body went hot. "The right hand doesn't know what the left hand's doing here." They'd stood in this room for two hours, watching reports come in on a number of stolen cars. A forest ranger had a large map hanging up on one wall and was putting red pins in it where the vehicles had been stolen. It was simple math in Dakota's mind: the escaped convicts were stealing them, swapping out the cars, throwing law enforcement off their trail and heading south, out of the park.

Grimacing, Shelby couldn't disagree. Cade Garner finally entered the large, crowded room. He wore a serious expression on his face and he went directly to the FBI agent, Collin Woods, who was running the show.

"We've got a new report of a Toyota Camry being stolen near the south gate of the park," he told Woods, handing him the paperwork.

Wood, who was in his mid-forties, short and lean, studied the report. He handed it to the forest ranger who was pushing red pins on the wall map. "Put it up," he ordered.

Cade studied the map. "These guys aren't staying in Yellowstone," he warned everyone. Going to the map, he traced his finger across the eastern gate highway. There were two red pins. At the main intersection, where the highway went south, there were now three red pins.

Woods scowled. "Vance Welton and Oren Hartley hid for two weeks near Norris Basin in this park. They aren't going to change their *modus operandi*."

Shelby moved her head, a silent gesture to tell Dakota to follow her. She was the only woman present. He gave her a bare nod in return and they moved around the group huddled around the table. Garner's face went dark with anger. His eyes flashed. He was a good sheriff's deputy, now number-two man in the Tetons County department.

"No?" Cade Garner jammed his index finger into the third red pin area. "That stolen car is only twenty-two miles from the south entrance to the park."

"You're assuming it's them," Woods said, impatient.

"Damn right I am," Garner breathed, holding his anger in tight check. He turned to Shelby. "You tracked these sick bastards before. Does this look like their M.O.?" he asked.

Shelby noticed the dismissive look Woods gave her. He was an arrogant little man in a black suit, white shirt and dark blue tie. She moved her finger along the highway at the east gate entrance. "Yes, it does, Cade. Look here." She brought her finger to Norris Basin, in the northwestern area of the park. "When I was tracking them, they had already turned south and were heading in the direction of the south gate entrance on foot."

"You can't be sure of that," Woods spouted. "You can't read their minds."

Dakota stepped around Shelby, glaring into Wood's arrogant face. "Listen, she's a tracker. In order to successfully track a target, you have to get inside the head of the escapee. She knows what the hell she's talking about." He loomed over the agent, who cowered beneath each of his carefully enunciated words. Woods took a step back, scowling up at Carson.

"And just who are you?" Woods challenged.

Dakota was the only man in civilian clothes, dressed in jeans, a red polo shirt and hiking boots in the room. He stood out like a sore thumb.

"Agent Woods," Shelby spoke up, her voice strong and brooking no argument, "this is Dakota Carson. Our commander requested his aid. He was a U.S. Navy SEAL, a tracker and sniper in his platoon."

Woods shrugged. "Whatever…we're not over in Afghanistan."

Cade Garner moved a step closer toward the FBI agent. "Agent Woods, you obviously don't appreciate what SEALs do. Mr. Carson has a lot of experience tracking in some of the worst places in the world, and successfully tracking down the enemy. We need him on this hunt for a thousand good reasons."

Quirking his thin mouth, Woods said, "Great. This is just what I need."

Dakota's right hand curled slowly into a fist. The little bastard. He had respect for all law enforcement but they'd been cursed with one bad apple. He gave Cade a warning look. This agent didn't know squat.

Most of the men were restless, wanting to do something other than standing for hours in this room trying to figure out the location of Welton and Hartley.

"Mr. Woods, with all due respect, Deputy Kincaid tracked these two sexual predators and murderers for two weeks here in Yellowstone. The dogs lost their trail a number of times, but she never did. Your presumptions about my team are baseless," Cade Garner said.

Shelby felt Dakota tense behind her. He came and stood at her shoulder. Automatically, she moved her hand back, warning him to remain silent. This was a turf war between Garner and Woods.

Woods shrugged. "The FBI has trackers, too," he flung out defensively to the group.

"They didn't find these two the last time," Garner reminded him acidly. "It was Shelby Kincaid, a sheriff's deputy. She was born here and she knows the land like the back of her hand," he said in a low voice.

"I wasn't on that case. I'm on this one and it will be different."

Shelby almost laughed. She placed her hand against her mouth so Woods wouldn't catch her smiling.

Garner drew himself up, his eyes slits as he surveyed the tense room. "Gentlemen, we've got two of the worst sexual predators in our county loose." His voice dropped to a warning rasp. "And I'll be damned if anyone is going to get caught up in the fact that our best tracker is a woman and damned good at what she does."

Garner turned, jamming a finger at the map. "My instincts are screaming at me that these two are already out of the park and heading south. I'm calling my commander, alerting him to just that and seeing if another car gets stolen between here and Jackson Hole. These guys have a plan, Agent Woods. And I'm not wasting one more minute of my time here in this damned room. We must follow the string of stolen cars. It's our only choice."

Dakota felt himself imploding with rage. He wanted to jerk Woods up by his expensive black suit lapels and pin his scrawny ass on that wall map. Ellie had been tortured and raped and had died at the hands of these two convicts. He felt Shelby's cool fingers pulling his fist apart, lacing them between her own. It broke the circuit of his building anger. She looked up, met his gaze, and barely shook her head. How did she know he was ready to kill the little weasel?

"Well, you go right ahead and call your commander," Woods said. "This is our command post."

Cade gestured to Shelby and Dakota to follow him. "Fine. You call me when you think you know what the hell you're doing. The evidence that Welton and Hartley are heading south toward Jackson Hole is as plain as those red tacks on the map."

Shelby kept her mouth fixed to stop her smile. Woods smirked, lifted his chin at an imperious angle as Cade spun on his heel and strode toward the door.

She turned and followed him. So did Dakota.

Once outside the building, Cade turned to them. He glanced at his watch. "Okay, there's nothing you two can do right now. If we can't find these two, you can't track them."

Dakota liked the way the deputy thought. "Why would they not hide in the park again? They managed to evade everyone for two weeks."

Cade's expression became grim. His gaze moved to Shelby. "I didn't want to say anything in there, Shelby, but my gut's screaming something else at me. It would explain why they're not trying to hole up in Yellowstone."

She frowned. "What?" Rarely had she seen her boss this worried. Or tense.

"Don't you see, Shelby? Those convicts are coming after you."

Shocked, she stared up at Cade. Her mouth dropped open for a second, considering the possibility. "I—never thought about that."

"I'm worried for you. You're the one who put them away. Vance Welton is well-known to get even, to take revenge on anyone who crosses him. You have his file, you know his background. It can't be lost on you that if he ever escaped, he'd want to finish business with you first."

For a moment, Shelby stood and allowed the idea to sink in. Dakota's hand on her shoulder felt stabilizing. "I wasn't thinking in that direction," she choked out. It made perfect sense.

Cade looked around the busy parking lot filled with tourists. Keeping his voice down, he took a step toward them. "Look, I hope like hell I'm wrong, Shelby."

"You're not," Dakota growled. "I came to the same conclusion a while ago."

Cade nodded, grim. "You're good at this, Dakota. You might not be in law enforcement, but you have one hell of a wolf nose on you. We have two things we must do. First, see if another tourist reports a stolen car on the south highway out of Yellowstone. That would be the Colby Bay Village area. Second—" his gaze burrowed into hers "—we need to get you to a safe house, Shelby. If

Welton and Hartley are around, they're going to watch and wait for the right moment to grab you out of your home."

Shelby automatically wrapped her arms across her chest. Vance Welton was a sexual predator from seven years old onward. There were two cold cases involving other young women in Cody, Wyoming. They had been kidnapped, tortured for weeks, raped innumerable times before their throats were slit. Law enforcement was sure this was Welton and Hartley's work. It was their M.O. Unfortunately, the law couldn't get enough evidence to prove it. And neither of the two would admit doing it during interrogation for Ellie Carson's murder.

Shelby had attended the trial for the murder of Ellie Carson for only one day, but it was one she'd never forget. Shelby shut her eyes, remembering the event. Remembering how the body of beautiful Ellie Carson flashed across a screen to show the jury just exactly what Hartley and Welton had done to her. A tremor passed through Shelby, the horrifying color photos never forgotten.

Dakota placed his hand on her shoulder. He saw the shock registering in her eyes and wanted to protect her. These two murderers would never get near her. "She's got a safe house, Cade."

"What?" Shelby twisted a look up at his hard, unreadable face. The man she knew was no longer present. This was the SEAL warrior and she could feel the tension radiating around him like a thunderstorm about to unleash its destructive power.

Cade looked at her and then over at Dakota. "Your cabin?"

"That's right. It's damn near impregnable. One way in and one way out. Most people can't even locate the road." He dug into Shelby's widening eyes as she realized what they were talking about. "You'll stay with me, Shelby. Those two gomers won't be able to find you. They might find out where you live, but you aren't going to be there. Not until we can apprehend these bastards."

Shelby stood mute for a moment, considering all the ramifications. She felt Dakota's fingers dig a little more firmly into her shoulder, as if to keep her from protesting.

What would it be like to live with him? Their connection was already fiery. Where was this going? Could she handle him and still be alert for Welton and Hartley? The fact that they might be tracking her shook her as little else ever had. "I just never thought..."

"That you'd become their target?" Dakota asked, holding her shaken gaze.

"I don't know if you remember his outburst because you weren't there for the entire trial," Cade said to Dakota. "After Shelby left the stand, Welton screamed at Shelby. He promised he'd get out and hunt her down. And he'd kill her just like he killed Ellie Carson."

Dakota felt an invisible KA-BAR knife slitting him from groin to neck, opening up everything between those two points. The serrated blade was used by SEALs precisely because it gutted and killed swiftly. Nothing was left alive after a slice or jab from this military knife blade. His heart contracted and he felt a new, different pain as he regarded Shelby. He'd forgotten that outburst in court, so mired in his own grieving at the time. His mind spun with anxiety—for her. Welton's threat in court did nothing but confirmed his intuition.

"I remember that...now..." His voice dropped to a rasp.

She couldn't hold on to the terror moving through her. "Y-yes. He said all those things." Opening her eyes, she gave Dakota a helpless look. "It didn't occur to me after Welton escaped that he was coming after me."

"Well, he's going to have to come through me first," Dakota said.

CHAPTER TEN

"ANOTHER CAR HAS BEEN stolen at Colby Bay," Cade informed Shelby and Dakota. They had arrived at the sheriff's department only minutes earlier, when a dispatcher gave him the news.

Shelby stood, hands on hips, her mind churning over the situation. "Okay, that confirms it's probably them. Is the car going to be checked for fingerprints?"

Cade sat at his desk, moving paperwork around. "Yes, as soon as I can get a forensics tech up there."

Dakota moved restively around the small room. He hated enclosed spaces like this. "What about the other cars stolen? Who's checked them for prints?"

Cade grimaced. "Agent Woods had his other FBI agent out doing it."

"Great," Shelby said, frowning, "we'll get those results when hell freezes over."

"Now, now," Cade murmured, grinning sourly, "we can't speak ill of our FBI cohorts. Woods is just not the ideal agent for this case. I'm sure they'll get their results to us. It's just a question of when."

Snorting, Dakota stopped pacing and growled, "Things would be done a helluva lot differently if a SEAL team were put on this op."

"I'm sure," Cade said. His gaze moved to Shelby. "We need to sit down and plan what's happening with you until we can apprehend these two."

Shelby held up her hands. "Whoa. What does that mean, Cade? I've already agreed to stay up at Dakota's cabin. Isn't that enough?"

"I'm inclined to take you off the duty roster, Shelby. I want you out of sight. Completely. Welton and Hartley know you work here. I wouldn't put it past them to watch this place."

"Oh, hell, Cade, I'm not going to stop doing my job! I'm not scared of those bastards! I know how they operate. Leave me on the job, because I don't think they'll try to grab me."

"Like hell they won't," Dakota snapped. He saw the stubbornness on her face. His heart lurched with fear for her safety. "You need to disappear, Shel." Dammit, she had to be protected! He knew those two criminals. His heart shrank in terror of them ever laying a hand on Shelby.

Every time he whispered her name like an endearment, her skin tingled as if he'd stroked her with one of his callused hands. She met and held his hooded stare. There was no question Dakota was the biggest, baddest guard dog she'd ever run into. "Look," she pleaded to him, "I will go stir-crazy up in that cabin of yours. I need to work! I have a very low tolerance for boredom."

Dakota shook his head, holding her glittering blue gaze. "I have to keep you safe, Shel. The only way to do it is stay at the cabin." He wanted to shake some sense into that head of hers. He didn't want to admit he was attracted to her, wanted her, but the end of the story was brutal. He was afraid he'd end up hurting her because the extent of his PTSD symptoms were severe.

Cade nodded. "He's right, Shelby. Until we can find out where these two are, you're in danger. I'm not risking your life. I know you'll hate being taken off the roster, but this is for your own good."

"Damn. This isn't fair."

"It isn't fair that those two gomers want to kill you, either."

Glaring over at Dakota, Shelby pushed her fingers through her hair in an irritated motion. "How long do I have to hide?" she demanded tightly of Cade.

"I hope only a few days," Cade said soothingly. "I'm sorry, Shelby, but you need to go with Dakota over to your house. Pack a few bags. He'll guard you. He knows how to watch out for bad guys. I'll breathe a lot easier once you get the hell out of Jackson Hole. A cabin off the grid and up in the Tetons is your best bet."

"Damn," she muttered, turning and jerking open

the door. She headed down the hall and pushed through the glass doors into the reception area. Outside, the day was sunny and bright. Anger moved through her as she went to the parking lot. Dakota was on her heels. She could feel him, not hear him. He walked like that wolf of his, undetected.

At her cruiser, she retrieved her assigned rifle and tracking gear and removed them. After locking it back up, she saw Dakota looking around the area. The sheriff's headquarters was opposite the courthouse, both on the same side of the street. She, too, was more alert than usual.

"Okay," she called to him, "come on." The idea of staying with Dakota was making her go shaky inside. Shelby felt as if she were suspended above a fire. Either way, she could get burned by this situation.

Dakota followed Shelby. He had memorized Welton's and Hartley's sick faces a long time ago. Seeing them older helped, too. Revenge flowed strong and palpable through him as he walked Shelby to her green Toyota Land Cruiser. She was angry and upset. She'd settle down once they got out of here. Right now she was a target. Were those bastards already here in town? Dakota wasn't going to take any chances. He wore his SIG Sauer pistol in a drop holster low on his right thigh, and it felt good to have it handy. He wished he had an M-4, the rifle SEALs carried out on missions. A pistol was a secondary weapon in the SEAL arsenal. A last-ditch stand between him and the bad guys. The M-4 would blow those bastards away with one shot each. His rifle was up at his cabin, and from now on, he'd be carrying it with him. He savored that possibility because he wanted nothing more than to avenge his sister's death at their sick, murderous hands.

"Coming?" Shelby called, sliding into the driver's seat. How different Dakota behaved. He was on guard and alert. The look in his eyes would have scared her if she hadn't been kissed by this man earlier.

Dakota climbed in. "They probably don't know what kind of vehicle you're driving yet. So let's take a slow ride around the block where you live. See if you notice any strange cars you don't recognize."

Shelby put the car in gear and drove it out of the parking lot. "That's a good idea," she admitted, the anger bleeding out of her voice. Glancing over at his set profile, she added, "You'd make a damn good cop, Dakota. You have the instincts of one."

His mouth barely twitched. "SEAL training, Shel. The training you get, the experience you accrue, always comes in handy."

She gripped the wheel a little tighter. The traffic was normal for this time of day as she headed in the direction of the hospital. "I don't mean to be a petulant child about this."

"But you are." He slid her an unwilling grin. She was frowning and he could see she was worried. "It's okay. I wouldn't like to be yanked off my job, either. But it's for the best."

"Yeah," she muttered, "I know."

"You made the right decision to come to the cabin."

"No, you and Cade made it for me." Shelby said nothing else, shuttling between anger and desire. Her body responded to his gruff voice and she felt an acute ache. How the hell was she going to live in that cabin with him? He only had a twin bed in there. The rest of her mind was focused on the escaped convicts. Her skin crawled as she recalled those stomach-turning photos of Ellie. *My God.* If they were really going to seek her out, treat her the same way, Shelby was relieved that Dakota was with her. The man was truly the right person to help protect her.

They drove slowly around the block. Shelby's house was a one-story, two-bedroom home with a white picket fence and a small yard. "I don't see anything out of place," she told Dakota after they'd swung around the block.

"Okay, let's go pick up whatever you need. But first, I'll check around the house before I give you the signal it's all clear."

RELIEF WAS SHORT-LIVED as Shelby drove her Land Cruiser up the steep, muddy road toward Dakota's cabin. She still wore her sheriff's uniform, and her radio on her shoulder came to life. Pressing the button, she heard Cade's voice.

"Shelby, all the stolen cars have been checked for prints. All that was found was the owner's prints. Nothing else."

"Roger that. Keep us in the loop?"

"Roger. Out."

"They're using gloves," she muttered to Dakota, paying attention to the curve that would take them up to eight thousand feet and his cabin.

"That's what I was thinking." He heard the concern in her tone. "How are you doing?"

Shrugging, Shelby said, "Scared. Angry. Wanting to find those two. Wanting my life back."

Dakota couldn't help himself and stared at her profile. His gaze just naturally fell to her mouth. He'd kissed those lips, felt the heat of her mouth bloom beneath his, felt her return his hunger in equal measure. His lower body tightened, reminding him just how long he'd been without a woman. He fought his need to protect Shelby from himself. How he wished he could kill the tendrils of need growing daily inside him.

"How's your arm doing?" Shelby asked, gesturing to his bear bite.

"Okay."

"No heat? Swelling?"

"None." And then he added drolly, "I'm being a good boy. I'm taking my antibiotics, Doc."

Giving a throaty chuckle, Shelby pulled into the driveway. "We need to pick up your truck."

"Tomorrow." Dakota saw Storm come trotting around the cabin, her yellow gaze pinned on the Toyota.

"She's beautiful." Shelby sighed, turning off the engine and opening the door.

"Yeah, she's all wolf," he agreed, climbing out.

Storm trotted up to Dakota and whined, rolled on her back, exposing her belly. The greeting was that of a subordinate wolf to the alpha male wolf. He leaned down and rubbed her belly, which she loved.

Shelby stood and watched them, a soft feeling moving through her. Dakota might have PTSD, but he was gentle with her and with the wolf. Storm leaped to her feet, tongue hanging out, the expression on her gray face one of unfettered joy that Dakota had returned home.

Looking around, Shelby studied where the cabin sat from the perspective of safety. The small clearing was surrounded by thick forest. The brook behind the cabin gurgled happily. She felt safe up here. Maybe it was the thick stands of fir. She glanced toward Dakota, who was rubbing Storm's broad, flat head, a smile tugging at the corners of her mouth. Maybe it was him.

Dakota pushed the door of the cabin open with his foot. He made a mental note to fix the lock. Before, it hadn't mattered. Now it did. He helped carry in one of Shelby's two suitcases. Throwing it on the unmade bed, he said, "You get the rack."

"What about you? Where are you going to sleep?" She looked around the chilly cabin. It hadn't been cleaned up since she'd arrived that early morning to get Dakota to the hospital. She picked up the chair and slid it beneath the table. The place was simple, the furniture spare.

"On the floor," he said. He noticed her concerned look. "The six months I was out with my SEAL platoon, we slept on the ground when out on missions. A wood floor is the Ritz." He allowed a hint of a smile.

"Not my idea of the Ritz," Shelby muttered. Looking around, she saw his dresser. There was no electricity. No water. It hurt her to think he'd remained up here for a year, alone. This was no way for a human to live.

He brought over a large steel bowl and set it on the dresser. He pulled out a towel and cloth and set them down. "Sorry, but the only bathing facilities are either climbing buck naked into that cold stream or washing up in here."

"I feel like I've regressed to pioneer days."

Dakota chuckled. "Believe me when I tell you, this is luxury compared to what I was used to having."

"It's hard to picture." She opened one suitcase and pulled out a set of jeans, a short-sleeved T-shirt and socks. It was time to get out of her sheriff's uniform and go civilian. Turning, she saw him filling a rusted pot with water from a nearby jug. The kitchen, if it could be called that, was a counter with one aluminum sink. The plumbing beneath went through a hole drilled through a log, to dump the water outside the cabin. "You making coffee?"

"Yes. Want some?"

It was all one room. No bathroom, either. "Yes, please." And then she smiled at him. "Hey, if I can have my coffee in the morning, I'm in heaven."

Dakota felt his heart expand in his chest over her husky laughter. He lit a magnesium tab on a metal hot plate and set the pot over it on a wire grate. This tab would create instant heat, enough to perk coffee. It also wouldn't create smoke that might alert Welton and Hartley if they were in the area. He doubted they were, but he was taking no chances by firing up the woodstove. They'd follow the white smoke and find Shelby.

"I'm going to change."

"Go ahead."

She sat down on the bed, unlacing her black boots. Dakota's back was turned to her. The white-hot magnesium tab was hard to look at directly because it glowed like a sun. The smell was terrible and she was glad he'd opened the window above the sink to let the noxious odor waft out of the cabin. She stood and shimmied out of her trousers. Unbuttoning the shirt, Shelby placed them aside. Her skin goose-bumped in the coolness. She reached for her green T-shirt and pulled it over her head. Would Dakota turn around and stare? No, she could see him deliberately dawdling at the counter.

"Are SEALs gentlemen?" she wondered, pulling on her Levi's.

"We're warriors with an ethos," he said, wiping down the counter with a damp rag. "We have a strict code of conduct."

"Sort of like the samurai warriors?"

He forced himself to look out the window, not turn around and watch her dress. "Something like that."

Thoughtful, Shelby said, "I didn't know that about the SEALs."

"We conduct ourselves to a higher bar of training."

"Unlike Welton and Hartley, who have no honor at all."

"They're scum," he muttered, steel lining his voice. He stopped wiping off the counter, his fist clenching the damp cloth.

"I won't disagree with you, Dakota. I'm dressed now. You can turn around."

He turned. Shelby looked damn good in those Levi's that clearly revealed and celebrated her long legs. The green T-shirt outlined her breasts and flat stomach. He watched like a starved wolf as she released her ponytail, her golden hair cascading softly about her shoulders. He had to turn away or he was going to do something he'd regret. "I need to fix the bed. I fell on it when I went septic with high fever. I broke one of its legs."

"I can help." Shelby held up her hands. "I'm good with tools, too."

"Why am I not surprised?"

She heard the teasing in his tone and saw the respect in his eyes. His left arm had to be tender and sore, even though he never complained about it. She had a hunch SEALs didn't whine about much of anything. Dakota was a poster child for them. They just sucked it up and kept on going no matter how much pain they were in. Like he said, pain was inevitable, but suffering was optional.

She pulled the bed out and noticed the bent leg. Feeling edgy because of herself, not him, Shelby tried to contain her feminine yearnings for Dakota. This was the wrong time and place to get caught making love, with Welton and Hartley looking for her.

Dakota dropped the damp cloth on the counter

and walked over to a corner where his toolbox was. There was anguish in his eyes. Was he remembering Ellie? Taking in a deep, ragged breath, Shelby wanted to help him in some way, to ease his grief from the past. But how? His kiss had been so damned healing for her. And yet, as Dakota walked toward her with the toolbox in hand, Shelby knew they needed to remain safe and undiscovered from the convicts who were at large. Personal needs had no place here.

CHAPTER ELEVEN

"WHAT WAS ELLIE LIKE?" Shelby asked as they worked together to repair the broken leg on the bed.

On his knees, Dakota glanced up toward her. Shelby was at his shoulder, holding up the bed so he could remove the broken leg. He could smell her, his nostrils inhaling her sweet scent.

"She was an incredible person," he began, his voice low with feeling. Taking a screwdriver, he began to methodically remove the screws that held the bent metal leg to the bed frame. "We were born and lived over in Cody, Wyoming. My dad was a farrier, a damned good one, always in high demand by ranchers outside the city. Ellie was two years older than I was."

Shelby watched him work. When she gently asked about his sister, his eyes grew light with fond memories. Good memories. His mouth relaxed as he worked. "Your dad shoed horses? What did your mom do?"

Dakota wanted to tell her everything. The care burning in her blue eyes made him open up more than he ever had to anyone else. "She was a full-blood Cheyenne Indian. She met my father and they fell in love."

Shelby knew how important it was to talk about family. "It sounds like it was a happy time in your life?"

Nodding, Dakota placed the fallen screw on a cloth beside him. He went to work on the second one. "My dad taught me how to hunt deer, fish, track and find my way through the mountains from the time I can remember. My mother stayed at home, cooked, cleaned and sewed. She made beautiful leather beaded purses and pouches." He sat up, hands resting on his long, thick thighs. "My dad had been in the U.S. Navy and he's the one who got me to thinking about trying to become a SEAL."

"And Ellie? How did she fit into your life?"

Momentary pain flitted through Dakota's heart. He looked down at his hands. "Ellie was an extrovert like my dad. I took after my mother, the strong, silent type." A slight smile tipped one corner of his mouth. "Ellie was incredibly beautiful. She had my mother's dark brown eyes. Ellie was outgoing and the most popular girl at her high school. She was kind, Shelby. She worked in the soup kitchens of Cody almost every weekend. She was an assistant kindergarten teacher at a women's shelter. She believed in helping those who had less than we did."

Reaching out, Shelby touched his slumped shoulder. The pain in his voice was almost unbearable.

"I'm sorry, I didn't mean to make you feel like this. I just wanted to understand you better, your family, was all."

An unexpected heat flowed through him. Did Shelby know how much her voice affected him? Made him want something he couldn't have? He set the tool on the floor. Against his better judgment he took her hand and cradled it within his larger one. "I'm finding I'm an open book around you." He met and held her gaze. Were there tears in her eyes? And he saw something else...desire. Instantly, he rejected the thought. He moved his fingers across her open palm, felt the softness of her flesh but also saw the small calluses across it, too. Shelby was a strong, confident woman.

"You remind me a lot of my mother. She was tough, strong and self-reliant. There wasn't anything she couldn't do." He reluctantly released Shelby's hand. What the hell was the matter with him? Wanting something he could never have.

"I thought you had some Native American blood in you," she said.

He snorted and touched his nose. "Yeah, my beak." He picked up the tool and focused on the bed once more. Because if he didn't, he was going to do something that could never happen between them.

"I like your profile. It's strong. Unwavering."

"That's my mother's genetic doing," he muttered. He leaned down as Shelby got to her knees

and positioned herself so he could take out the last
screw on the bent leg.

"There," he growled, triumphant. The four screws
were finally removed. Sitting up, he looked over at
Shelby. He felt care radiating off her. "You can let
the bed down. I'm going to find a piece of wood
the same length as the leg, and fix it so you have a
bed tonight."

Shelby set the bed down. Dakota offered her a
hand to get up. Reaching out, she curved her fingers into his. He drew her to her feet as if she were
a feather. The muscles in his right arm tightened
and she felt his monitored strength as she stood. It
took effort to let go of his hand.

"How's your left arm feeling?" she asked, pointing to the dressing around it.

Dakota stepped aside, picked up the toolbox and
set it on the table. "It's okay."

"No pain? Swelling?"

"There's no infection," he assured her.

Shelby sat down at the table, watching him
put the tools back into the beat-up metal toolbox.
"You've had a hard life," she offered in a low tone.

"Who hasn't?" Dakota saw the shadow in her
eyes, her face set. He ached to touch her golden
hair that fell in a soft curve around her face and
shoulders. How could he have thought she was
one-dimensional? One couldn't always trust first
impressions. The realization that she was like his

mother sent warmth through the cold grief he still held over her passing. His mother had been incredibly strong. When the family fell apart over Ellie's murder, it was she who had gathered all of them within her unwavering embrace.

Shelby picked up the mug and saw there was still some coffee left. She sipped it. "I think I understand why you're so protective. When I first met you, you were really tough and hard."

Closing the toolbox, Dakota walked it over to the corner and set it down. "I still am." He sat down in a chair opposite Shelby and picked up his cooling coffee. "I always will be."

Looking over the cup she held between her hands, she said, "Because you're a SEAL?"

"Yes."

Shelby saw Storm lying near the door. The wolf's ears twitched as they spoke in low voices. She realized the female wolf was listening in her own way. "Tell me about Storm." Shelby wanted to stop digging into his old wounds regarding his family. His light brown eyes softened as he turned and looked over at the wolf.

"I was out laying my line of rabbit traps last April when I ran up on a grizzly who was digging into a wolf den. She'd already killed the mother, a black wolf, who was trying to defend her newly born pups. The grizzly had just come out of hibernation and was starving. She probably picked up the scent of the newborn pups, followed it and discovered the den."

Shelby said nothing, her hands around the mug. The grief had left his eyes. "She killed all the pups, too?"

"All but one. When I unexpectedly came upon her, I startled her and she took off. I went over to see if anything was left alive. The mother was part of the Snake River wolf pack. I'd seen her and the pack from time to time, running their territory across the valley. The mother had given her life to protect her pups. I heard a whine and got down on my hands and knees to search the torn-up den. I found a little runt of a gray pup buried in a lot of dirt at the end of the den tunnel. Drew it out and there she was." He hitched a thumb over his shoulder toward Storm and smiled.

"What happened next?"

"I checked the pup and she was dirty but unhurt. I tucked her into my jacket and brought her back to the cabin. I'd just gotten some groceries from town and had some cow's milk. She was so tiny her eyes weren't even open yet. I had an eyedropper and warmed up the milk, put some sugar and salt in it and started to feed her." He smiled fondly. "She was one hungry pup."

Shelby drowned in Dakota's gold-brown eyes. When he was happy, she saw the gold tones in them. Her heart lifted as she held his gaze. "And you didn't call Game and Fish?"

"Is that the deputy sheriff questioning me?"

"No, not really. Your secret's safe with me," she said. He should have handed the pup over to the state to be cared for. Knowing how alone Dakota was, she understood why he hadn't; even he needed company. The company of a wolf. He'd lost everything else: his sister, his parents. He'd lost being in his SEAL platoon, something that gave him a sense of family. "I'm glad you happened upon the situation. Storm looks happy to be with you."

"She saved my life in that grizzly fight the other day," he said, drinking the rest of his coffee. "She's a year old now, and I think she's going to be missing her own kind pretty soon. I expect her to disappear some day. She goes out and finds food for herself and sometimes she's gone for days at a time. I don't know whether she's looking for her pack or she's just hunting."

"Storm never liked dog food, huh?" Shelby grinned.

He grudgingly returned her smile. "Couldn't get her to eat it. She refused. I finally figured out she needed raw, red meat. I'd just skinned a rabbit and cut some of it up for her. She gobbled it down and that's when I realized I'd be hunting for two of us until she got old enough to hunt on her own."

The rumble of his laughter moved through Shelby as if he was touching her physically. The lightness in his brown eyes made her feel good, made her want him all over again. "Storm seems like a wonderful companion." Looking around the cabin, she murmured, "I couldn't live out here alone."

Dakota moved the cup between his large, square hands. "Shock and trauma leave scars, Shel. I'm like that wolf—happy to be free to roam in the woods. I feel calmer when I'm out here." And then a corner of his mouth drew inward. "I don't expect you or anyone to understand." Yet his fingers positively itched to release the mug and, instead, frame her face, slide his fingers through those golden strands and kiss her senseless. The memory of that kiss in her kitchen burned through him. Dakota wanted more. He wanted Shelby. All of her.

"I know they do," she said in a quiet tone. "Dr. McPherson wants you to come back to the clinic. She says she can help you."

Dakota snorted. "How? By medicating me up to my friggin' eyeballs so I don't know my name? Therapy?" He straightened. "Sorry, but that's not my gig. Talk isn't my thing. And I'll never use drugs."

Tilting her head, she asked softy, "Do you feel better talking to me about your past? Your family?"

"Hell, you're different. You're no shrink poking and prodding into my brain like an elephant." He met her smile with one of his own, absorbing her dancing blue gaze. Shelby was so clean, less touched by life. He was battle-scarred in comparison to her. His life had gone from happy to a war at age seventeen when Ellie was murdered. When she died, he lost a piece of himself. And joining the SEALs and going to war only reinforced the war elements that ran as a continued theme throughout his life.

"Jordana McPherson will not poke or prod you, Dakota. Nor will she necessarily prescribe drugs. She just wants to give you a saliva test to check your cortisol levels. There's new research available that shows high cortisol is found in people with PTSD. It's just a test...."

"I'll think about it," he growled, none too excited about the prospect.

"She was right, you know," Shelby said, reaching out and sliding her hand over his. "You went from one war into another."

Dakota nodded, picked up her hand and held it. "Yeah, there's always a war going on inside me, Shel." And that was why, no matter how damn badly he wanted her, he could never have her. "And with Welton and Hartley on the loose and in the area, you'd better believe I'm on war footing. I'm going to find those two and put an end to their lives."

A small shiver moved up her spine as she witnessed the sudden hatred and animal-like focus come to Dakota's eyes. She couldn't blame him. Shelby had no other siblings in her family now, and she tried to imagine how she'd feel if the situation was reversed. If Jason was murdered instead of Ellie by those convicts. How would she feel then?

"I hope someone identifies or sees them," she whispered, her voice off-key.

"They'll make a mistake," Dakota promised her. He studied each of Shelby's fingers, the nails clipped short on her no-nonsense hands. "Where did you get all these calluses?" He grazed them with his index finger. There was such hidden pleasure in touching her.

"My parents have a home on the outskirts of town. I help my dad cut and chop wood for the winter." Her skin tingled hotly as he traced each of the calluses across her palm. Throat going dry, Shelby wanted to explore Dakota in the same way he was exploring her. The kiss had never left her and even now, as she licked her lower lip, she wanted to taste him again.

"Your dad taught you to track, hunt and chop wood?" He forced himself to release her hand. "Did he want a son?"

"Fair question," Shelby said, reclaiming her hand. Her flesh still had wild, heated shocks moving through them afterward. "The answer is no. My dad wanted me to be able to handle any situation that came up. He never believed women were weak, just the opposite. I loved going out hunting with him. I didn't like killing things, so I was happy learning to track and identify the different animal tracks, instead."

"And he's a tracker?"

"He was. When he retired as commander of the sheriff's department, he had arthritis of the spine. It really hampers his movements now." Sadness tinged her tone. "He can't hunt or fish very much. Or chop wood anymore. I really feel badly for him. Arthritis runs in his side of the family."

Nodding, Dakota forced his hands around the coffee mug. "Your dad should be proud of you. You're smart, educated and you don't take grief from anyone." His mouth curved ruefully. "Even me and I know I'm a handful."

Meeting his warm gaze, Shelby felt her insides turn weak with need. "You are, but you're not mean. You're wounded, Dakota." Her voice dropped to a whisper. "There's a huge difference."

He hadn't thought of himself in that particular light. She didn't know how dangerous he could become when his PTSD got out from beneath his steel control. Looking around the cabin, he said, "We've got a lot to do to make this place work for two people." As he rose to his feet, Dakota wondered how the hell he was going to sleep with Shelby only a few feet away from him. Oh, he didn't mind sleeping on a wood floor. Hell, that was good digs compared to sleeping out in the rocky, freezing mountains of Afghanistan. Now, that was a bitch.

What really ate at him was how close Shelby would be to him. He'd be able to reach out a long arm and touch her. His lower body grew hot with longing just thinking about it. Yet, as he put the cup in the sink, Dakota knew it wasn't right. Yes, they'd kissed. But would it have led to something else? To bed? He wasn't sure and he wasn't going to use this situation to trap Shelby and force her into a corner. Dakota was smart enough to respect her. Plus, he had to remain alert and protect her, not get distracted. Distraction got a person killed damned fast.

Still, as he moved around the cabin, he chafed. So often, he'd wake up at night screaming, caught in the throes of a nightmare from a SEAL mission. He wasn't sure what he'd do if that happened tonight. The nightmares released all his carefully closeted emotions, grief and rage. He knew from being in the hospital, wounded, that nurses were careful around him precisely because of what he'd endured. If he was asleep, they would pinch his toe to awaken him. He'd automatically come up swinging. They knew his hands were lethal weapons, and that he could kill with one blow if they got too close to him.

Worried, his mouth quirking, Dakota wasn't sure what to do. Should he warn Shelby about his nightmares? She was the last person he wanted to accidentally hurt. The last one.

CHAPTER TWELVE

CURT DOWNING WAS in his office at Ace Trucking when the door opened. It was dark outside and he was rushing to finish off some paperwork. His stomach grumbled; it was 9:00 p.m. and he still hadn't eaten dinner. His back to the door, he twisted around. His eyes grew to slits. The door closed, two men were standing and looking at him. "What the hell are you two doing here?"

Vance Welton grinned, glad that the blinds were closed. The small office was ensconced deep within the main trucking bay. "Hey, boss, long time, no see." He gestured to his partner. "You remember Oren Hartley?" His yellowed teeth were revealed when he smiled. "We worked for you at one time. We need some help."

Turning in his chair, Curt stared disbelievingly at them. "You stupid bastards! The whole damned state is looking for you two!"

"Yeah," Vance said, shoving his hands in the pockets of his jeans, "we know." His smile became broader. "Been stealing cars to keep the cops and

FBI off our asses. We need a set of wheels that's legal. Figure you can loan us a truck for a while?"

Scowling, Curt sat there feeling the danger surrounding the two escaped convicts. Both looked grim. Pistols were stuck into the waist of their jeans, hidden by shirts that were too big for them. Curt always kept a Glock pistol in his drawer. Now he wished he had it sitting on his desk. "Yeah, you worked for me. But I don't owe you anything, Welton. You were a lousy truck driver anyway."

Vance's brown eyes grew thoughtful. "Well, boss, considering I was trucking your heroin, marijuana and cocaine all over the West, you don't have much room to talk."

"Just what the hell does that mean?" he snarled, hands curving into fists.

Welton shrugged and looked around the small, warm office. "Read between the lines if you want. We need a set of wheels that won't come up stolen."

"And you're leaving town?"

"Sort of," Welton said, then glanced over at Hartley. "We got some unfinished business here in Jackson Hole to attend to first and then we'll move on. Don't worry, you won't be implicated. If the cops see your truck, they'll think we're some of the hired drivers from your company."

"And if I don't agree to this?" Curt snarled, tensing.

Vance fingered the handle of the pistol in his

waistband. "Well, now, it would be a shame for your men to discover you dead in your office tomorrow morning. Wouldn't it?" He added a feral smile to go with his threat.

Inwardly Curt was enraged. In his business as a regional drug lord, he dealt with scum like this all the time. His mind flicked over the possibilities. "You have business here?" He jabbed his finger down at the floor.

"We do."

"Mind telling me what it involves?"

"Can't."

"Won't?" Curt growled.

Vance moved his hand over his triangular-shaped chin. He felt the stubble of hair growing out on his face. "The less you know, the better off you'll be."

"But if you're caught in one of my trucks—"

"We're not gonna get caught. And we intend to change our looks. It will be hard for anyone to identify us."

Nostrils flaring, Curt felt evil around Vance. His small, close-set eyes never left him. He was a sexual predator, a murderer and a sociopath. "How long are you going to be hanging around here?"

"As long as it takes. Need to do a little hunting…"

Curt shook his head. "You're putting me in a helluva spot, Welton. If I give you a truck and you get caught, those damned sheriff's deputies and the FBI are going to climb down my ass." He jerked a hand in a gesture toward the truck bay. "I've got too much to lose and you know it."

"I always liked seeing you sweat," Vance said, continuing to smile. "If you don't give us a truck and five thousand dollars, all in twenties, I'll make an anonymous call to the sheriff's department I'll tell them how you smuggle drugs all over the West." His brows moved upward. "You think they'd like to hear from me?"

Rage tunneled through Curt. "You son of a bitch!"

"Thank you. Now fork over the keys to one of your many trucks that are parked out there." Vance thrust out his hand. "And the money, too. We need some operating funds."

Getting up, mouth set, Curt knew better than to push Vance. He knew his prison record. His hand rested over the butt of the pistol in his waist. Walking to the Peg-Board hanging on one wall, Curt jerked off a set of keys. He turned and tossed them at Oren Hartley, who caught them.

"There's a dark green Chevy truck at the end of the first row. Take that one."

"No company sign on the door?" Vance demanded. "We want to blend in, not stand out."

"No, that's why I'm giving it to you. All my

other trucks have *Ace Trucking* painted on both doors."

Going to his desk, Curt pulled open a drawer on the right-hand side. "This is it, Welton. You can't ever come back here and ask me for anything else again."

"We'll see," Vance murmured.

Curt pulled out the cashbox, set it on his desk and opened it with a set of keys.

"Look at all that cash," Oren said, gawking into the box. "Hooooeeee, that's a chunk of greenbacks."

Curt counted out five thousand dollars in small denominations. He shoved the bills to the edge of the desk.

"Thanks, boss," Vance said, picking them up. He took half and gave Oren the other half. "Stuff it into your pockets," he ordered.

"Now get the hell out of my life," Curt snarled.

"Gladly," Vance said, opening the door. "Later, gator."

Curt sat down, fuming after they'd left. The door was still open and he stood and slammed it shut. *Dammit!* Pushing his fingers through his sandy red hair, he got up and angrily paced the office. What the hell could he do? If he went to the sheriff's, he could tell them Welton and Hartley held him up, stole money and a truck. The downside, and it was a steep cliff, was Welton, who had driven for him for a year, would turn him in. He'd take a plea bargain and turn state's evidence against him and his drug operation. It was rare that Curt felt so damned helpless.

As he finished up his paperwork, Curt could only hope those two bastards wouldn't get caught in his truck. And what the hell was this about some business in Jackson Hole? They had no ties to this place! Cursing softly, he jerked open the left drawer and dropped in the receipt bag that would go to the bank tomorrow morning. What were those two up to? It would be smarter for them to hightail it out of Wyoming and disappear.

"WHAT ARE YOU DOING?" Shelby asked, having just put the sheets and covers on the bed. Dakota had his sleeping bag tucked beneath his arm, heading for the door. It was 10:00 p.m.

"Going to sleep outside."

"What?" She stared at him, uncomprehending. "It's below freezing out there at night, Dakota." Part of her deflated. She wanted him close.

"I want to keep you safe," he growled, hand resting on the doorknob.

"You're guarding me from the outside?" She studied his darkening eyes. What was going on here? All evening, she'd seen Dakota close up, unavailable, as he worked to make the cabin hospitable for her. He'd dusted, cleaned the floors and swept down the cobwebs from the corners.

"You ever been around a combat soldier?" He hated bringing up her dead brother, Jason, but he had to.

"Only Jason." Brows drawing down, she said, "What's he got to do with this?"

"When Jason stayed with your parents, did he ever wake them up at night?"

Shelby thought for a moment. "Well…yes… sometimes." Tilting her head, he stared hard at him. "What's this got to do with us?"

"Your brother had PTSD. The dark is when the nightmares stalk us." He tried to soften the growl in his tone because he saw her distressed by the fact that he was going to leave the cabin. "I had a good friend over in Afghanistan, a Green Beret. He was a top soldier, but he'd seen four rotations of combat in that country. The last time he came home after his tour, he had nightmares." His mouth tightened. "His wife tried to wake him up one night when he was in the middle of one. He kept a pistol under his pillow." His voice lowered. "He shot and killed her, mistaking her for an enemy who was attacking him in the nightmare."

Gasping, Shelby's eyes widened. "Oh my God…."

"It wasn't pretty. He got tried for manslaughter and spent five years in prison. When I heard about it, I remember the firefight that probably pushed him over the edge. The Taliban had come over the hill. There were seventy of them and ten Green Berets. It ended up in hand-to-hand combat. He was the only survivor in that skirmish and it scarred him."

Shelby stood quiet, feeling terrible for the soldier and his wife. "You think you're going to have a nightmare tonight? And you're afraid you'll hurt me during it? That's it, isn't it?" Her heart pounded.

The shadows deepened in his eyes and he nodded.

"Okay, if you wake up, I promise I will not come out of this bed to help you. That way, you can stay in here."

Shaking his head, Dakota rasped, "You don't understand, Shel. Sometimes I wake up and I sleepwalk. I'm fighting my own ghosts from my Afghan tours." He held up one of his hands. "I can easily kill with one of these." He hated that tears flooded her eyes. Just as swiftly, they disappeared. "I don't want to hurt you. You're the last person on this earth I'd want to harm. Do you understand?" Dammit, she was waging a good campaign of reason against him. If he stayed in the cabin, he'd take her. He'd take her and love her until neither of them could move afterward, so completely exhausted. He'd been so damn long without a woman. And most women didn't appeal to him anyway, but she did.

A lump formed in Shelby's throat. "Okay…" Taking a step forward, she whispered, "You have to see Dr. McPherson. I've heard of her working with other vets who have had similar issues. She's been able to help them, Dakota." Swallowing hard, Shelby felt the heat of tears pushing into her eyes. God help her, all she wanted to do was take those few steps and throw her arms around Dakota and hold him. Hold him against the night terrors that she clearly saw in his gaze. For a moment, he looked sad, but quickly covered it up.

"Yeah, I think I will see her. But not right now." He moved his shoulders to get rid of the accumulated tension in them. "The woodshed is near the creek. Storm and I will be out there."

"What if it snows?"

He held up his down sleeping bag. "This is specially made for SEALs in cold climates. It looks pretty ratty, but it keeps me plenty warm."

"Damn, Dakota, I didn't mean to force you out of your own cabin," Shelby muttered, frustrated. She put her hands on her hips. "Maybe I should stay at my parents' home."

"No."

The swift response stunned her. "What? You think Welton will try to find me there? He doesn't know my parents live here."

"Welton is a sociopath," Dakota began heavily, "and you can't ever assume he's stupid. Most of them are damned brilliant, Shel. I worry about your parents, too. I called Cade Garner a few hours ago and asked him to warn them. It's up to your dad to decide what he wants to do. Frankly—" he rubbed his jaw "—I told Cade to ask them to leave town until we can verify if these convicts are in the vicinity or not."

Her throat tightened. "I didn't even think in that direction. Do you know what Cade found out? Are they going to leave?"

He nodded. "I talked to him earlier this evening on my cell. Your dad wanted you to come with them, but Cade told them you wouldn't do that."

"He's right about that," Shelby muttered. "I want to track those two and land their asses back in federal prison like I did before."

Dakota respected her decision. "I'm having a helluva time looking at you and grasping the fact you tracked them down." Giving her an uneven grin, Dakota added, "That's a backhanded compliment, Shel. Old dogs like me have to learn new tricks. Tracking isn't a gender skill. I'm just too used to working with the men of my SEAL team. It just never occurred to me a woman could do it, too."

Her shoulders slumped, the tension bleeding out of her. "Tomorrow, we need to start sniffing around, Dakota. I want to find them. My gut tells me they're going to hole up in the Tetons."

Nodding, he said, "Bingo. Welton hid in the mountains of Yellowstone. The last stolen car has put him in our vicinity. We'll go see Cade tomorrow and start creating a mission plan to locate them."

"Are you really going to sleep outside every night?"

"Yes. It's better this way." *For you. For me.* He struggled and said, "I don't like it, but I couldn't live with myself if I harmed you, Shel." He held her steady gaze. She was upset and concerned. Not for herself, but for him.

"Well," she groused, trying to lighten the tension, "I'll miss you."

"Yeah?" It made him feel good for the first time in such a long while. She had the capacity to reach him in a place he thought had died when he was seventeen.

A slow, heated male smile touched the corners of his mouth. Shelby recalled the scalding desire he'd sparked within her before and she responded powerfully to that glittering look in his eyes. Now he was the wolf stalking her. It excited her, made her want to beg him to stay. It was a selfish and foolish thought, not worthy of herself. Or him. He was putting his life on the line to protect her.

"You realize when we pick up their trail, Dakota, we'll be out in the woods for maybe days on end."

He saw the challenging light in her eyes. "Yes, that occurred to me."

"Unless we're humping two tents, we'll be sharing one. Together." She set her jaw, hands on her hips.

He studied her, the silence intensifying between them. "That thought didn't escape me."

"And you aren't going to sleep outside the damned tent, Dakota. I won't let you."

"No?" The heat in her eyes made him feel good about himself as a man.

"No. It will be just you and me. I'm not afraid of you. I'm a law enforcement officer. I can take care of myself."

As he met her steady, challenging gaze, his mouth curved faintly. "Let's cross that bridge when we get to it." He twisted the doorknob. "Remember, if you hear me yelling, do not come out and rescue me."

"Okay, but I won't like it, Dakota. I'm not a weakling. You think you're so dangerous that no one on this earth can help you."

"Talk to the nurses at Landstuhl Medical Center in Germany. I sent one flying across the room one time. She was new to the hospital and they failed to warn her not to come running to my bedside if they heard me screaming at night." He shook his head. "I broke her arm. I felt really bad about it after I woke up."

Shaken, Shelby said, "If you scream and you wake me up, I won't guarantee you anything, Dakota. How do I know if Welton and Hartley aren't holding you prisoner? You could be in real trouble and need my help."

Grimly, he rasped, "Those two would never get within a hundred feet of me. They'd be dead in a heartbeat. You stay inside this cabin and do not go out that door until morning. Understand?"

CHAPTER THIRTEEN

SHELBY JERKED AWAKE when her cell phone began ringing near her head. She'd placed the iPhone near her pillow, in case the sheriff's department or her parents called. Blinking, she sat up, the covers falling away from her pink flannel, long-sleeved nightgown. She focused her drowsy attention on the iPhone. As she picked it up, she saw it was dawn.

"Shelby here," she whispered, rubbing her eyes.

"Shelby, it's Cade. Sorry to wake you up so early, but we need your help."

"You got a line on Welton?" she mumbled, rubbing her face.

"No. Not yet. We just got a call from Yellowstone Forest Rangers HQ. They've got a camper who is missing. Apparently his wife brought her husband, who has Alzheimer's, to the park because he loved being in the woods. When she awoke this morning, he was gone. She has no idea where and there are thousands of acres of woods surrounding them."

Shelby sat up, her feet touching the cool wood

floor. She heard a knock at the door. "Hold on, Cade…" She pulled the cell away. "Come in," she called.

Dakota entered the cabin, concern written on his features. Storm squeezed by him, wagging her tail.

Shelby said, "It's Cade. They've got a missing man up in Yellowstone."

Nodding, Dakota put the rifle in the corner after shutting the door. He focused on the phone conversation as he lit a magnesium tab, opened the window and got the coffee going.

After finishing the call, Shelby got out of the bed, the pink nightgown falling to her slender ankles. Dakota felt his body respond. The gown was old-fashioned, with ruffles across the bodice. It was pink with tiny white roses across the material. There was grayness in the cabin, but even in low light, he saw the wheat and gold colors of Shelby's hair tumble around her shoulders.

Shelby was hotly aware of Dakota's gaze upon her as she went to the table and pulled a notebook from the pocket of her shirt. Once she wrote down the information on the missing man, she glanced up to meet his hooded gaze. There it was again, that connection between them. He was dressed like the night before. Had he slept in his clothes?

She gave Dakota the intel on the missing man. Moving over to the bed, she pulled on a clean pair of thick socks for hiking. It was cold in the cabin and she wanted to get warm.

"And Cade wants me to go along?" he asked, placing two mugs out on the counter as the coffee percolated on the heating grate.

"Yes. Will you?" She lifted her head after putting on the thick socks.

"You're going nowhere without me until we find those two gomers," he said.

"Turn around. I need to get dressed."

"I'd rather watch."

"Another time and place, Dakota."

"I'll hold you to that, Shel." He turned, facing the window.

Shelby grabbed civilian clothes. She never tracked in her sheriff's uniform. Even though it was early June, it was cold in the area. Taking a dark brown cable-knit sweater, she pulled it over her head. A set of heavy corduroy trousers of the same color completed her uniform. She pushed her fingers through her mussed hair. "Okay, you can look now."

Dakota did. The dark sweater brought out the color of her hair. His fingers itched to investigate those shining strands as she pulled out a brush and comb from the opened suitcase on the floor. The chocolate-colored trousers did nothing but remind him how long and beautifully sculpted her legs were. Scowling, he turned and poured hot coffee into the awaiting mugs.

"Here, breakfast."

Taking the cup, she thanked him. "Did you get any sleep?" she asked.

Dakota sat down at the table, coffee between his large hands. "Some."

"Why do I not believe you?" She pulled her hiking boots from the suitcase. "You look like death warmed over."

"And I never thought this cabin would look so good as when you were in it." He sipped his coffee, watching her reaction over the rim of the mug.

Grinning, Shelby pulled on one boot and then another. She met his dark, assessing eyes. "I slept like a baby. Probably because I knew you and your wolf were keeping me safe from the bad guys."

"Close to the truth," Dakota murmured. When she stood up and smoothed the corduroy down across her thighs, his body reacted. "Come and get some coffee in your veins. We'll talk tracking strategy."

Groaning, Shelby nodded, pulled out the chair opposite him. Storm came and sat next to her, resting her head in her lap.

"Does Storm like me?" she wondered, sitting down and gently patting her head.

"She's taken a shine to you."

"Is that unusual?"

"She's a female alpha wolf. She may see you as a female beta wolf."

Picking up her coffee, Shelby chuckled. "Is she worried I'm going to take her mate?"

His brows moved upward for a moment. "Could be."

"Do I have to roll over on my back and expose my belly to her to convince her that you're safe with me?" A warmth exuded from Dakota. It enveloped her. His light brown eyes gleamed with unspoken desire. For a moment, her gaze fell to his well-shaped mouth. A mouth she was already familiar with—and wanted to taste again. Only longer and more deeply.

"Let's get back to business," he growled. "Have law enforcement or the rangers started a search for this guy?"

"They're just starting because they need light." Shelby glanced toward the window. "I feel sorry for the wife. She and her husband used to come to Yellowstone every year for two weeks and camp. He was a birder. It gave him such joy to be in the woods."

There was real concern and sadness in her blue eyes. "Why are you so touched by this situation?"

"I try to put myself in the wife's place. How would I feel? They've been married for thirty-five years. That's a long time. And I can't imagine her terror when she woke up this morning and he wasn't at her side. That's hard on the heart, Dakota."

"Anyone ever tell you that you're a softy beneath that sheriff's uniform?"

Shelby took his gruff teasing in stride. "I think that if you turned this around and it was one of the men in your SEAL platoon lost, you'd have a similar emotional response. Don't you?"

Her intelligence was wide and deep. He liked her ability to help him understand in ways he never had before. "Okay, I see your point."

"So, I'm not some 'softy' as you put it. We're going to have to deal with the wife. She's going to be upset and anxious."

"Guilty feeling, too, I'm sure."

"Yes. See? You're not as hard-hearted as you'd like the world to think."

"Maybe not." Dakota gave her a soft grin.

"If one of your men was lost, you'd do everything in your power to find him."

"I'd go to hell to find him if I had to, no question."

"Right." She finished off her coffee and set the mug aside. "Let's get saddled up. We can stop inside the south entrance at Grant Village and grab some food. This could be an all-day, all-night kind of track."

Dakota rose. "We'll leave Storm here. I don't like her around groups of people. They'll think she's a wild wolf and start getting weird about it."

"Can she track?"

"If I give her a piece of fabric the person wore, yes. She's good at finding a trail. Cuts my tracking time down."

She smiled at the gray wolf. "We could use her today."

"I don't like running into Fish and Game types with a wild wolf trotting at my side. They'd want to take her away from me."

Shelby grabbed her knapsack and pulled on her thick, warm dark green coat. "No kidding. You'd get fined up to your butt and back, too."

"Duly noted," Dakota said drily, pulling his rucksack out of the closet. He reached inside and pulled his H-harness off a hook.

Shelby stopped packing her knapsack and watched Dakota. The odd-looking piece of gear settled around his shoulders and fastened it around his narrow waist. "That's a nifty-looking piece of equipment. How many pockets have you got in that thing?"

"It's my H-gear. All SEALs wear it. We call it second-line gear." He pulled open a drawer at the counter. "I got fifteen pockets in this thing and I can carry ammunition, protein bars, a tourniquet and anything else I might need on this hike."

Impressed, she saw him filling each one. "That's a lot of weight if you're stowing mags of ammunition in it, isn't it?"

"It's not unusual if I'm wearing my first, second and third line of gear to be carrying sixty-five pounds on my body, and that includes my rucksack."

"Phew, that's a lot." But then, she was coming to realize SEALs were not the typical American male at all. Dakota was strong, tall and powerful, but he wasn't muscle-bound. He was a finely honed athlete who was in amazing shape.

"Normal weight for us to hump on a multiday mission," he assured her. He took a sheathed knife from his ruck and strapped it around his left thigh. On the other thigh, he already wore his SIG Sauer.

"I feel like we're going to war," Shelby said, locating her gloves in the suitcase.

"Don't kid yourself. We are. There's nothing to say Welton and Hartley aren't snooping around up there, either," he warned her.

Mouth quirking, Shelby said, "Yeah, I already thought in that direction."

He picked up his rifle, a modified M-4 that he routinely carried on SEAL missions. This was a civilian model of the military weapon he used to have. The only downside was that he couldn't slap a grenade launcher below the barrel. Grenades were frowned upon out here in the civilian world, but they could come in damn handy if he had to use them.

"How's your arm doing this morning?" she asked. "Do you need the dressing changed?"

"No, it's fine. It's healing well. You can help me change it tomorrow or whenever we get off this track."

"Just remember to take your antibiotics with you. I don't know how long we're going to be out there looking for this guy."

"Are you always such a mother hen?"

"Nah, just special for you, Carson." She pulled the knapsack over her shoulder. There was a shadowy grin on his unshaven face.

Pulling on his camouflage jacket of green, dark brown and tan, he met her smile. "Let's go Down Range."

Shelby pulled the door open. Dawn was coming, light infusing the area. Storm bounded out the door and disappeared into the surrounding woods. She opened the rear of the sheriff's cruiser and stowed her gear. So did Dakota.

"Is Storm off hunting?"

"Yeah, every morning and night."

Shelby retrieved the keys from her jacket pocket. "What will she do if we're still tracking tonight and don't get back here?"

Dakota placed his H-gear next to his rucksack. "Nothing. She comes and goes as she pleases. She always comes back at some point."

After climbing into the driver's seat, she started the vehicle and then called the sheriff's department to let them know they were on their way to the campground in Yellowstone. Dakota climbed in and closed the door. She appreciated him being along.

Shelby pulled out and turned around near the cabin. "I'm looking forward to working with you. First time I've ever tracked with a SEAL. I'm sure I'll learn a lot from you."

"It's a little different from how you track."

"How so?" Shelby asked, driving down the long, narrow, winding road toward the valley. The sky was lightening, a pink color following the shadow of the night.

"We're tracking gomers. It's kill or be killed."

"Do you think Welton and Hartley have anything to do with this missing guy?"

"No. My gut tells me they're in the Tetons. I don't think they're stupid enough to hide in Yellowstone again. They got caught by you the last time. Welton won't make the same mistake twice."

Her skin crawled with momentary fear. They were probably hunting her right now. "I just hope we can find this guy alive. The nights are below freezing up at that altitude."

Dakota could hear the worry in her voice. "Alzheimer's is a bitch. We'll find out more from his wife." He noticed Shelby's thin brows knit and the worry in her profile as she turned onto the main highway that would eventually lead them into Yellowstone. Across the road was a small herd of buffalo, their breath like misting shots from their nostrils as they hungrily grazed on the early grass coming up from the long winter. Their shaggy brown coats kept them warm in any type of weather.

"Did you get any sleep last night?"

He turned his attention to her. "Not much. I got it in snatches."

"Nightmares wake you?"

"Always."

"You're probably so sleep-deprived you're used to it." It hurt Shelby to realize he suffered all the time. Jordana often talked about PTSD symptoms, that insomnia was a major component. Over time, it added another horrific layer of stress upon the person.

Dakota managed a dark chuckle. "Stop worrying. When my SEAL team was deployed over to Afghanistan for six months, no one got much sleep. We'd be operational around the clock on some missions. You learn to gut through it. The thought of being killed keeps you alert and awake."

"For a day or two?"

"Sometimes longer."

Shaking her head, she muttered, "I think I'm deciding that you guys who join the SEALs are supermen. You'd have to be."

"There's a six-month course everyone goes through," he told her. "It's called BUD/S. And it's hell on earth. It weeds out the wannabes from the rest of us who want it bad enough to work through any kind of pain and training they throw at us."

She shook her head. "Then what drives you SEALs, Dakota?"

"Heart. Teamwork. Family, I guess." He looked around the empty highway. "We're looking to belong to something bigger than ourselves. To be a part of something that's important."

Hearing the wistful note in his voice, she glanced over quickly to see his face soften for a moment. "Maybe the P.C. response would be that you're patriots? But really, underneath, you want to belong?"

"Yes," he said, "and our patriotism is strong. The bottom line is we know we can protect America and her people."

"You lost your entire family," she said. "Did the SEALs become your family instead?"

He felt his way through her deep insight. Taking in a breath, he released it and said, "Looking at it from that perspective, yeah, I got my family back. But it's more than that, Shelby. We're warriors. We want our gun in the fight. We believe in what we're doing—getting rid of the gomers on this planet. We like combat. We're never more alive than when we're in a life-and-death dance with the bad guys. We feel as a platoon, no one is better than we are. We're training eighteen months of every two-year cycle. Then we're deployed overseas to hunt and make a difference in the war effort for six months."

She brushed a strand of loose hair over her shoulder as she considered his quiet, impassioned words. "I couldn't possibly do what the SEALs do." She met his glance. "Truly, Dakota, you are a hero in my eyes."

CHAPTER FOURTEEN

SHELBY WAS EAGER TO get on with the track. They'd arrived, talked to the distraught wife about her husband, Tony Banyon, who had wandered off sometime during the night. A number of other people, volunteers, were looking for him, too. Dakota got them on the same page with a plan. Every group would work in a grid pattern for maximum coverage.

The sun was just rising as Dakota picked up a trail outside the camp. No one else was a trained tracker, so the officials allowed them to follow what they found. The rest of the groups would begin searching other grid-assigned areas. Their breath was white, the temperature in the twenties. Shelby let Dakota take the lead, his gaze fixed and moving in front of him. The woods were thick and the light bad because of the forest canopy above them.

The pine-needle floor was brown and soft. It had snowed two days earlier, melted and Shelby felt it was a good time to track. A man's footprint would leave a minuscule depression even in the soft, spongy brown needles. She could see Dakota was quickly following the slight depressions as it led deeper into the woods.

They had tracked for an hour, up and over a small hill, when he held up his fist. She halted beside him, breathing hard. "Is that a signal you just gave me?"

He turned, looking over at her. Shelby's cheeks were a bright pink from the exertion of the climb. "Sorry. Yes."

"Is that nonverbal SEAL talk?" she ventured, appreciating his nearness. Dakota looked almost invisible in the camouflage gear. He blended in almost to the point where he couldn't be seen. Only his face made him stand out against the mottled light and dark of the woods.

"It is. Don't you deputies have hand signals?"

"No. What does it mean when you raise your forearm in a fist?"

"Stop."

"I did. I'm pretty good at this." Shelby gave him an evil grin.

Heat flowed through his sweaty body as he saw Shelby's teasing smile. He almost leaned down to kiss her. Almost… Turning, Dakota pointed down the hill. "This guy, from what I can tell, probably left about two o'clock yesterday morning. He seems to know where he's going. He's not wandering around in circles. People who are really lost walk around in circles."

"It looks like he stops and rests for a bit, and then moves on," she agreed.

"Poor bastard," he breathed, shaking his head.

"At least he took his coat, hat and gloves."

"You can still freeze to death from hypothermia in this stuff, Shel. Real damn fast. It takes no prisoners."

"You were in the mountains of Afghanistan. You would know."

"Yeah, and we were operating at twelve thousand feet, twenty below Fahrenheit and the wind blowing like a banshee." He touched his gear. "I'm wearing five layers of specially designed cold-weather gear. That poor guy doesn't have anything near that to survive in."

"I don't think we'll find him alive, Dakota," Shelby said softly.

"I don't, either. Helluva way to die."

"I wonder if he did this on purpose."

"What? Walk away knowing he'd freeze to death out here?"

"Yeah. Maybe he had enough of his mind left to know how much of a burden he was becoming to his wife. Maybe he couldn't stand seeing her suffering and working so hard to keep him safe. I've seen other suicides like this."

Dakota could see the raw concern in her blue

eyes. He was losing control. And God, that was the last thing he needed right now. Control to keep his hands, his mouth, off Shelby. Her trembling words, the grief on her face, did something internally to him. He couldn't name what it was, only that it happened. Taking off his glove, he said roughly, "Come here...." He slid his hand along her clean jaw. Tilting her head up slightly, he moved close. "You have the softest heart, Shel..." He leaned down, curving his mouth across her parting lips. He'd seen the look of surprise and then heat and desire enter her eyes as he'd shifted, captured her and kissed her.

Shelby had been aching to continue the first interrupted kiss they'd shared days ago. Momentarily startled by his unexpected move, she stepped forward, sliding her arms around his broad shoulders, drawing him against herself as she met and moved her lips against his plundering, commanding mouth.

His breath was punctuated against her nose and cheek, his callused hand feeling raspy, fingers sliding down her jawline and curving around her nape, drawing her hard against him. She felt the full force of his hunger and she responded, matching his desire with her own. There was something incredibly haunting and vulnerable about Dakota; she felt it, couldn't put it in words. Yet, as their lips moved together, she felt him quiver. He rocked her lips open and they tasted each other. She pulled him as close as they could get with all the gear on between them. His beard was harsh against her cheek, but she didn't care.

The heat built explosively between them. She glided her tongue boldly against his. Instantly, he groaned, his fingers capturing the base of her skull, holding her so he could plunder her more deeply. There was such need erupting between them, Shelby realized. She ached to somehow get closer to him, to his flesh. Never had she had a kiss like this. It was rough, unbridled and primal. But so was she.

Gradually, Dakota came out of the lust haze and need for Shelby. He realized he had probably bruised her soft lips. She wasn't afraid of him. No, she was just as assertive as he'd been. Easing the pressure of his mouth against hers, inhaling her feminine scent, a mix of sweetness and pine, he reluctantly broke contact.

He barely opened his eyes, but instead drowned in the blue luster of her glistening eyes. Dakota brushed her wet mouth, wanting to ease any pain he might have caused her. He hadn't intended to hurt her. Hell, he hadn't intended to kiss her at all! He was shattered in another way, unable to control his needs for her. His body trembled inwardly, the ache increasing between his legs. There was no disguising his feelings for her. Her flared hips rested against his. He knew Shelby could feel his hunger in real time. Placing small, gentle kisses against her cheek, brow and finally, upon her mouth once more, he rasped, "I wanted to finish that kiss we started at your house." That wasn't a lie. Hell, he was thinking about kissing her every friggin' minute of the day. He felt like a drug addict. He felt trapped, his heart and body screaming for her and his mind imprisoned in PTSD screaming he had to stop—or else.

Her mouth curved softly into a smile. "I did, too."

"I'm sorry if I hurt you." He touched her lower lip with his thumb, moving it gently across the swollen, glistening surface.

Shelby shook her head, tried to struggle out of the all-consuming kiss. "No…you didn't hurt me." As she looked up at his scalding gaze, her body exploded with a need that shocked her. "It was mutual, Dakota. I wanted you as much as you wanted me."

Though he didn't want to let her go, Dakota knew he had to. Their five minutes of rest were over. Releasing her, he stepped back. Studying her in the silence, a few birds calling somewhere beyond them, Dakota memorized her oval face, those fierce blue eyes that shone with desire for him alone. Somehow he had to keep his hands off her. Somehow… "We need to keep going."

Nodding, Shelby said, "I'll take over the tracking."

"I could use a break." Tracking took every ounce of a person's concentration. His body clamored for more of Shelby's kiss and he struggled to establish control over his body. She was like a missing key to his heart and soul. How could he stop her effect on him when she'd already melted his control with just one damn kiss? Shelby had opened him up in ways that rocked his dark, wounded world. There was nothing shy or reclusive about her kiss—or her.

As she moved past him to pick up the trail, Dakota's mouth twisted with pain and frustration. Whatever they shared, whatever it was, made him feel whole. And that was a joke, because he was broken in so many ways. Shelby appeared in his life, and his goddamn heart thought that she could transform him. His mind knew otherwise, that the effects of trauma didn't just disappear.

Dakota kept his attention on the surrounding area. Everything seemed quiet, the woods always making him feel embraced by nature. He took the radio from his belt and checked-in to Ranger HQ, giving them an update as well as their current GPS position. Because the woods were so thick, the cover impossible to penetrate, it would do no good to use a helicopter to find the poor gent. Ground tracking was the only way to find Banyon.

After signing off, Dakota watched Shelby track.

She was good. Every once in a while, she'd kneel down, study a depression, look around before moving on. That was the only way to find out if the lost man might be somewhere ahead. Tracking was not done quickly. Sometimes it was, depending upon the spore or print. Here, Dakota knew pine needles, especially if dry, were hell to track in, slowing everything down to a near crawl.

Shelby moved silently, the woods making the area dim and dark. There were rocks here and there, fallen logs, but for the most part, Tony Banyon seemed to have a destination in mind. She felt bad for him. She half expected to find him huddled by a tree. But that didn't happen. The man seemed to be in good physical condition because his stride was even, not choppy or unbalanced. She tried to keep her mind on her work, but her body was like a starved animal, her lower area between her thighs wanting to be satisfied. Dakota's kiss had forced her to acknowledge she missed having a man in her life. He reminded her fully that she was a woman with healthy needs. Up until now, she could ignore them. Dakota was like a match striking against her, flaring her dormant body back to explosive life. And she'd felt his arousal earlier, wanted him in every way.

At the end of the slope of the hill, an hour later, Shelby stopped. Dakota came soundlessly up behind her. It felt like a warm wave embracing her from behind. She looked to her right, amazed at how silently he could move. His face was set, gaze scanning the area down below them. "This guy is moving out. And he knows where he's going. He's got an objective in mind."

"Yeah," Dakota growled, "but where? The wife said he did a lot of birding in this area and knew it well." He gestured to the steep slope that led down into an even thicker area of woodlands. Taking out his map, he had her hold two edges of it. "About ten miles ahead, there's a meadow. I'm hoping we can find him alive. If we do, we can get him to that meadow where a helo could come in and pick us up."

Shelby was no stranger to reading a topographical map. "Our GPS is putting us in a northern trek with Tony." She shook her head. "I'd swear he knows where he is."

"Maybe. Remember, the wife said he'd walk ten or fifteen miles a day with his camera and binos, binoculars, because he was a birder."

Shelby absorbed Dakota's overwhelming male nearness. She tried to ignore the desire banked in his brown eyes that seem to burn right through her heart and lower body. When he'd kissed her earlier, she'd seen gold in the depths of them, too. Her mouth continued to tingle off and on from his hungry kiss. "It's 11:00 a.m.," she muttered. "And if his track continues toward that meadow, it's a long way from here to there."

Tracking was an art coupled with a lot of patience. Dakota nodded. "We can't just assume he's heading there, though." He gestured to the darkening woods in front of them. "This area has heavy woods. We're going to have to be careful and watch to see if his tracks don't suddenly peel off in another direction."

"Yeah, the depressions are getting more and more shallow. It will be easy to miss a print."

"That's because the needles are drying out."

"Damn." Shelby sighed, studying the map one more time. It was hard, slow work if pine needles completely dried out. They would be forced to slow down even more and start looking for one or two pine needles being turned the wrong way to indicate someone had stepped on them. "This isn't good."

"Not for him, it isn't."

Shelby glanced up. "I wish like hell we didn't have this kind of tree cover. I wish we had a military helo available with thermal imaging on board to detect his body heat. I just feel like he's going to die."

He reached out and slid his hand across her shoulders. "I know. But that kind of helo isn't available."

Shelby folded the map and handed it back to Dakota. They'd already made six miles into the forest following him. There were patches of snow on the ground along with only a few open areas. Early June weather meant a mix of rain, sleet, snow and sunshine. A few slats of light made their way down to the ground, bright yellow spots in the gloom of the forest. "Can you track for a while?"

"Yes." He took the lead. It was going to be a long, hard day as spring storm clouds continued to gather around them. The rangers had warned the volunteer group this morning that a swift moving cold front would sweep through the area at sunset. And that was bad news for Tony Banyon.

DUSK WAS FALLING and the storm chased them. Shelby couldn't hide her frustration that they still hadn't found Tony. All afternoon, they'd called out his name about every quarter mile. They would stop, hoping to hear a reply. Nothing. The sky was a gunmetal gray, the winds blowing hard and sharp. Spits of sleet already began to cover the area. Dakota called a halt to their search because it was getting too dark to track. Shelby reluctantly agreed.

They were a mile from the meadow. Dakota had already picked out an area of heavy brush that would give them protection against the growing gusts of wind. She helped by clearing the space with a long, fallen branch, smoothing it out for their tent. Her stomach growled with hunger.

Dakota finished off the radio transmission with HQ, giving them their GPS coordinates. They would stay and ride out the storm. He turned and saw that Shelby had chosen a good place for their tent.

"This is a fast-moving storm," he warned her. "Weather guy just said it will hit this area right now."

Shelby straightened. "It's already starting."

"He said the storm should clear off by tomorrow morning," Dakota growled. "The snow is going to cover Tony's tracks. We'll make a best guess tomorrow morning and then head toward the direction of the meadow as soon as we get enough light." His mouth turned grim. "I hope we run into him." It would be too late, but he didn't say it. He could see the truth on Shelby's face.

"Yes, first light," she whispered. "It's the best anyone can do under the circumstances."

Opening the ruck, Dakota pulled out the desert camouflage tent. He wished he could somehow ease her worry. Shelby was the type of person who cared deeply about everything and everyone. His job right now was to get her mind off the man who was lost somewhere out beyond them. He tossed her some of the stakes that would keep the tent from flying away in the gusts of wind.

For the next ten minutes, they worked quickly and without speaking. Darkness was falling rapidly now. Shelby straightened, studying the tent. "This is military issue?"

"Yeah. SEAL stuff. What? You're looking at it like it's not very protective?"

She saw the shadows on his face as he knelt at the front and opened the Velcro flaps. "No," she said slowly, "I'm thinking that it's cramped. How do you get two people in there?" Her heart started a slight pound as she considered his closeness in such a confined space. Until this moment, her mind and heart had been on Tony and his situation.

"You do," he said. "This is cold winter gear. SEALs sleep two to a tent because body warmth will keep them from freezing to death." Looking up, he pointed toward the tops of the trees around them. "We're going to get hammered tonight with heavy, wet snow. The temperature will drop below zero." Her brows moved down as she stared with a question in her eyes.

"Are you going to have nightmares tonight? Turn over and think I'm the enemy?"

It was a fair question. Dakota pulled over his rucksack. He took out two MREs. Opening his jacket, he pulled two magnesium tablets from one of the pockets of his H-gear. "You have a choice," he told her quietly, gesturing for her to come over and sit down with him and eat beneath the protection of the overhanging tree limbs.

Shelby brought her pack over and sat down

cross-legged on the pine needles. It was almost dark. Their breaths turned to white vapor as the temperature fell rapidly. Dakota expertly set the MREs on two small metal grates and lit the magnesium tablets beneath them. He'd already cleared the area so no fire could start as a result. Rubbing her gloved hands together, she said, "What are my choices?"

Hitching a thumb toward the tent, Dakota rasped, "If you're worried I'll try to kill you in there during the throes of a nightmare, I'll sleep over there." He pointed to a group of bushes that would provide protection against the wind and snow. How he hoped she wouldn't ask him to leave. He understood her wariness but he'd never wanted a woman more than Shelby. He could feel his body turning traitor on him, his massive control dissolving in the heat of his need to feel her warm, firm body against his flesh. His mind just wouldn't stop. Nightmares be damned. Shelby had fractured the massive wall he'd hidden behind. Dakota had no answer for why or how she did. Only that she did. It left him starved for her, shaky, needy and his control slipping by the minute as they sat together. He prayed she'd take the first choice. She had to.

Shelby could barely see the outline of heavy bushes near the tent. The magnesium tabs were so bright, it was like sudden sunlight piercing the dark, ruining her night vision. She stared into his hooded eyes. Her body responded with aching need to that heated look. "What's my other choice?"

"Let me lie with you, love you and we'll spend the night in each other's arms. I promise, we won't be cold...."

The words, barely above a whisper, flowed hotly through her. She stared at him. His eyes were hard and intelligent, his mouth pursed. The beard had deepened and accentuated his high cheekbones, strong nose and full mouth. "You're serious?" she asked.

A slight twitch pulled at the left corner of his mouth. "Never more serious."

Her eyes widened momentarily. *Just say yes, Shel.* He'd willingly sleep outside in his specially made sleeping bag and survive nicely out in the coming snowstorm. And he didn't want her to decide based on worry he'd freeze to death. He knew her well enough to know because she cared so deeply, she'd make a poor choice. He was hoping his bluntness would scare her enough to make the right decision.

"Wouldn't you freeze out here?" She gestured toward the brush.

"No, Shelby. I took winter training up at Kodiak Island, off Alaska. We were out in the rain, snow and cold for three weeks. Trust me, I can survive any kind of storm conditions." He watched her consider the situation. There was no question he wanted her. The real question was: did she want him?

"I'll think about it," she muttered. "Are those MREs hot enough to eat? I'm starving to death."

CHAPTER FIFTEEN

COLD SLEET BEGAN to pummel the area as they quickly finished eating their MREs. Shelby stared through the near darkness at Dakota. "You know I don't want you out in this miserable weather," she said.

"Don't worry about me tonight, I'm tired." It was the truth. But right then his body caught a sudden burst of energy. Desperate energy. Why hadn't Shelby taken the first choice? He surrendered inwardly. Maybe it was a year's worth of being alone and lonely that snapped his control where she was concerned. Maybe...just one night... just one and he'd get her out of his blood. "I figured you'd choose door number two. You have such a soft heart, Shel. You feel sorry for any poor son of a bitch. Even me." It was more truth than teasing. No one needed a broken, scarred vet in her life. He'd only make it more miserable.

Shelby muttered defiantly, mouth quirking, "You're such a bastard, Carson."

He came over and smiled down at her. All

around them the sleet continued to thicken, the sound like tiny pebbles striking the limbs and pine branches. "It worked, didn't it?"

She could see the fatigue in his eyes. "Yes. And you're getting your ass into that tent. I refuse to lie awake worrying about you out in this crappy weather."

Without hesitation, he got down on his knees, opened his sleeping bag and pushed it inside the cramped quarters. "You're such a marshmallow, Shel."

His shoulders were broad and she could literally feel the heat rolling off his body as she knelt beside him and pushed her sleeping bag into the tight space. "Yes, I am," she said. "But so are you."

He barely twisted a humored look in her direction. The chips of ice had stuck to strands of her hair. "No, not me. Somehow, soft and SEAL aren't synonymous. No one has ever called us marshmallows, either."

Laughing, Shelby turned around, leaned back on her heels as she opened her pack to locate food. "They both start with an *s,* smart guy. You put on this fierce, tough front, but in the end, you have a big heart, Dakota."

His eyes narrowed intently upon her. Instantly, she felt that stalking energy around him. The night was nearly complete. "For example," she went on conversationally, pulling out two protein bars, "you saved Storm. You could have let that grizzly finish the job, but you put yourself in jeopardy by standing your ground. The bear would have known Storm was hiding in that burrow."

"Get inside," he growled, gesturing to the opening in the tent. "We don't need to chat out here and get wet if we don't have to."

Shelby grinned as she moved into the tent. She caught the glint of acknowledgment in his eyes regarding her argument. The two bags were right next to each other, the tent high enough to sit up in, but that was all. Dakota dragged in their packs and stowed them at the door after he squeezed his bulk into the tent. The Velcro on the openings were quickly closed. The pelting of the ice crystals continued. She handed him a protein bar after he sat cross-legged on top of his bag.

"Dessert?"

She was dessert, but he didn't say it. "Thanks," he said instead, taking the bar. As they touched fingers, he relished their brief contact.

Just then, Shelby's radio went off. She pulled it out of her pocket and answered it.

Dakota listened to the conversation, his brow dipping over the news. When she placed the radio above her head and near the sleeping bag, Dakota saw the concerned look on her face. She pushed the hood back, her hair mussed. "So, someone identified Vance Welton?"

The tent became warm very quickly, and Shelby unzipped her coat and shrugged out of it. She would use it as a pillow later. "Yes. Good thing Cade had photos of those guys put on television. It worked."

He could barely see Shelby, but he could feel her. Unconsciously, he inhaled her feminine scent. "How are you feeling about this development?"

"Considering it was my neighbor who saw him walking by my house, shaken," she admitted, unhappy. Shelby busied herself by untying the laces to her boots and shoving them off her feet. Getting on her hands and knees, she placed them at the end of the tent, near the entrance. She sat cross-legged once more, facing Dakota. "It bothers me a lot. I'm just glad my mom and dad decided to leave town until this is over." A cold shiver made its way up her spine.

Hearing the edge in her voice, he added, "Shel, we're going to find them and we're going to put them back behind bars where they belong."

"Count on it," she said. "I'm more worried about the women in town, Dakota. These guys are rapists and murderers. They're loose, like wild animals."

"Tomorrow," he assured her, "at first light, we'll start working our way toward the meadow and hope we run into Tony." It would snow all night and there was no way they could find him in the dark as a snarling storm whipped around them. They could get lost and die of hypothermia themselves. Under any other conditions, Dakota would have pushed on through the night trying to find the man.

"I wish we could do more to help Tony, but I know we can't. It's depressing." She finished off her power bar and located her canteen by touch. Opening it, Shelby drank deeply. The cold water soothed her anxiety about the radio call. "I can hear the worry in Cade's voice. He's thinking what we're talking about. No woman is safe with them prowling around," she said.

Dakota savagely pushed down his grief over his sister's death. "And we need to assume that Hartley is around, too. They worked as a team last time. It would be stupid to think Welton is working alone."

Capping her canteen, Shelby shoved it in a corner. "Where are they staying? That's what we need to find out."

"A better question is, did they steal another vehicle? Is someone missing a car or truck in Jackson Hole?"

"It's the right question to ask," she agreed. "It could give us a lead, a place where they might be hiding." The heat in the tent amazed her. She shed her sweater, down to a silk camisole. Modesty no longer an issue, Shelby shed her jeans and stuffed them down at the entrance along with her boots. With thick socks on her feet, her silk briefs and camisole, she pulled open her down sleeping bag, slid down inside it and faced him. She was glad Dakota was with her. Shelby felt fearful even though she knew the convicts were fifty miles away. Tomorrow, they had to return to Jackson Hole after, hopefully, finding Tony. Shelby knew she'd be anxious and alert going back home.

After finishing his protein bar, Dakota shrugged out of his winter gear and stripped down to his boxer shorts. He rolled the coat into a makeshift pillow. Wildly aware of Shelby's nearness, he reined in his desire for her. Right now she was worried and she had a right to be because Welton and Hartley were trying to find her. He could hear the veiled nervousness in her husky voice. She was struggling not to be affected by the news, but hell, she was human. And she'd already seen the carnage these two convicts caused up front and close before.

"Comfy?" he asked her.

"Yes. It's incredibly warm in here. This is an amazing SEAL tent you have!"

"The SEALs get the best of everything," he told her. "This sleeping bag is a product of the best minds around the world creating it for us so we could survive minus forty below if we had to." He opened it and slid in, using the Velcro to close it up to retain his body heat. After punching the jacket into a pillow, he lay down, facing Shelby. He could smell her damp hair and could hear her soft breathing. *So close.* Shelby was inches away from him.

"You guys deserve the best," she told him.

He reached out, his fingers making contact with her naked shoulder. He felt the warmth of her flesh beneath his callused fingertips, and it sent a keening ache through him. "Listen, stop worrying, Shel. We're going to find these gomers." He grazed her damp hair. Nostrils flaring, he inhaled her scent, honey mixed with pine. The combination was like an aphrodisiac to him, sending a sheet of fire burning through his hardening lower body. Her brow was wrinkled beneath his exploring thumb and he gently smoothed out the lines. "Go to sleep. I'm here...."

She closed her eyes. Dakota filled the tent with his size. She felt his protection like a warm blanket, erasing her fears and worry. Exhaustion came over her and the anxiety loosened its grip as she focused on his fingers stroking the curve of her neck and sliding across her shoulder. "Thanks, Dakota. It means a lot."

Dakota waited until he was sure Shelby was asleep. As tired as he was, he couldn't sleep. His mind was focused on the fact that Welton had been identified just outside her home. Lying on his back, hands tucked behind his head, he listened to the sleet finally go away to be replaced with soft, huge white snowflakes plopping gently on the sides of their tent. The wind was picking up and he could hear the gusts singing through the Douglas fir. That sound was like a lullaby to him. Despite his hunger for her, in moments, his lashes dropped and he fell into a deep, dreamless sleep. In the end, the strain upon their physical bodies won out.

SHELBY AWOKE WITH a scream. She launched into a sitting position, caught in a nightmare where Welton had her by her throat and was choking her.

Instantly, Dakota jerked awake. Fully awake. Without thinking, he sat up, reached out and found her in the darkness. "Shel…it's okay," he rasped, dragging her into his arms. "It's just a nightmare. You're safe…."

She gave a cry of relief. She didn't resist him, but instead collapsed in his arms, her head coming to rest against his shoulder.

"Oh…God…" A low moan tore out of her throat, her hand pressed against her neck. "Welton was choking me."

"Shh, it's just a bad dream," he whispered, pulling her next to him. He smoothed her mussed hair, his fingers threading slowly between the dry, silky strands. "He can't hurt you, Shel. I won't ever let that happen. You're okay, you're safe."

His moist, heated breath flowed across her cheek and ear. The trembling that had held her captive began to dissolve as his lips lightly grazed her cheek, her brow and hair. "I never have nightmares, Dakota. Not ever."

"Don't worry. The nightmares don't kill you. I

have them every night. I don't know what I'd do if
I didn't have them."

"You're sick," she mumbled, smiling a little as
his teasing short-circuited her terror. Shelby burrowed her face into his shoulder. His male scent ate
away at the edges of her bad dream. She heard his
rolling chuckle. The sound surrounded her and she
slipped her arm around his slab-hard belly. Sometime during the night, he'd opened his bag and the
material was bunched up around his waist.

"No, just being honest," he rumbled, smiling a
little into the darkness. He savored the feel of her
body against his, the curve of her waist as he slid
his hand across the swell of her hip. Automatically,
as if he were soothing a fractious, frightened horse,
he trailed his fingers from her shoulder down the
length of her spine to her hips. The camisole was
a thin barrier and he fought to ignore the silky motion beneath his fingertips. When she burrowed
closer to him, her hips nuzzling against his, he
knew she was silently asking him to love her. Dakota grew hard. Wanting her, knowing it wasn't the
right time, he forced himself to keep his ministra-
tions light, not intimate. Perspiration popped out
on his brow and across his shoulders as he wrestled
control over his own body. At the same time, another part of him screamed its need to make her his.

Shelby ran her hand up across his naked back,
feeling a number of long scars beneath her finger-

tips. Had to be war wounds. How much pain had Dakota endured? Wherever she traced, his flesh tensed. The nightmare had been so violent, so real. Shelby wanted to do something to make it disappear. Without thinking, more out of instinct, she lifted her chin, rose on her elbow, sought and found Dakota's mouth in the darkness.

When her lips touched his, he was startled. Her mouth was soft and searching, cajoling him to respond. He placed massive control over his body, but he was like a primal animal, wanting to take her hard and fast, stamping his maleness into her. His other side wanted to make her a partner, not something to be used. He gritted his teeth, lifted his hand, found her left shoulder. He eased Shelby onto her back, her body against his.

"Shel, is this what you really want?" His voice was husky with concern. He saw the fear banked in her drowsy eyes. Was she running away from the nightmare or running toward him? When a person thought she was going to die, there was an equal, violent will to prove she was alive. Having sex was one helluva way to confirm life over death.

"Yes, I want you," she breathed, feeling his hand around her back, drawing her up on her right side. "Now. And to answer your question, yes, I'm protected. No more questions." She eased out of his sheltering embrace, pulling off the camisole and quickly dispensing with her silk panties and socks.

Dakota pulled open his sleeping bag to allow her next to him. Her hips touched and then pressed against his. She had to know how much he wanted her. And when her hand ranged down to his waist, fingers easing beneath the waistband of his boxers, smoldering heat built rapidly within him. She pulled and tugged the rest of his clothes off his body.

Shelby felt the hard strength of his erection pressing insistently into her soft, rounded belly, her own body flexing, aching for him. Dakota slid his arm beneath her neck, drawing her fully up against him. His hard length sent wild shocks rippling down into her womb. Her core grew hot and moist instantly as the beat of his heart thundered against her breasts. Yes, this was what she'd been wanting. Him. All of him. And it had never seemed so right as it did right now.

"Kiss me," she breathed against the hardened line of his mouth.

His massive control began to crack as her soft lips waged a sweet campaign against him. She sought and found his mouth. Her fingers tangled in his short hair, trailing around the nape of his neck, pulling him down upon her. There was nothing shy or hesitant about Shelby, and Dakota curved his mouth hotly against hers, feeling the returning pressure of her lips, feeling her womanly smile beneath his. She was warm, responsive and when she pressed her hips against his, a groan broke free from deep inside him.

The moment Dakota lifted his hand, his roughened fingers cupping around the curve of her breast, Shelby lost the real world. Her flesh tingled, shards of electricity racing across her skin as those fingers caressed and explored her tightening flesh. The hunger of his mouth plundering hers, his thumb and index finger teasing the nipple into a hardened, needy peak, broke the nightmare and her whole world burned around her. His hips ground into hers, pushing her onto her back, his weight coming down upon her.

Everywhere she moved her fingers, his flesh tensed his muscles leaped beneath her as she mapped out his body, memorizing it and him. It filled her with satisfaction as a woman knowing her feminine power could physically affect him so powerfully. Her fingers grazed across his powerful chest, touching the dark strip of hair and following it down the center of his body that disappeared into his groin. His entire body tensed. There was an urgency to mate with this scarred warrior, this man who held her carefully, as if she were fragile china that might shatter in his embrace. His arms around her, his lips burned a trail of fire from her jaw, neck and down to her breasts. Her world exploded and she became mindless as his mouth settled upon the first nipple, his tongue lavishing it, suckling her, sending her deeper into a need she'd never felt so intensely before. Her body tightened and nearly convulsed as the shocks flew wildly down to her core.

Hips restless, Shelby moaned as his mouth captured the second nipple, his hand brushing her rib cage and easing toward her waist. His fingers sought and found the apex of her thighs, and a softened cry of pleasure tore out of her throat. His large palm flattened out over the area, his fingers moving downward. Somewhere in her cartwheeling mind, she understood Dakota wanted to please her. This wasn't a man taking sex from a woman for selfish gratification. No, this was a man wanting to awaken her body fully, then meet as equals. As his fingers tangled in the heat and wetness of her, she moaned his name, pleading for more of him. Heart racing, her breath coming in ragged gasps, she pushed against his hand, wanting more. Wanting him.

Dakota felt her silkiness, her slick warmth, telling him she was ready. In one moment, he pulled her over him as he settled on his back, her curved, damp thighs straddling his narrow hips. He could hear her gasping for breath, trembling violently as he brought her hips forward. A little cry tore from her as he moved against her heat, slowly entering her, giving her time to adjust. Gritting his teeth, he wrapped his large hands around her hips as she flowed down onto him, hot and slick. The last of his control disintegrated as she moved with him, her fingers digging convulsively into his chest as he established a wild rhythm between them. Dakota arched his hips against hers and heard her cry of pleasure tremor through her throat. He captured her hips fully against him, bringing more pressure to bear within her, pleasuring her, driving her to the edge of rapture and into his arms.

His hands were relentless, and he thrust deeply into her. He drove Shelby to the edge of mindlessness, her body quivering, spasming as he felt her begin to clench around him. An explosion occurred deep within her body and Shelby gave a hoarse cry, her back arching, head thrown back. The rivulets of fire raced outward like circles on a pond, each one more intense, more pleasurable, than the last within her quivering, taut body. And when he leaned upward, his lips capturing her hardened nipples, more explosions released wildly within her.

Lost in the darkness, the heat and feel of her body dissolved. Dakota eased her off him and moved her onto her back. His weight felt wonderful against her body and he nudged her thighs open to receive him again. Waves of glittering sensations blossomed hotly within her core as he moved powerfully within her. He took her swiftly, thrusting deep, stamping her with his maleness, claiming her in the only way a man can claim a woman. Shelby lifted her hips, knowing it would send him over the edge of pleasure. Dakota suddenly tensed. His hands curved into fists on either side of Shelby's head, his back flexing, violently trembling. A low animal growl rolled out of his chest, the delicious sound reverberating through every cell of her body. She wrapped her long legs around his narrow hips, her face pressed against his neck, their breathing chaotic, sweat slick between them. He released powerfully into her body. More scalding explosions occurred within Shelby, and all she could do was cry out hoarsely and cling to Dakota, who held her a willing prisoner within his arms and against his body. She tasted the sweat across his temple, her mouth searching and finding his. Their mouths clung together, sharing joy, sharing the fire continuing to erupt between them. The coolness of the below-freezing temperature did nothing but make her keenly aware of the sleekness of their burning bodies moving in primal unison with each other.

Collapsing against him, Shelby sobbed for air. Dakota slowly eased off her and brought her against him. Their bodies glowed against each other, their hips fused, their legs entangled. She nestled her head against his shoulder, her fingers moving against his sandpapery cheek, sliding across his damp, short hair. She kissed his corded neck, feeling his powerful pulse beneath her lips. Shelby smiled weakly, leaning up, drawing Dakota's head toward her so she could kiss him one more time.

His mouth ravished hers, but then became tender and coaxing. Her body was satiated as never before, Shelby curved her hand against the hard line of his jaw. This time, she moved her lips softly against his. His hands skimmed slowly down the breadth of her body and she could feel him memorizing her, gentling her with his touch alone. Shelby discovered a new level of emotion opening up her thundering heart. Fierce feeling flowed through her, taking her to another level of happiness she'd never experienced before.

Once Dakota eased out of her, Shelby nestled against his chest, he drew the sleeping bag over them. He made sure she was completely covered, his large hand coming to rest, finger splaying outward against her hip. It was a claim of possession. A man taking his woman, protecting her, loving her.

She closed her eyes and whispered, "I never want this to end." And then she fell asleep, utterly spent and cocooned within Dakota's arms.

CHAPTER SIXTEEN

THE NEXT MORNING, A quarter mile away from the meadow, they discovered Tony Banyon. He'd curled up, knees to chest, next to a Douglas fir and died of hypothermia. Shelby's heart broke as she took off her glove and held it to the man's neck, looking for the pulse she knew she wouldn't find. His skin was faintly bluish-gray. No pulse.

"He died at least four to five hours ago," Shelby whispered, straightening. At the height of the storm. There was no possible way to have found him in time. She saw something gripped in his gloved hand and gently eased it out from between his frozen fingers. As she read the scrawled note, her heart broke even more.

"It's a suicide note," she whispered, handing it to Dakota. Tears came to her eyes. "We were right. He knew what he was doing all along. He didn't want to be a burden to his wife any longer." Her voice broke and she stared down at the man. "This is so sad...."

Dakota read it, his mouth pursing. He handed

the note back to her and shrugged out of his rucksack. He pulled out a dark green blanket and gently
placed it over the older man's body. "He didn't have
a chance out here and he knew it," he muttered
darkly. Dakota honored his courage to look into
death's face and surrender to it. Not many men
could do that.

"That's a special kind of bravery," Shelby
agreed, her voice raspy with tears. She pulled out
her radio, cleared her throat and called HQ, giving
them the information. The head ranger would pass
on the contents of the note to the wife. Shelby was
glad she didn't have to give the wife the contents
of the note. She wasn't sure she could remain de-
tached. A helicopter would meet them in an hour
in the meadow. She looked over to see the mask
on Dakota's face, his eyes dark with suffering for
the man and his wife.

"At least this guy died in a place he loved," he
muttered.

"Yes…" Shelby managed, her voice a bit stran-
gled. Emotionally, she was thinking of the wife,
their long marriage and to have it all come to a sad
end like this. She stuffed the radio back on her belt.
"We need to transport him toward the meadow."

"I'll do it. Can you carry my ruck?"

Nodding, she hefted his heavy rucksack strap
over her left shoulder. They had a good amount
of distance to the meadow with knee-deep snow

slowing their pace. It was nearly 7:00 a.m., the sky a light blue with scattered clouds left in the wake of the swift-moving storm from last night. She watched Dakota as he gently brought the man's body into a fireman's carry across his broad, capable shoulders.

"Let's go," Dakota said, barely turning his head to catch her gaze. There were tears glistening in Shelby's eyes. He was touched deeply, too, but forced his reaction away, the way he always did. The man was small, weighing only about a hundred and thirty pounds. Dakota could easily carry him through the forest. They arrived at the oval, and the helicopter flew in ten minutes later.

Shelby sat with Dakota in the helicopter, holding his gloved hand. Dakota wished he could take away the anguish he saw in her eyes. Shelby was easily touched by human suffering. And he loved her even more than before. Dakota wasn't looking forward to driving back to Jackson Hole. They would get dumped into another kind of brutal storm, one that promised either life or death.

"ANYTHING NEW ON WELTON?" Shelby asked Cade Garner as they arrived at the sheriff's department. They had returned midday from Yellowstone after filling out a lot of paperwork on Tony's death at Ranger headquarters. Dakota stood relaxed at her side.

Cade was at his desk, papers strewn around it. "No. Your neighbor, Cat Edwin, who works at the fire department, spotted him."

Frowning, Shelby sat down in front of his desk. "She didn't see a strange or unknown car?"

"Nothing." Cade grimaced. "We're running their photos on local television with the evening news and we'll continue to do it every day. We're going to have to catch a break."

Dakota took a chair and sat down. "We know Welton is focused on Shelby. And he was caught in front of her home."

"Which was stupid of him, but lucky for us," Shelby said almost choking on her growing fear. Being stalked wasn't something she would ever get used to.

"But it shows he's that cocksure he isn't going to be recognized," Cade warned her.

"That's what you want," Dakota said, "because that kind of brazen behavior will eventually get him caught."

Shelby pushed her damp palms against her jeans. "I'm more worried that Welton and Hartley are going to kidnap another unsuspecting woman, Cade. That's what has me going. I feel like I can take care of myself where those two are concerned, but what about all the innocent women who live here in Jackson Hole?"

Cade nodded and became somber. "I'm worried

about it, too. I don't have unlimited manpower to devote a couple of deputies to find these two. We talked about strategies yesterday after Welton was spotted. If I had extra people, we could go to the local banks and grocery stores to look at video to see if we can spot them that way. They have to eat."

"Let me volunteer for that duty, then," Dakota said, giving Shelby a glance. "It's easy enough for me to sit and watch videos to try to spot them."

"I can deputize you," Cade said, liking the idea.

"But you'll have to be interfacing with a lot of people," Shelby warned, worried about his PTSD symptoms.

Dakota shrugged. "I lived with PTSD symptoms for years out in Afghanistan. I'll deal with it here." His eyes locked onto hers. "Your life is on the line. And these two are wolves walking among sheep. Ellie died because they were loose. I don't ever want another woman caught in her position. Not ever."

The low growl in his voice convinced her. There was pure hatred in his eyes for the two convicts. She glanced at Cade, who gave him a nod of approval. "If Cade can make it happen, that's fine with me." She stood up. "I'm going to get back on the rotation schedule, Cade. I can't sit up at Dakota's cabin twiddling my thumbs. I need to be out on the beat."

"Go get cleaned up and then come back in this

afternoon after lunch. I'll put you back on the duty roster."

"Welton and Hartley know she works here. Aren't you worried about that?" Dakota asked.

"Yes, but look, Shelby is a seasoned deputy. She has a cruiser, she knows the lay of the land around here and she's going to remain alert," Cade said.

Shelby reached out and touched Dakota's shoulder. "I'll be okay."

Mouth quirking, Dakota stood. He wasn't so sure, but that conversation would be in the cruiser on the way to his cabin.

"See you later," Cade called as they left his office.

The midday sun was warm with a breeze that made Shelby keep the knit cap on her head. She noticed Dakota scowling as he walked with her. He was scanning the area. But so was she. Climbing into the black Tahoe sheriff's cruiser, she waited until he got inside before starting the vehicle. Her body still glowed from their lovemaking last night.

"I can't sit and wait," she told him, backing the SUV out of the parking slot.

"They're actively looking for you."

"So?" she said, putting the cruiser in Drive and guiding it out of the parking lot. "Where else can they find me other than at my house?"

"They're hunters, Shel," he said, worry in his tone. Dakota ran his hands through his short hair.

"You can't get complacent. I worked with sniper teams in the SEAL platoon from time to time and they never relaxed or took downtime when on an op. For them, the enemy was out there 24/7. To assume the enemy slept wasn't something they took for granted, either. When they were out hunting, one man slept and the other stayed awake. They never both slept at the same time for fear of being caught by surprise."

The streets of Jackson Hole were wet with melting snow from the storm that had roared through the area last night. The same storm that had caught them. It was impossible not to be affected by Dakota—every part of him. Her body still felt his hands moving across her, remembering her, pleasuring her. He fulfilled a hunger in her that no man ever had. Shelby glanced over at him, his profile set, mouth thinned, telling her he was worried for her.

"I promise you, I won't get caught flat-footed. You keep forgetting I was the one who found their trail and tracked them for three days before I caught up with them at Norris Basin."

Reaching out, Dakota slid his hand down the curve of her thigh. He remembered her strong legs straddling his hips. Even though he wanted her all over again, he knew he had to get a handle on his desire and remain alert. "You've already proven yourself," he said. "You're the hunted now. This is a different mind-set, Shel. An involuted game turned upside down and you're the target. If I had my way about it, you'd stay at the cabin and not be seen anywhere near this town."

She lifted her hand and placed it over his. "I think you're seeing me through the eyes of a man who isn't used to working with women who are as good at what they do as you are."

His brows rose a little as they sped through a long curve of four-lane traffic through the center of town. "You're good all right." His lower body throbbed with need for her. She was a fierce, asser-tive lover, and that was when he realized just how confident Shelby really was. It was a surprise, but one of the best he'd had in a long time.

Laughing softly, Shelby gave him a tender look before returning her attention to her driving. "What are we going to do, Dakota?"

"About us?"

"Yes."

He stared at her full lower lip, hotly recalling her mouth skimming his chest, her kisses burning his flesh with such intense pleasure. "You and I aren't going to like my answer. Until Welton and Hart-ley are caught, nothing changes up at the cabin."

"What? You're going to sleep outside?"

"Yes. I'm the lightest sleeper in the world, thanks to my experience. And if those convicts get lucky and find where you're staying, I'm your first line of defense."

Scowling, Shelby muttered defiantly, "I knew you were going to say that."

He patted her thigh. "This is the kind of war my platoon fought over in Afghanistan. While the terrain changes, the enemy's mind-set doesn't. They want you, Shelby. And if Welton is ballsy enough to be caught out in broad daylight in front of your house, that tells me he's arrogant and on the hunt."

"A war," she said, unhappy. They crawled through the central plaza area, rife with tourists from around the world drawn to the famous Western town.

"It's a mind-set you have to embrace and understand. I worry that maybe you're overconfident, Shel. Yes, you tracked those two down, you hunted and captured them, but the tables are turned now. You can't afford to rest on yesterday."

As she sped out of town, up a long, easy hill with the elk refuge fence and land on the right and a huge black, rocky hill rising thousands of feet into the sky on the left, Shelby knew he was right. "Look, I'm scared. Okay? But I can't let fear run me, Dakota. If I allow it, I'll freeze and I'll get distracted. Both those things can put me in their crosshairs, and we know it."

Though he wanted to stop the car and hold her safe, he said nothing. Shelby was highly intelligent and she was a good law enforcement officer. "I wish," Dakota groused, "I could somehow transfer my years of experience over in Afghanistan into your head. Welton and Hartley remind me of the Taliban. They are damn good hunters. They knew the lay of the land and we didn't. They'd grown up in those mountains and knew them far better than we ever did. And those were all advantages they had over us. We lost some good SEALs because of it."

They crested the hill, the Tetons shining with a new coat of overnight snow on their slopes to the left. She never got tired of seeing them, their gray-blue granite flanks gleaming in the bright, over-head sunlight. "I wish I could do a Vulcan mind meld with you, too." She gave him a soft smile. The look in his eyes was one of raw concern. His sister had died at their hands. And after making love with this warrior last night, Shelby felt his fierce, unrelenting protectiveness around her.

Shaking his head, Dakota said in a low voice, "Dammit. I can feel them around, Shelby. I can feel them hunting you."

"THAT BITCH ISN'T at her house," Vance griped to Hartley. He'd just returned from getting food from the local supermarket in Jackson Hole. Hartley was continuing to put up plastic across the three windows in the broken-down cabin to stop the cold drafts. The hammer, nails and large roll of plastic lay on the yellowed kitchen counter.

Oren stopped what he was doing and came over to help unload the bags of groceries. "Were you able to get near the sheriff's HQ?"

Opening the refrigerator, Vance said, "No. I checked it out. The sheriff's department is about a hundred feet from the courthouse and they're on the same side of the street. On the other side is nothing but row upon row of houses. And they're all pretty close together with individual fences up between each one. I can't walk between them." He scratched his short hair growing back on his head. "As soon as I'm done here, I'm going over to the address of someone with her last name. I think it's her parents."

"Two for one?" Oren asked, taking the cans and stacking them on an open shelf to the left of the kitchen sinks.

"Maybe. Maybe she's holed up with them."

"Then what?"

"I want her. If we're stupid enough to blow the brains of her parents out, the cops will know it was us. And I want to keep a low profile and hunt her down. I don't need cops swarming all over this place because we shot them."

"But if you can't get her?"

Smiling a little, he said, "Then we'll go back

and target her parents. It's just another form of pay-back."

"And then we'll hightail it out of here?"

"Damn straight." He had sexual dreams every night that gave him an erection without fail. He took care of it on his own, but not as he wanted. Remembering Ellie Carson, how soft and young she was, he itched to be inside another woman. But not just any woman. Shelby Kincaid was going to be tied up on that bed in the corner, splayed out, naked, and he was going to make her bleed. Just as Ellie had. He could still remember her whimpers, her begging him to stop hurting her. For now he had to bide his time. He finished putting the groceries away.

"You keep gettin' this place cleaned up. It's damned cold up here at night. I'm gonna slip back into town. There's a gun dealer outside the town, and we need a couple of good pistols and two rifles," Welton said.

Oren Hartley returned to cutting out large, rect-angular pieces of thick plastic for the next window that needed to be fixed. "Be careful. You know they do background checks."

"That's okay." He patted the back pocket of his jeans. "Our new IDs are in place. That dude with the Garcia drug cartel did a nice job on our new license and social security cards. Worth the two thousand it cost." Welton smiled a little, feeling good about their steps toward throwing the cops off their trail. He rubbed his jaw. The prickly growth had given his triangular face a fuller look. As he pulled on a dark blue baseball cap, his camouflage was in place. Few would be able to identify him as a convict on the run.

"Be careful out there," Hartley drawled.

"Always," Welton called over his shoulder. He shut the door to the cabin and looked around. A rutted dirt road led up to the cabin. He could see one of the Tetons shining with a coat of overnight snow through the tall Douglas fir that surrounded them. They had happened upon the broken-down cabin by accident. The road had been hidden by overgrown brush. Luckily, Welton sensed it was a good path up the slope.

As he walked across the muddy ground to the truck, Vance congratulated himself. They'd successfully evaded law enforcement. Even Shelby Kincaid wouldn't be able to pick up their trail. Snickering, he climbed into the truck and shut the door. The cabin was an unexpected gift because it was clear to him whoever had owned it hadn't been back to it in a decade or more. The log walls were splintered, peeling and hadn't gotten a coat of shellac to protect the outer logs from the long, hard winters in the area. The windows all had caulking that had frozen, dried and fallen out, leaving wind whistling through the cracks. There was electricity to the place. The refrigerator was at least fifteen or so years old, but it still worked. A new tank of propane fired up the stove so they could cook their meals.

As he backed out and turned around, the wheels spinning in the mud, Welton drove down the steep slope. Moose Lake was far below, a popular hiking destination for tourists. Between the thick forest, he could catch occasional glimpses of the smooth blue surface of the small lake.

There was a spiderweb of dirt roads all across the eastern slopes of the Tetons. He'd scoured them relentlessly since finding the cabin, wanting to know what the odds were of a stupid tourist finding them by accident. The good news was there were no hiking trails above or below their cabin. The slope was steep, littered thickly with pine needles and thousands of Douglas fir standing guard to hide them.

As he slowly crawled around the curve, there was a window, a break between the firs. He could see down where the slope met the valley floor. Moose Lake was off to his left and he saw a gravel road leading from it to the main highway through the national park. Braking, Welton got out and stood observing the traffic. He was always interested in who was up and moving about. He picked up a pair of binoculars and scanned the main highway. His heart began to beat harder as he locked on to a black Tahoe SUV, a sheriff's cruiser, coming north.

Eyes squinted, Welton watched the cruiser drawing closer. He was too far away to see who was in it, except the outline of two people. Was this part of the ongoing attempt to find them? What got his attention was that it slowed down, took the Moose Lake turnoff and headed toward him. Fear trickled through him. Had the cops identified him? Seen him in the truck? Mouth dry, Welton watched intently, wishing like hell he had weapons on him.

To his surprise, the cruiser slowed and made a turn onto another less-used gravel road that led north of Moose Lake. The sunlight was overhead and for a split second, he thought he saw a glint of blond hair on the driver. What the hell? He remembered the color of that hair. Damned if it wasn't Shelby Kincaid! Hands tight around the glasses, Vance felt excitement mix with fear. The cruiser disappeared beneath the cover of the fir, gone from sight.

Welton stood there, his mind whirling with questions. Had Kincaid found them? *No, impossible.* He'd been damned careful to be in his cap and dark glasses. His beard had grown enough to hide his pointed chin. Rubbing his mouth, Welton looked at the area where the cruiser had disappeared. There was a narrow road there, he knew. He got into his truck, opened the glove box and jerked out a map

of the Tetons. Opening it, he hunted for the red X
he'd put on it, indicating their cabin. Once he found
it, he moved his finger down. There were several
capillary-like dirt roads north of Moose Lake. He
hadn't had time to explore the northern area beyond their cabin.

As he lifted his head, the sun slanting into the
window of the truck, he thought for a moment. So,
what was Kincaid doing in this neck of the woods?
He knew she was a damn good tracker. The last
thing he needed was her snooping around. Maybe
she was heading up to Lake Jackson to get a latte?
Maybe that's all it was.

Slowly continuing down the steep incline, Welton felt glee over his discovery. There was nothing more exciting to him than stalking a woman.
And now he was going to check out those minor
dirt roads that crisscrossed the slopes of the Tetons,
just to make damn sure Kincaid hadn't found them.
He fantasized about capturing the bitch and grew
hard. He could almost see the expression on her
face when she realized he'd gotten to her.

CHAPTER SEVENTEEN

"SHELBY, GOT A MINUTE?" Cade crooked his finger as she walked by the open door to his office.

She'd just gotten into uniform and came back to the department when he called her in. "Sure. Got my schedule ready?"

"I'm working on it." He handed her a piece of paper. "Check this out. I've been ratting through every file known on Welton and Hartley, and look what popped up."

Frowning, Shelby stood near his desk, reading the information. "They worked here? For Curt Downing?"

"Yeah," Cade growled. "Our homegrown regional drug lord is connected to them. Small world, eh?"

She read the rest of the information. "Yes, but that was nearly a decade ago. Downing hired them as truck drivers for his newly established trucking company here in Jackson Hole."

"Hey, it's a lead. I'm going to put an undercover agent over there to keep watch," Cade said.

"I didn't think we had the manpower to do something like that."

Cade smiled a little. "I got a call from the FBI earlier. They have a hand in wanting these two bastards taken down as swiftly as possible, too. They're assigning four FBI agents to me. They'll be here by this evening."

A little relief trickled through Shelby. "That's good news."

"And more good news. I'm getting volunteer deputies from surrounding counties coming in to start searching for these two. I can't have civilians doing it, because they're armed and they'll kill."

Nodding, Shelby handed the paper back to him. "How many men?"

"Ten. It's a good number. I'm going to meet with them and the FBI agents tomorrow morning in the conference room. I'd like you and Carson to be present. You and he know the trails and roads of the Tetons like few do."

"Dakota knows the Tetons better than most," she agreed, thinking out loud. "He's been hunting, fishing and trapping on their slopes. If anyone knows the back roads, the old, broken-down cabins, it's him."

"Which is why I want him here. These deputies coming in will go undercover, appear to be tourist hikers in the Tetons. It's good timing, because this is when the tourists come in, after the snow melts." He smiled and looked up at Shelby.

"How are you doing? This has to be damned stressful on you."

"It is but I'm not going to whine. I feel better being on the job. I'll be looking for those two as I work the town and surrounding highways."

"Let Dakota know we'll be convening at nine tomorrow morning," he said.

"I will," Shelby said. "Am I on duty right now?"

Grinning, Cade said, "Sure are. We've got an extra cruiser out there. Why don't you just keep your eyes and ears open here in town? We've got the photos of those two on TV. I'd like you to go over to the supermarket and talk to the store manager. Dakota said he'd go over and watch the store videos once he got his dressing changed over at the hospital on his bear bite. Those two have to eat and I'm hoping someone's seen them."

"I'll start with grocery stores and then check at the gas stations. I'm assuming they have a set of wheels."

"Good plan. Let me know if you get anything."

"You'll be the first to know," Shelby promised. She would head to her locker, pick up her weapon and belt. She felt a tad better that she was allowed to go back to work, but then her mind turned to Dakota. On the way to his cabin earlier, she'd convinced him to see Dr. Jordana McPherson. It was time for him to get his bear bite looked at by the physician. Shelby also persuaded him to see her about his PTSD symptoms. Would he? Damn, he was one stubborn man. Her steps slowed to the locker room. She couldn't stop thinking of their night together. They had been starving for each other. Was it just about sex? She had no answers. At least, not yet. For now she had to focus her mind on Welton and Hartley.

"YOU HEAL UP FAST," Jordana McPherson congratulated Dakota. He sat on a gurney as she cleansed the bear bite wounds and gave him a fresh, clean waterproof dressing to cover the forearm.

"Good, because I need to use that arm."

"You were lucky the bear missed a major nerve." She pressed her latex-gloved index finger near one of the puncture wounds. "If that had happened, you'd have lost complete use of your hand."

"Don't even want to go there, Doc," he rumbled. Dakota sat in a cubicle in the E.R. There were very few emergencies under way from what he could see. Jordana's touch was quick and professional. The red-haired nurse at her side handed her the new dressing.

"There, you're good to go for another five days," Jordana said, smiling.

Dakota waited until the nurse left. He slid off

the gurney and rolled down his shirt. "Doc, you got a minute?"

She was pulling off the gloves and dropping them into a receptacle. "Yes, it's quiet as a mouse around here."

"Can we talk in private? Go to your office?" He knew as head of the E.R., Jordana would have an office that afforded privacy. "Sure, follow me."

They left the cubicle and went down a hall.

In her office, Dakota closed the door behind him. Jordana's desk was clean and efficient, like her. He sat down once she took a seat. "You said you could help my PTSD symptoms?"

Nodding, Jordana said, "Yes. We've got more research available, Dakota."

She opened a drawer and handed him a small box. "This is a saliva test. If you'll follow directions and send it in to the company, they'll send me the test results. Basically, it's checking your cortisol levels four times in one day. It gives me a baseline to see what's going on with that hormone in your body."

He frowned at the box. "I'm sure my cortisol is through the roof."

"More than likely," she said, her voice soft with compassion. "By any chance, are you doing this because Shelby pushed you?"

Dakota met her gaze and saw merriment in her eyes. "Is it that obvious?"

The doctor chuckled. "I've been trying to get you to come in and take this test ever since I met you a year ago."

"Guilty as charged, Doc." He held the box in his hand, resting it on his thigh. "Shelby doesn't take no for an answer."

"I think you've met your match. I don't know which of you is more bullheaded."

"She is."

Nodding, Jordana gestured to the box. "Look, there is an adaptogen created by a pharmaceutical company that can lower cortisol levels back to normal. That's good news for people with PTSD. It's a one-month cycle of taking the adaptogen and then you stop. We retest you after three months to find out where your cortisol level is."

"So," Dakota said, looking at the nondescript cardboard box in his large hand, "you can make my PTSD symptoms go away?"

"Some of the symptoms, in most cases. That, or dialing them down tremendously so you don't suffer from them 24/7." Tilting her head, Jordana held his gaze. "Would you like to sleep at night, Dakota? Get rid of insomnia? Anxiety? Not jump at your shadow?"

"Sure I would."

"We can do that with this adaptogen treatment. Once you follow the protocol, which is twenty-four hours in length, send in the kit and I get the information back from the company, I'll have one of my nurses call you for an appointment. Then you'll come in and we'll get you on that adaptogen and change your life for the better. How does that sound?"

"Like a miracle," Dakota admitted. "I've had PTSD for a long, long time, Doc. And I won't get drugged up to my eyeballs to dull the symptoms. I may only have half a life, but it's all I got. I'm not going to let a drug take what's left."

"I understand," she murmured, giving him a sad look. "Shelby did the right thing in goading you to get tested."

Dakota felt his heart open just thinking about her. "When I first met her, I thought she was a Barbie doll."

Laughing lightly, Jordana stood and pulled her white lab coat on. "Shelby is deceiving in that way. She's beautiful and I've seen more than one guy project that image on her. Just because she has blond hair doesn't mean she's one-dimensional."

"Far from it," he agreed, standing.

"You two must get along." She walked around her desk, placing two pens in the breast pocket of the lab coat and picking up her stethoscope.

Of all the people he'd met in the year since he'd come home, Jordana was someone Dakota always trusted. There was compassion in her eyes, in her touch and proof of her care of others. Much like Shelby, he realized. "Yes, she's one of a kind," he admitted.

"I think she's good for you. Matter of fact, I think you're good for Shelby, too." Jordana halted at the door and looked up at the craggy vet.

"She's special, Doc."

Smiling, Jordana reached out and squeezed his upper arm. "Take care of her, okay? Cade Garner called me earlier today to let me know what was going on in trying to find those two convicts. I worry for Shelby. I know she can take care of herself, but she's potentially got two murderers hunting for her, wanting revenge."

"I've got her back, Doc. Don't worry."

Jordana opened the door. "Good. If nothing else, Dakota, you're the biggest, baddest guard dog she can have."

"SEAL power."

Jordana knew of his military background. She let her hand drop from his arm. "Exactly. Use it to the hilt, Dakota, because until these dudes are captured, Shelby is in danger." She frowned. "And so is every other woman around here...."

"I know, Doc. I'm sure Cade will keep you updated."

"Yes, he's been good about that. We've already warned our women employees to be careful and be much more alert. We have male security guards escorting our nurses to their cars at night now. We can't be too careful."

DAKOTA HEARD A VEHICLE coming up the road. So did Storm. The wolf went to the door, ears up, alert. The sun was beginning to set in the west. He glanced at his watch and saw it was 7:00 p.m. Shelby got off duty about this time, and it had to be her. Opening the door, he walked out into the shadowed woods that surrounded the area.

Shelby drove up in her green Toyota Land Cruiser. She parked and climbed out, no longer in uniform. Storm raced up to her, wagging her tail.

Laughing, Shelby turned and met Dakota's hooded eyes. "How did your day go?" She fondly petted the wolf's broad head.

"Okay," he said. "I found a videotape of Welton going in and leaving the supermarket. So that's good news. Cade has sent a deputy over to work with the manager and get the grocery clerks up to speed. If he was there once, he'll be back."

"Yes, Cade told me about it before I left after my shift was over." She smiled. "It's a step in the right direction."

Dakota nodded. "What's in there?"

"I brought us dinner." She reached in and brought out two sacks. "Chinese," she said, handing him one of the two sacks.

"Smells good," he told her.

"Better than eating a can of cold beans," she said, wrinkling her nose and drowning in his slow, heated smile. Just touching his fingers, remembering them grazing her flesh, giving her such pleasure, made her go weak for a moment.

"Let's get inside," he said, looking around. It was as normal as breathing for Dakota to scan the area, listen to the sounds or see if anything looked out of place. Satisfied it was safe for the moment, he followed Shelby into the cabin.

As she set her sack on the counter, Shelby asked, "How is your arm? Did you talk to Jordana?"

Dakota shut the door and locked it. "Yes to all the above. My arm is healing up fine."

The cabin was grayish-looking inside. Dakota didn't want a lantern turned on because it would make the cabin a target to anyone trying to locate her. He took no chances.

"Good. And you're going to take the cortisol test?" She pulled out several cartons and set them in a line on the counter. Just looking at him, Shelby felt her body hotly respond to that predatory gaze of his. There was no question, Dakota was a hunter.

He set his sack on the counter. "Come here," he rasped, pulling her into his arms. "I've missed the hell out of you today." He leaned down, curving his mouth over her lips.

Moaning as his mouth slid and rocked her lips

open, she felt his hands splay against her soft pink angora shell. She moved her hips against his, wanting him in every way. She drowned in the hunger that exploded between them.

Her arms slid around his shoulders. She tasted sweet, a hint of chocolate. Smiling to himself, his hand raking through her loose blond hair, capturing her, he tilted her head just enough to kiss her thoroughly. Her breath was rapid, moist against his unshaven cheek. Her moan was caught in his mouth and he absorbed the sound, her breasts pressing against the wall of his chest. He wanted to take her here. Now. It would be so easy to pull her to the bed, undress her and love her. God, how he wanted to do just that. In the back of his melting mind, he knew it wasn't wise. Danger lay somewhere out there. Someone was hunting Shelby and wanted to not only hurt her, but kill her.

Reluctantly, he tore his mouth from hers. Opening his eyes, Dakota saw her blue eyes filled with desire. He'd seen that look in her eyes before. Last night. He held her, his thumb moving across her wet lower lip. "Damn, you make me feel like a starved wolf, Shel." He leaned down, grazed her lips, felt her smile beneath his mouth. Her slender fingers moved up the hard line of his jaw and framed his face. But he forced himself to pull away from her mouth.

"I'm starved for you all the time," she whispered, giving him a wicked look.

"As much as I want to drag you to the bed and make love with you all night long, we can't."

Nodding, Shelby lost her smile. "I know…."

Dakota reluctantly released her, cursing the circumstances. The ache in his lower body was painful. Damn, how he wanted to bury himself in her, love her, fly with her. It was a shattered dream. At least, for right now.

"I keep thinking we could go to a hotel room somewhere in town," she said huskily, touching the side of his temple, seeing a small white scar across the area. It hurt her to think how he'd gotten it. In battle, for sure. She looked up and fearlessly met his slitted eyes, felt his heat even standing inches away from his powerful, tense body. "Want to?"

"You're a damned tease."

"I know. You've turned me into one. Can I help it if you're the best lover I've ever had?"

"You're the wild woman, not me. Do you know that?"

She grinned. "Only with you, Dakota. It's you. You make me lose every inhibition I ever had."

Lifting his hand, he slid his fingers across the crown of her golden hair, taming some of the strands back into place. "As much as I want to go to that hotel, we can't. We could be seen, Shel. You know that."

"It's hell being trained in law enforcement," she griped good-naturedly. She stepped back, putting enough distance between them so she wouldn't be tempted to continue touching him, learning his body, feeling him react and pleasuring him. "I'll be a good girl for now. Come on, let's eat while the food is still hot."

"The only food I want is you. And you'll never get cold."

"Damn, Dakota, you're making this tough." Shelby saw a slight grin leak into the line of his sensual mouth. A mouth she wanted to kiss, explore and have tease and tantalize her forever.

"We're good together, Shel."

"Too good." Taking a deep breath, she picked up a container and pressed it against his chest. "Food. Let's eat."

"Can I have you for dessert then?"

CHAPTER EIGHTEEN

SHE WAS LATE. After a quick glance at her watch, Shelby left the sheriff's office. The sun was behind the hills in the west. All day, law enforcement and the FBI agents had been arriving and gearing up to find Welton and Hartley. She'd been in meetings off and on, her head aching from giving info to the men who would begin combing the Tetons. Rubbing her brow, she headed toward where she'd parked, in an auxiliary parking lot behind the courthouse. What a long day.

Shelby hurried down the sidewalk, the area that now looked like a used-car lot because of the extra activities. She had called Dakota and he'd suggested they meet at Mo's Ice Cream Parlor at the main plaza for dinner. As she walked past the three-story gray-brick courthouse, she smiled softly. Ordinarily, she knew he would never eat in a restaurant; the noise was too much for him. Yet Dakota was putting himself outside his comfort zone for her. There were few options for a good hot meal at his cabin, so he'd opted for Mo's.

Turning into the asphalt parking lot, Shelby hesitated. Where had she put her Land Cruiser? The place was packed. The lights in the lot had not come on yet, making it harder to spot it. Her mind was still on the presentations she'd been giving to different groups. And she wasn't in her normal parking spot, which contributed to her confusion.

She remembered she'd parked the Toyota near the gray-brick wall in the sixth row of seven. She quickly threaded between the aisles. Fruit trees had been planted near the wall, taking away the urban look. Approaching her vehicle, she pulled out the key. Shelby slowed, as she always did, and focused on the interior of her Land Cruiser. It wasn't impossible that one of the convicts could be hiding in there and waiting to jump her. She inspected the inside closely, finding nothing out of place.

Satisfied, Shelby opened the car door to climb in.

A hand suddenly clamped her mouth, yanking her backward off her feet.

Shelby hit the asphalt hard. Nostrils flaring, she tried to scream, the hand pressing hard against her mouth and nose. Pain shot through her head as she violently struck the pavement. Eyes wide, she saw it was Oren Hartley. His blue eyes were slits as he maneuvered around her, his fist cocked.

Shock rolled through her. He held her down on her back, his knee pushed into her chest. A scream drowned beneath his hand as he cocked his arm, fist coming straight for her head.

Her face exploded with pain. A cracking sound went off through her head as his fist connected solidly with her cheek and nose. She was stunned, partly conscious from the strike. Adrenaline surged through her. Somewhere in her graying senses, Shelby realized no one would see the act. The Land Cruiser was parked next to the other tall SUVs. She was in trouble.

Gasping, she saw Hartley grin. His teeth were yellow. Grabbing her by the collar of her uniform, he got off her. She sobbed for breath, warm blood spreading across her lips and chin. Shelby wasn't even aware her nose had been broken, but she had a feeling it might be. As soon as Hartley removed his knee, she instinctively kicked out. Her boot connected with his groin.

Grunting, Hartley released her, his hands flying to his crotch. He leaned over, his mouth open in a silent scream of agony, eyes wide with surprise.

Shelby scrambled to her knees and got one last look at the murderous expression in the convict's eyes. He limped backward one pace, gasping, unable to straighten.

It gave her the split second she needed. As she scrambled to her knees, her ears ringing with sounds, pain reared up through her face. Shelby snapped off the restraining strap holding her pistol. In one motion, she whipped the pistol up and aimed it at the staggering convict.

"Freeze!" she yelled, both hands around the butt of her pistol.

"You bitch!" Hartley snarled, trying to make a lunge for her.

Shelby fired.

Hartley crumpled with a scream, grabbing for his left calf.

As she shoved herself to her feet, dizziness struck her. Shelby kept the pistol trained on the convict now writhing on the ground with a leg wound. Pressing the button on her shoulder radio, she called for backup, giving her location. She'd shot Hartley in the calf and she'd done it on purpose. The bastard wasn't walking away this time. Worse, she knew he probably wasn't alone.

Shelby warily looked around, gasping for breath, her pulse pounding with fear. Was Welton close by? She saw no one else. And help was on the way. Never once did she remove her focus on Hartley, who was moaning and cursing, his hands wrapped around his bleeding calf. He wasn't going anywhere.

As soon as help arrived, Shelby sat down in the opened Land Cruiser door and pulled out her cell phone. As she called Dakota with trembling fingers, she watched as Hartley's hands were cuffed behind him. An ambulance arrived, its lights flashing.

"Hello?"

Gulping, wiping the blood from her nose, Shelby rasped, "I'm in the courthouse parking lot. Hartley tried to take me down. Everything's all right. He's in custody. Can you get over here?"

"Stay there, Shel. I'm on my way...."

Nodding, she felt the shaking begin in earnest. One of the sheriff's deputies, Tom Langley, walked over to her.

"You need to be patched up, Shelby. Are you able to get to the ambulance or do you want some help?"

She managed a grimace toward the forty-year-old deputy. "I—I'm okay, Tom. Dakota's on his way. Just get that bastard over to the hospital."

Langley nodded grimly. He reached out, his hand on her shoulder. "You're looking pretty roughed up, Shelby. You want me to stay until he gets here?" He looked around. "I'm worried that Welton could be hiding nearby."

"You're right," she muttered, wiping her nose, looking at her hand that was now red with her blood. "Yeah, stay. I can use your help."

Dakota found Shelby sitting in the driver's side of her Land Cruiser, the door open, the deputy standing vigilant guard. Night had fallen, and he was alarmed at how bad she looked under the sulfur lights. He nodded to Tom, thanked him and eased his bulk between the opened door and Shelby. His eyes slitted as he saw her nose was puffy, bleeding and her cheek swollen. It broke his heart in two.

Dakota reached out. "Let's get you to the E.R. You've got a broken nose."

Shelby looked into his deeply shadowed face. There was rage banked in his eyes. "Hartley jumped me. He must have been hiding on the other side of my SUV."

Sliding his hand around her arm, he gently pulled her out of the vehicle. "Don't talk, Shel. You're looking pale. Can you stand?"

Nodding, she stood and had never felt safer as when Dakota's arm went around her shoulders. She leaned against him, feeling her knees grow mushy as the adrenaline began to leave her. She was glad he was strong and tall. He locked the SUV up with the key.

"I screwed up," she muttered as he led her to his pickup truck. "I should have gone around the Land Cruiser, looked—"

"Stop talking, Shel. Conserve your energy." He opened the door of the pickup and helped her inside. He worried as her eyes went cloudy. She was in shock. After buckling her in, Dakota closed the door. As he searched the parking lot, now crawling with deputies, a white-hot rage tunneled through him. Where was Welton? Had the bastard slipped away when their attack failed?

Shelby lay back, eyes closed, while he drove the short distance to the hospital. On the way over, she told him what had happened. The quiet anger swirled around Dakota. He didn't talk at all, but his mind seemed to operate at warp speed. Was this the SEAL reaction? The man who had survived years in hostile environments? Her nose and face ached so much Shelby couldn't think very far beyond that.

"Stay here," Dakota growled, opening the door. He'd parked the SUV at the doors of the E.R. "I'll get a gurney. Stay put."

The warning in his voice reverberated through Shelby. Not to worry, she didn't want to go anywhere. Her head hurt. Her nose ached like hell. Tipping her head back, Shelby closed her eyes as some of the fear and realization that she'd almost been kidnapped seeped like a poison through her. She tasted fear and had never felt as vulnerable as she did right now. The only thing between her and those two convicts willing to capture her was Dakota.

"SHE'S GOING TO be okay," Jordana reassured Shelby and Dakota. Standing in an E.R. cubicle, she'd finished looking at the X-rays.

Shelby sat up on the gurney. "That's good," she muttered, barely touching her nose. The swelling had begun in earnest. At least the bleeding had stopped.

Jordana nodded. "I use homeopathic remedies to stop the swelling." She placed some white pellets in Shelby's hand. "Take these, let them melt in your mouth. Hopefully, it will stop you from looking like a raccoon by tomorrow morning."

Grinning lopsidedly, Shelby did as she instructed. "Thanks, Jordana. So, my nose is fractured?"

"Yes, hairline. No surgery needed. It will be sensitive for a month, but you'll heal up fine." She checked the swelling on her left cheek and quickly cleaned it up. "You've been roughed up, but you got off a lot better than Hartley."

"I wanted to blow his head off," she admitted, giving the doctor a quick look.

"I understand," she soothed, adding some antibiotic ointment to the scratches on her cheek. "Dr. Collins is taking care of him. You shot him in a good spot. No major damage, but he's not going anywhere fast. You clipped his wings." Her lips twitched and she held Shelby's dark stare. "Right now they're taking him over to another wing of the hospital, up on the sixth floor, with two deputies guarding him. I heard Cade Garner just got here and he's going to interrogate him."

"Hopefully to find out where Welton is holed up," she muttered. "Thanks, my cheek feels better."

"You're welcome. I'll send a nurse to get you a

prescription for any residual pain you have with your broken nose. I'd try a couple of aspirin first, however."

Shelby nodded and then looked up at Dakota. She continued to feel the harnessed rage vibrating around him. He'd said little, and it was starting to worry her. Reaching out, she covered his hand with hers. His was so scarred-looking compared to hers. "How are you doing?"

Dakota looked down at Shelby. Her face was bruised. He could see purple shadows beneath her eyes, all thanks to Hartley breaking her nose. Lifting his hand, he gently eased some gold strands away from her cheek. "Okay. I'm more concerned about you."

"I'm coming down from the attack. I feel like so much jelly held together by skin at this point, if you want the truth."

Dakota allowed his hand to come to rest on her slumped shoulder. "You handled the situation fine."

Seeing the pride in his darkened eyes, she couldn't help but protest. "I should have checked out around my Land Cruiser. I checked inside, but not around it. It was a rookie's mistake. My head was still wrapped around all those briefings I gave the law enforcement guys today. I was distracted. I should have been focused."

He heard the censure in her husky voice. All he wanted to do was hold Shelby. Hold her and keep her safe. But she wasn't safe and Dakota knew it. "Listen, why don't you lie here on the gurney and rest for a while? I need to go talk to Cade. I have a plan, but I need his help on it. Okay?"

Though she gave him a quizzical look, Shelby did as ordered and lay back down on the gurney, the pillow feeling good behind her aching head. "What plan?"

Dakota watched her with that enigmatic expression. He had his own agenda. Trying to ease the worry in her eyes, he leaned down and tenderly caressed her lips. He eased away. "I'll tell you more, later."

CADE GARNER HAD JUST come out of Hartley's hospital room when he saw Dakota come striding down the hall. Nodding to the two armed deputies at the door, he went to meet him.

"How's Shelby doing?" he asked, putting his notebook in his pocket.

"She's okay," Dakota said, looking beyond the deputy to the room where Hartley was kept under guard. "You get anything from Hartley?"

Cade shook his head. "He's not talking. Smart-assed bastard. He lawyered up. Now I have to give him his call to get an attorney tomorrow morning."

"Let me talk to him," Dakota said, drawing him aside.

"I can't do that. I want to, but it's against the law."

Hand slowly curling, Dakota stood glaring at the door where Hartley was inside. He wanted the son of a bitch dead. "Okay," he rasped. "I need to get Shelby somewhere safe. I know your family ranch has a number of cabins on it you rent out every summer to tourists?"

"Yes, my parents have rentals." He quirked his mouth. "You're worried that Welton knows where your cabin is?"

"It could be compromised, and until I know for sure, I need Shelby somewhere safe."

"Well, maybe safer," Cade said, frowning. "It would be better if both of you were at our ranch. She's going to need a full-time bodyguard."

Dakota silently promised she was going nowhere without him from now on. "She's going to want to go back to work."

"I need her, Dakota. She's the one who tracked Welton and Hartley in the first place. Everything's in motion now. I can't take her out of the equation, and you know that."

He didn't want to hear it, but agreed. "Okay, but I'm in the mix."

"I want you with her," Cade said. Looking at his watch, he said, "I'll call my parents and find out which cabin you can have. Let me get back to you later tonight by cell? It won't take too long."

"I appreciate it," Dakota said, meaning it. He knew the deputy was up to his ass in alligators with the search moving forward plus trying to squeeze intel out of Hartley as to Welton's whereabouts. The deputy turned and walked down the hall toward a set of elevators.

Dakota stood for a moment, checked out the area. The room was at the end of a hall. The nurses' station was around the corner. There wasn't much activity on this floor; plus, it had been cordoned off to keep reporters and nosy people away from it. He studied the two deputies and knew both of them.

Looking at his clock, he decided to get down to the E.R. and keep Shelby company. It was where he wanted to be. As the rage moved lethally through him, Dakota stared at the door one moment where Hartley was, memorizing it. He was going to get to that son of a bitch and, one way or another, get the information on Welton's whereabouts. His mouth hardened, and he kept going down the hall.

DAKOTA HAD MADE SURE Shelby was comfortable in the cabin on the Garner family ranch. It was near 10:00 p.m. A wrangler kept guard outside the cabin. Dakota drove back to the hospital. Everything was quiet. It was time.

Only one deputy was at Hartley's door when Dakota arrived on the sixth floor. He checked out the nurses' station. One woman was hard at work on the computer, entering info. Turning, he headed down the tiled hall. Deputy Gary Epson raised his head.

"Hey, Gary, how's it going?" Dakota asked. The man was twenty-one, fresh from law enforcement training.

"Hey, Dakota, fine. How's Shelby doing?"

"Fractured nose, roughed up, but she's going to be all right."

"That's good news." Epson looked around, a worried look on his face. "Hey, I gotta get to the bathroom. Can you stand here for a few minutes? My partner is down at the cafeteria grabbing a bite to eat. I'm not supposed to leave, but nature is calling. Would you? Hartley's cuffed to the bed, so he isn't going anywhere."

Dakota nodded. "Sure, go ahead. Your secret's safe with me."

He waited until the deputy disappeared around the corner. He knew the restrooms were near the nurses' station. Turning on his heel, he entered the room swiftly and silently.

Hartley was sitting up, wearing a blue gown, his one leg wrapped in a white dressing. He looked like a skinny jaybird. Dakota quietly shut the door and closed the distance on the convict. He didn't have much time and he was going to make the most of it.

CHAPTER NINETEEN

"Hey!" Hartley yelled. "Who the hell are you?"
He saw the tall, dark-haired man with eyes like
slits heading straight for him. It was his posture,
his shoulders hunched, head leading his body, his
hand curled into a fist at his side that scared the
hell out of him. Fear shot through him. He had no
way to escape the stranger.

Without a word, Dakota's fist shot out like a
striking snake. It connected solidly with Hartley's
fear-etched face.

The blow sent the convict slamming into his
bed, jerked sideways by the cuff holding his left
wrist to the railing. He cried out once, slumped to
the floor, his nose bleeding profusely.

Without a word, Dakota leaned down, grabbed
the guy by his shoulders and hauled his ass up on
the bed. He pushed him down.

Eyes wide with fear, Hartley cringed away from
the man. "Who are you?" he shrieked, trying to get
away from him.

"Your worst nightmare," Dakota hissed. He

yanked Hartley back, slamming his head into the pillow, his long, greasy hair between his fingers. Savage pleasure hummed through Dakota as he saw he'd broken the man's nose. It was crooked and bleeding heavily. He put his face inches from Hartley's and snarled in a low growl, "I'm Ellie Carson's brother. Ring a bell?" He tightened his grip on the man's hair.

Hartley gasped, the name hitting home. His eyes widened even more, his mouth opening. "Oh God…"

"I want to know where Welton is. I'll give you one chance to answer me or I'll kill you. Got it?"

Hartley saw murder in the man's narrowed eyes, the way violence surrounded him. His nose was bleeding heavily, the blood spilling down his lips, chin and splattering onto the blue gown across his chest. Hartley knew the man would carry out his threat. "He's in a cabin off a dirt road. Th-there's no road name."

"It has a number, asshole. All forest service roads have a number. What is it?" he snarled, his breath puncturing across Hartley's frightened features.

"I—uh…uh…"

There wasn't much time. Dakota knew the deputy would be back very shortly. He raised his right hand and slowly curled it into a fist. "I can kill a man with one strike."

Welton made a mewing sound, trying to move, but Dakota had him pinned. Escape was impossible. "Y-yes…the number is 420."

Dakota smiled. "Smart move. I broke your nose because you broke my woman's nose earlier this evening."

Hartley blinked once. He'd hidden a shiv that the deputies had not found, beneath the bed, just in case. His hand reached out, feeling for it, found it with shaking fingers. Hartley knew he was a dead man. His fingers wrapped around the four-inch shiv. With a grunt, he wrenched up his right arm, aiming to sink the shiv into the man's chest.

Dakota saw the flash come up in Hartley's hand. His reaction was automatic. In blinding seconds, he bunched his fist, striking Hartley in the temple, sending broken bone splinters into the man's brain. He never even felt the shiv penetrate his lower arm.

Hartley slumped suddenly, dead in his hands.

Son of a bitch! Breathing hard, Dakota held the little bastard's limp body. Remorse flowed through him. He didn't need this. Although Hartley sure as hell deserved to die, Dakota knew this would be a messy detail. *Dammit!* The bloody shiv lay nearby. Blood was dripping from his left forearm, near where he'd received the grizzly bite. The drops congealed on the floor near Hartley. Mouth tightening, Dakota turned and knew he had to do the right thing. Cade Garner would have to be notified. He'd just killed a man in self-defense, and the weapon and his wound would prove his story. Still, Dakota hated the complexity that this would cause. Right now all he wanted to do was go find Welton. But that wasn't going to happen. He'd have to wait.

As he walked out of the room, Gary, the deputy, was returning. It was going to be a long night. He pulled out his phone to tell Shelby what had happened. She wasn't going to be happy, either. No one would be.

WAS HE IN TIME? Dakota stood quietly as he stalked Welton's cabin. Would Welton know Hartley was dead? Cade Garner was keeping the information off the airwaves in hopes that he could nail Welton at the address Hartley had given him. He moved like a shadow near the road leading up to the cabin where Welton was supposed to be. He wore dark clothes, a black bandana around his head, dark green and black face paint, his eyes adjusted to the thin wash of moonlight through the forest. Without a sound, he trotted up the curve.

Ahead, Dakota saw the silhouette of a cabin. He halted and knelt down behind some brush, waited and watched. His breath came sharp and fast, mouth open so no one could hear him breathing. In his left hand he held his M-4. He had a Nightforce scope on it and he could see through the dark with it. His SIG Sauer was strapped low on his right thigh, the restraining strap released so he could smoothly pull it out and use it if he had to.

Dakota heard and saw nothing. There was no vehicle around, either. Was Welton here? Had he somehow realized he was being hunted? Unsure, Dakota moved like the shadows around him, soundlessly, as he checked out around the ramshackle cabin.

Nothing.

His senses were on high alert. He drew close to the house. The porch was grayed by weather, several boards sticking up that needed to be nailed down. Moving silently, Dakota made it to the door. Gloves on so no one could lift fingerprints on him, he tested the knob. It moved. It wasn't locked. He slowly looked around, his ears keyed to the sounds of the night. Nothing seemed out of place.

In an instant, Dakota slipped through the door, M-4 jammed against his shoulder, the barrel pointed toward anything that moved. After swiftly entering the cabin, he cleared it. The place was empty.

Dakota continued to look around and made sure the only door had nothing behind it. Everything was quiet. Welton was not here. Turning, he began a quiet search of some clothes strewn across the empty bed. It took him ten minutes to search through everything. Welton was either out on the prowl or had been nearby when Hartley had jumped Shelby and then disappeared.

And then it struck him. Dakota realized that Welton might have tracked Shelby back to his cabin after that incident. *Damn!* With a soft hiss, he turned on his heel, leaving the cabin and hurrying down the narrow road toward his well hidden truck far below.

BY THE TIME Dakota had driven up to his cabin, it was 2:00 a.m. The moon was low on the western horizon. Not taking any chances, he parked his truck near brush at the base of the road. He ran silently full tilt up the road, M-4 in hand. If Welton was up there, he'd know shortly. His breath came in quiet gasps, and as he neared the cabin, Dakota spotted no vehicle. And no one seemed to be around.

Moving into the shadows, the trees and brush hiding him, Dakota kept his M-4 up and ready to fire. He used the Nightforce scope to detect any thermal heat movement of a human being hidden nearby. *Nothing.*

As he moved parallel to the front door, he saw it was ajar. He never kept the door open. Kneeling, he waited and watched. The crickets were chirping. They always stopped singing if they were disturbed by human activity. His instincts screamed that Welton had already been here, not found Shelby and had left. *Damn!* Quickly moving, Dakota checked out around the cabin before entering it. When he did, he found the place tossed. Everything was on the floor, the mattress torn apart. His mouth turned into a snarl as he surveyed the mess. Welton had followed Shelby!

There was a whine at the door.

Head snapping up, Dakota saw Storm quietly enter the opened door.

Relief flowed through him as the wolf came over, licked his gloved hand, tail wagging. Dakota petted her head, so glad Welton hadn't found her. The convict would have killed Storm without a second thought.

"Good girl," he murmured, running his hand over her back.

He took off his clothes and put them and the gloves into a bag. After washing his hands and face, he drew out a new set of clean clothes.

Once dressed, Dakota went outside and noticed a half-eaten rabbit on the ground near the porch. Storm hunted every night. In this case, hunting had saved her life. He paced soundlessly across the porch. The road was powder-dry dirt. There could be footprints from Welton imprinted in the soil. A new kind of satisfaction thrummed through Dakota as he carefully retraced his own footsteps. He'd come up here tomorrow morning and find what kind of shoe or boot Welton was wearing. It was one step closer to finding the murderer.

SHELBY AWOKE SLOWLY. Her headache was gone. And her nose wasn't aching. She turned over in the luxury of a queen-size bed. Reaching out, she felt a warm spot where Dakota had lain earlier. Sunlight lanced around the edges of the window where the dark burgundy drapes were drawn. Pulling herself up, she felt achy and sore. The door was open and she could hear the clink of pots and pans out in the kitchen.

She pushed her hair out of her face and forced herself to sit up. Her bare feet touched the pine floor, grounding her. The smell of coffee laced the air and she lifted her nose, inhaling deeply. It smelled good. She was surprised she could smell anything at all with a broken nose. Sitting there, she felt her heart move powerfully with love for Dakota.

"You're up...."

Dakota stood in the doorway, dressed in body-hugging Levi's and a black T-shirt. She gave him a drowsy smile. "How did you know I was smelling the coffee you were making?"

His heart wrenched as he looked into her cloudy blue eyes. There was still swelling on the left side of her nose and a crescent of purple beneath her left eye two days after the attack.

"I felt you wake up," he said, walking over and handing her the bright yellow mug with steaming coffee.

"Thanks," she murmured, meeting his hooded gaze. He had shaved, his hair gleaming from a recent shower. "You look good," she said, sipping the coffee. "How long have you been up?"

"Not long." Dakota sat down on the bed next to her, careful not to slosh the coffee out of the cup in her hands. "You awake enough to hear some news?" he asked. Her blond hair was badly mussed and needed brushing. Lifting his hand, he slid the strands gently across her shoulders. The pink flannel gown she wore was soft-feeling beneath his fingertips. She closed her eyes for a moment, enjoying his touch, absorbing it into her bruised body. He kept his rage over her attack on a leash. Right now his focus was on her.

Shelby knew yesterday evening when Dakota had come back to the cabin that he'd accidentally killed Hartley. And she'd persuaded him to have the puncture wound looked at. A clean white dressing was on his forearm. Dakota had regretted killing Hartley. He'd wanted to see the bastard go to death row and suffer a very long time before they pumped him full of chemicals to finally take his miserable life.

Shelby glanced at the clock on the bed stand. It was 9:00 a.m. This was two days in a row she'd slept in late, and she knew it was because of the shock and trauma she'd endured.

He moved his fingers around her nape, her skin

warm, the silk of her hair tangling between them. "Cade's talked to the county prosecutor about what happened with Hartley. And he's not pressing charges against me." He heard Shelby gasp. Her head snapped up, her eyes widening as she stared over at him.

"Thank God," she whispered, pressing her hand against her pounding heart.

Dakota explained the judgment by the prosecutor. It would be seen as defending himself. He wouldn't go on trial and he wouldn't go to prison, a relief to him. As he continued to touch her, he felt the tension dissolve in her shoulders.

He'd left their bed at one o'clock this morning, looking to find Welton. And then Dakota had driven to his cabin to find it had been ransacked. By 3:00 a.m. he'd returned here to sleep with Shelby at his side. He hadn't slept much, his mind churning over what Welton might try next. At 5:00 a.m., he'd awakened and allowed Shelby to sleep as long as she wanted.

"After I drove up to our cabin last night, I found the door standing open." His voice deepened. He knew this would upset her. "Welton knew where we were."

Setting the mug down on the bed stand, Shelby could sense the anger in his voice and in his eyes. She turned, her knees pressed against his right thigh. "But…how…?"

"I suspect he followed you. He might have been hiding nearby when Hartley jumped you. Or he might have seen your cruiser on the highway below my cabin by chance. I just don't know." Dakota tenderly leaned over and kissed her wrinkled brow. "Don't worry, we're safe here, Shel. By the time I got up to my cabin, he was gone."

Shelby smelled warm and sweet. Dakota wanted to continue to kiss her, but the timing was all wrong. "I woke up at five this morning and I decided to drive back up to my cabin. It was too dark to search for tire tracks or footprints. The good news is that I found his footprints this morning. Cade sent up a forensics team and they made impressions. That will help in tracking him."

"Things are moving fast," Shelby said more to herself than him. As his hand moved gently across her shoulders, she sighed.

"You look upset," Dakota said, kissing her temple. "What's going on in your head?"

"I sat here after I got up thinking I could have died out in that parking lot. I guess it's shock hitting me."

The tremble in her softly spoken words tore at him. "Come here." He brought Shelby into his arms, gently holding her. She came and nestled her head against his shoulder, her brow against his jaw. When her arms went around his waist, Dakota drew in a deep, ragged breath. He wanted to love her, tenderly, erase the fear he knew was lingering within her about her own brush with death. Pressing a chaste kiss to her hair, he said in a low tone, "You defended yourself. You saved your own life, Shel. You're a well-trained law enforcement officer and you got the upper hand."

She released a ragged sigh and closed her eyes. "I was so shocked by the attack. So...scared..." Shelby opened her eyes and eased back just enough to meet his gaze. There was turbulence—and desire—in his light brown eyes. "Do you know what made me fight back with everything I had?"

"No. What?"

"When Hartley slammed me to the ground and I was semiconscious, I realized that I loved you, Dakota." She smiled softly and slid her fingers across his sandpapery cheek. "I don't know when it happened or how it happened, but lying there with his knee crushing my chest, seeing the look of murder in his eyes, I knew I loved you...."

Whispering her name as if it were a prayer against her lips, Dakota took her with all the tenderness he possessed. He curved his mouth against her parting lips, wanting to somehow infuse her with his strength and love. He knew he could love her, heal her and help reclaim her life once again. But not right now.

Welton was on the prowl and Dakota could feel the convict, feel his murderous intent toward

Shelby. If he admitted his feelings, he couldn't go back. He couldn't survive losing Shelby. For now, all he could do was drown in the returning splendor of her kiss, the heat between them. As he sat on the bed with this fierce, independent woman who had fought to live, he knew without a doubt, he loved her, too.

CHAPTER TWENTY

"SHELBY, I NEED your help," Cade Garner called on the phone. "We've got a tourist in Tetons National Park whose three-year-old boy walked away. He's lost. I need some good trackers. Are you available?"

After two weeks of being holed up at Cade's parents' ranch, Shelby was more than ready. "Yes. Have you contacted Dakota?"

"I have. Drive on in. I'm putting you back on the roster and you'll be a deputy again."

"Thank God," she muttered. After hanging up, she quickly traded her shoes for a good pair of hiking boots. Going into the bush to hunt for a missing child would require some different clothing. The sun was streaming across the valley as she climbed into her Land Cruiser and took off. The day was bright, cloudless and warm.

For two weeks, Shelby had stayed on the ranch, a relatively safe place. Dakota had been hunting for Welton every day in the Tetons. He'd found the convict's tracks, but it was a dead end. No one knew what kind of a vehicle he had. Forensics had taken impressions of the tires of a vehicle down at the end the road, but they were a variety that a good half of Jackson Hole residents had on their vehicles. There was no way to find him in that avenue of investigation.

Touching her cheek, she noticed that the scratches she'd acquired were gone. The swelling around her nose had disappeared. In a mirror, Shelby looked normal, no hint of the violence done against her. But she could still feel its effects. Frowning, she drove at the maximum speed limit, wanting to get back to work.

"HEY, GOOD TO see you," Cade called as Shelby entered his office.

Dakota was with him looking at a wall map of the Tetons.

"Nice to be here. Thanks for letting me go back to work. I was slowly going crazy out there." She grinned. Her gaze moved to Dakota, and she saw the worry banked in his brown eyes. Probably for her. He wanted her off this case for good, but Cade had refused to release her. Her body responded to Dakota's hooded, smoldering look. This morning, before he left for work, they had made long, tender love. As much of a warrior he was, she'd discovered over the past two weeks how gentle he could be with her. Her love for him grew daily.

"What do you have?" Shelby asked, moving to where Dakota stood.

"Three-year-old boy, Bobby Parker, walked away from his parents' campsite this morning. The mother was watching him, went into the tent for two minutes, came out and he was gone."

"Poor Mom," Shelby murmured. "Kids at that age are so fast."

"I'm more worried about a grizzly finding the kid," Dakota muttered. He punched the wall map with his index finger above where the camp was situated. "I was over in that area two days ago. I ran into two male grizzlies. One was a cinnamon color and the other was a dark brown. One had a collar on it for tracking purposes and the other did not. I reported both to the rangers and gave them photos. What's bad about this is that brown grizzly is a newcomer. No one knows its behavior or its pattern of where it's going to go to find food. He's a wild card in this track."

Mouth compressed, Shelby said, "That's not good news."

"Bears at this time of year are starving," Cade said, scowling. "I have Charlie, the Tetons Forest Service supervisor, on this. He's assigned three rangers to try to locate the whereabouts of this new bear. He's worried the grizzly might mistake the child for a baby elk and kill it."

A cold shiver ran down Shelby's spine. "It's not a good situation."

"So you two are going in with major weapons in hand," Cade warned them. "Carry your rifles and a pistol."

"I'm staying in my civilian gear," she told Cade.

"Good. Just show your identification to the parents once you arrive. I'm gathering another group of searchers and volunteers right now, but I need you on this now."

Dakota nodded and walked around Cade. "We'll get over there now."

Shelby said, "I'll pick up a radio for Dakota at the desk."

"Good. Test them out before you start tracking with our dispatcher. Make sure they have fresh batteries in them."

"We're good to go," Shelby said, walking out with Dakota.

In the hall, Dakota looked over at her. She wore a bright red long-sleeved blouse beneath her dark green jacket. "You sure you're ready for this?"

She could hear the veiled worry in his deep voice. "I am." Shelby reached out, caught his fingers for a moment and squeezed them. "I have to get back to work, Dakota. I'm fine. I'm healed up."

"If I had my way, you'd be chained to the bed." A hint of a smile lightened his dark expression.

"I know you're worried for me, but you can't

hide me away in a castle. I need to work. I can't let what Hartley did stop me from living. You know that."

"Yeah," he groused, giving her a frown. "You're hell-bent to get back to your deputy work."

"Look, this is a lost child. We'll be tracking together. And we have radios. I really don't think this kid disappearing is Welton's work. It's an accident. And we should be able to find him pretty quickly. I hope." She had tracked lost children before in the Tetons, and each time she found them alive and well.

Dakota halted at the dispatcher's desk, where the woman handed him a radio. He thanked her and they walked toward the front door.

SHELBY CALMED BOBBY'S frantic parents at the campground. While she took the information for a report, Dakota had already identified the child's tennis shoe tread and was following it into some brush located at one end of the large campground. By the time she reached him, he waited to show her the track.

"There's no reason why this kid would plunge into this kind of brush," Dakota growled, pointing at the broken small twigs and branches.

Shelby knelt nearby, studying the scene. "Is it possible the child heard a sound in the brush? If he did, he might have gone through it to investigate."

Scowling, Dakota saw the trail of tiny branches and torn green leaves in the wake of the child's exploration into the brush. "Good call."

"Or maybe there was a baby elk on the other side of these willows?" Shelby stood up and craned her neck, but she couldn't see over or through the thick brush.

"Let's go on the other side of this area and see."

The warmth of the morning climbed. Shelby shrugged out of her green jacket and tied it to the pack she wore. The pine needles were dry and cracked beneath the soles of their boots as they made it to the opposite side of the willow stand. She watched Dakota slow to a stop. He searched the area. Moving quietly to his side, she saw what he was looking at. There were some disturbed pine needles near the exit point in the brush. Moving forward, she leaned down, studying more closely.

"The problem with pine needles is that they destroy the track on the sole of a shoe," she muttered. She turned to glance up at him. "What do you think?"

"I think the depression is a little too deep for a three-year-old kid," he said. Kneeling down on one knee, he examined it intently for a moment.

Shelby looked around. "But there are no other prints anywhere else."

Rubbing the back of his neck, he growled, "I know."

"Maybe the boy was running?" She pointed to the heel area of the depression. It was deeper than the toe area.

"Running toward what?" he said, unhappy. Dakota had a bad feeling about this. He was jumpy anyway because of worry about Shelby.

Slowly rising, Shelby walked parallel to the footprint and searched for other depressions. The problem was there were a lot of rocks up the face of the mountain along with dry pine needles scattered and thinning out across the area. "I'm spreading out to look for bear spore...." She hated even saying it. A grizzly could have been sniffing around this side of the willows, the child could have heard the bear and gone through the brush to investigate. A quick, cold shiver raced through her. Automatically, she prayed that the grizzly did not find the child.

Dakota took steps in the opposite direction, carefully looking near the edge of the brush for any sign of bear spore. *Nothing.*

"Dakota?" Shelby called. She knelt and waited for him to come over to her. His face was hard and unreadable.

"Look, scat."

He leaned over, hands on his knees, next to her. "Yeah, but that's old bear scat. At least two days."

"I know," she said, disappointed. "But what it does prove is there is grizzly in this area." Her voice trailed off and she stood up.

Dakota reached out, pushing a few gold strands away from her healed left cheek. "Don't go there," he said. "Not yet…"

Her skin tingled in the wake of his grazing touch. Despite how hard he looked, the lethal power that swirled around him, she reacted to his tender look and his finger trailing down the line of her jaw. "You think it's a grizzly?"

Shrugging, he studied the steep, rocky hill above them. "It's a lead, Shel. That's all."

She rested her hand on his broad chest, the heat of his skin emanating from beneath the dark brown shirt. There was a change in his eyes, and the line of his mouth softened. "We need to find this boy…."

Leaning down, he curved his mouth across hers. Shelby's response was heated and filled with promise. He slid his hand against her jaw, tilting her head slightly, and deepened their kiss. He inhaled the sweet scent of her as a woman, tasting her, absorbing her. Reluctantly, Dakota eased away, her eyes drowsy and filled with desire. "Let's keep going. We got good daylight. Kids are fast but they tire out, too. We'll probably find him within a mile of the camp."

Mouth tingling, Shelby yearned for another time and place with Dakota. She could never get enough of this warrior whose scarred hands were tender, sending her into realms she'd never gone before.

"Okay," she said, her voice softer than normal. "We have to find the boy before it's too late…."

"Let's hold out hope for him, then." He wrestled inwardly with his feelings for Shelby. Dakota was plagued with worry over his PTSD and, some night, hurting her. He felt as if he had one foot in heaven and one in hell. And with no quick, easy answers to fix it or fix himself. *Damn.*

Shelby moved away from Dakota, feeling heat, the power exuding from around him, the invisible rippling effect making her dizzy with need. Dakota could look at her a certain way and she would feel her body blossom in anticipation of his touch or kiss. Getting hold of her emotions, she turned and pointed to the edge of the hill. "I think the boy might have tried to find an easier way up this hill. What do you think?"

"Don't know. You take that side of it and look. I'm going to go up the rocks."

Shelby nodded. Trying to find the trace of a footprint on rock was nearly impossible. Yet she saw Dakota shift gears to the black lava rock face scattered with brown pine needles. She had the rifle over her shoulder as she went nearly a tenth of a mile to the right of where he was tracking.

Dakota would look up every once in a while to check on Shelby's location. There was no brush on the hill, just Douglas fir, like soldiers standing at attention. He'd then shift back to looking for a few pine needles out of place among the millions that were not. It was tedious, intense work to try to find those three or four needles.

Shelby followed the curve of the hill. To her left, Dakota was about halfway up the rocky face. She was finding no depressions in the floor of the forest. Disheartened, she was leaned over, moving slowly, head down, gaze fixed and moving from right to left.

She felt more than heard movement to her right. *What?* Lifting her head, she twisted and looked. A brown grizzly male, nearly seven hundred pounds, was less than a hundred feet away from her. Fear shot through Shelby. The bear whuffed—a warning.

Without hesitating, she jerked the rifle off her shoulder. It was instinctive to flip off the safety. She knew from long experience to keep a bullet in the chamber at all times.

The bear charged, roaring.

Dakota jerked upright, hearing the roaring sound. Suddenly, to his horror, he saw the brown grizzly hurtling toward Shelby. Without thinking, he pulled his pistol out in one smooth motion. Shelby stood her ground, jamming the butt of the rifle into her shoulder, aiming and firing.

The bear was hit in the shoulder with the first shot.

In seconds, it would be on top of her.

Dakota leaped to one side, hands on the SIG, firing one, two, three, four shots into the angry, charging bear. He didn't miss.

Shelby fired a second shot, not even hearing Dakota firing his pistol to the right of her. The bear leaped, its long curved claws aimed right at her head. She twisted her body, pushed herself to the left, firing the rifle as she fell toward the ground.

The grizzly swiped at her, roaring, his mouth open, teeth bared. Shelby landed hard. Rolling, she tried to get away from the bear. It landed with a heavy thud next to her. Eyes wide with terror, she saw it lift its paw, blood running out of its one eye. She gasped and dug the toes of her boots into the floor of the forest, lunging away from the grizzly.

She was breathing hard, the strap of the rifle tangled around her left arm. Dakota raced up, his pistol aimed at the dying bear. His face was a mask of intensity. He lifted the pistol and fired a cartridge at point-blank range into the bear's thick skull. The round went in and the bear groaned, slumped and then lay still.

Dakota released the emptied magazine from the pistol, pulled out another magazine from his gear and slammed it into the SIG. He then turned on his heel, holstered the pistol and quickly moved to Shelby's side. Her face was pale, her eyes wide with terror.

"It's all right," he soothed, picking her up. He

untangled the leather strap from around her left arm. "Are you okay?"

Shelby's knees were weak. She reached out and grabbed for his arm. "I never expected this...." she rasped hoarsely, gazing at the dead bear less than ten feet away from her. Shaken, she heard her voice trembling. "I must be under some kind of dark cloud. God, that was close." She felt his arm slide around her shoulders, drawing her up against him.

"Too damned close," Dakota rasped, pulling her hard against him, his gaze never leaving the bear. Grizzlies were known to look dead, but rise and attack again.

Closing her eyes for a moment, Shelby leaned heavily against him. "The bears have it out for us." She remembered Dakota being attacked earlier in June.

"They're nothing to mess with at this time of year. They're hungry and they're willing to defend their territory. That bear was here before. It's his territory." He pressed a kiss to her mussed hair. "You were in his territory and that's why he charged you."

Shelby slid her arms around his lean waist, breathing raggedly from her brush with death. "Thanks...thanks for being there. Why did you use your pistol and not the rifle?"

He moved his hand across her back, feeling her

trembling in earnest now. Dakota recognized it as the adrenaline surging through her body. "Couldn't get it off my shoulder fast enough, Shel. When you're in a situation like this, you go for the second line of defense, the pistol."

Shaking in earnest, Shelby nodded. "Thank God you were there. I hit the bear in the shoulder the first time. My second shot bounced off its skull. I couldn't believe it!"

"You were caught flat-footed," Dakota said, his voice low with feeling. "You did the best you could. Bear skulls are the thickest in the world." He knew if he hadn't been with her, the bear would have killed her. Inwardly, his gut clenched. To lose Shelby after he'd found her would be like tearing his heart out of his chest. He'd never felt this way about any woman. Holding her tight, he pressed small kisses along her hairline and cheek. "It's okay, Shel. It's okay."

As he held her, Dakota began to realize how much Shelby was helping him to heal. It wasn't anything she did consciously; it was just her. He squeezed her gently and released her, checking her expression. Dakota was always stunned that his touch could soothe her so quickly. Was that love? A part of him didn't want to go there, but his pounding heart did. As he drowned in her blue gaze, he felt an incredibly powerful ribbon of blinding emotions explode through him. The sensations heated, healing and lifting the darkness that always haunted him. How could a man like himself, filled with demons, ever learn to love? Somehow he had.

CHAPTER TWENTY-ONE

DAKOTA HEARD A small cry. It was the child! *Where?* He twisted his head toward the sound. It was coming from over the hill where the grizzly had attacked Shelby.

"Did you hear that?" Shelby whispered, giving him a look of disbelief.

"Yeah, stay here." He left her standing there, running across the rocky, slippery area toward the sound in the distance. Dakota trotted past the dead grizzly and broached the hill. His sharpened gaze caught the three-year-old boy near a stand of willows, a small limb in his hand. He was frightened, tears making paths through the dirt and scratches on his face.

Relief sizzled through Dakota as he slowed and walked up to the boy. Kneeling down, he said, "Bobby?"

The boy sniffed and scrubbed his eyes. "Y-yes. I want my mommy...."

"I'm going to take you to her. My name is Dakota. Are you hurt at all?" He saw the boy's eyes were red-rimmed. He was dirty from crawling through the willow stand.

"N-no, but that bear was following me." He lifted his hand and pointed at the dead grizzly up on the hill. His squeaky voice became stronger as he lifted the stick to show Dakota. "But I picked this up. I was going to hit him and scare him off with it."

Smiling a little, Dakota took the stick and set it aside. "You're a very brave boy, Bobby. Are you thirsty?" He pulled the canteen from his belt, opened it and handed it to him.

Without a word, Bobby put the canteen to his lips and drank.

Dakota watched water dribbling from the sides of the child's mouth as he slugged down the liquid. Finally, when he'd had enough, Bobby shyly handed the canteen back to him. Capping it, Dakota said, "Ready to go?"

"Yes, but I can walk."

Straightening to his full height, Dakota grinned at the plucky child. He held out his hand. "Okay, ready? My partner is on the other side of the hill. We're going to pick her up and then take you home. Your parents are very worried for you."

"Okay," Bobby said, slipping his small hand into his large one. "I'm hungry."

"I bet you are. Let's go find Shelby and then we'll see if I've got a protein bar you can have."

Bobby brightened. "I like protein bars!"

Smiling to himself, Dakota checked his stride to match the child's steps. He took the radio from his belt and called in to Cade Garner, reporting they'd found Bobby Parker. Dakota could hear the relief in the deputy's voice. Cade would then have one of the deputies staying with the parents at the campground give them the good news.

Shelby's eyes widened as Dakota reappeared at the hill with Bobby walking at his side. She grinned, sliding the leather strap of the rifle over her left shoulder. Bobby waved to her, as if he were on some kind of exciting grand outing. Shelby waved back and met them halfway. She knelt down and introduced herself to the child. Touched by Dakota's gentleness with the three-year-old, she smiled up into his eyes. There was a softness in them she'd not seen before. Clearly, Bobby liked holding on to his large, scarred hand.

"Let's take Bobby home."

Shelby stood and walked to the other side of Bobby. She gently held the boy's other hand, feeling a rush of relief that the child had not been killed by the grizzly.

"THAT GRIZZLY WAS stalking the kid," Dakota told Shelby later as they drove back to the Garner Ranch.

"I got that."

"He was stalking Bobby when you happened

upon them. The grizzly saw you as a threat to his forthcoming dinner." Dakota slid a quick glance toward her. She looked shaken and pale from her run-in with the bear. Anyone would be. When an animal of that speed and weight attacks, there are seconds between surviving and dying.

"It scared the hell out of me." Shelby pushed her fingers through her dirty hair, wishing for a hot shower.

"You reacted right away," he said, complimenting her.

"Yeah, but I couldn't shoot worth a damn."

One corner of his mouth crooked. "Listen, you did what you could under the circumstances."

"You were cool as a cucumber. I hit the ground and saw you running and firing at the grizzly. Every shot hit that bear. You didn't miss."

"I had to hit him."

She heard the low growl in Dakota's tone, saw the look of anxiety in his gaze as he caught hers. "You moved so swiftly. You were completely focused on that grizzly. I've never seen someone move and shoot like you did."

"SEAL training," he said, reaching out and capturing her hand. There were several scratches across her fingers where she'd hit the sharp volcanic rocks.

"You shot the bear in the eye. That's damn good

shooting." She remembered he'd shot the other bear that had bitten him in the arm with an eye shot, too.

Dakota swelled with some pride. He felt good beneath her praise. "Thanks. I was a sniper, so I'm not half bad at hitting a target. The grizzly was moving so quickly I fired six shots into him before I got his eye and brain."

"I couldn't hit the broad side of a barn in that battle," she muttered, shaking her head.

"Stop being hard on yourself. You were startled, the grizzly was too close. You were lucky you got that rifle off your shoulder to shoot at all." He squeezed Shelby's fingers gently and saw some of the self-indictment leave her blue eyes. "Let's get you home. I think a shower is in your future." He caught her lips pulling into a wry smile.

LATER, AFTER A shower and clean clothes, Shelby combed her damp hair. Her hands were scratched and bruised. She got off lucky. She could smell bacon frying out in the kitchen. Dakota was making them a late lunch of his favorite food, breakfast. Resting her hands on the sink, she stared into the foggy mirror. She loved this ex-SEAL. He'd just saved her life. Never would she forget the swift, blurred movement of his hand as it went for the pistol slung low on his right thigh. Or how quickly Dakota had moved, that pistol always level as he ran, firing into the grizzly. And yet, when it was all over, he was solicitous, caring for her. Later, he was incredibly gentle with little Bobby Parker. He was a man of depth and he intrigued her. The whole situation hadn't rattled him at all. Never mind that he'd already captured her heart.

Setting the comb aside, Shelby left the bathroom and padded down the hall to the kitchen. The smell of bacon frying and pancakes in another large skillet filled the air. "It all smells so good," she said, inhaling.

Dakota turned over the pancakes and looked over his shoulder. Shelby was dressed in a simple pink T-shirt, jeans and moccasins. Her damp blond hair hung in straight strands around her shoulders. "Go sit down. I'll serve you." He quickly flipped the pancakes onto a large platter, lifted the bacon out of the skillet and turned off the stove. Worried, he saw darkness in her eyes. Leftover shock, he was sure. Shelby had had two near misses with death. First with Hartley and now this. How was she really holding up emotionally? Dakota would tread carefully and continue to silently assess her well-being.

"Looks great," Shelby said, meaning it as he placed the plate in front of her.

"Figured some good breakfast food would go down easy," he said, watching her rally and pick up her knife and fork. Would she eat? Dakota wasn't sure, but he sat down with his own plate and dug hungrily into four stacked pancakes slathered with melting butter and Vermont maple syrup.

Shelby pushed the pancake around, chewed on some bacon, but discovered she really wasn't hungry. The day was bright, the sunshine slanting through the kitchen window. Sighing, she muttered, "You went to all this trouble and I just can't eat, Dakota…." She set the flatware aside. Instead, she picked up the coffee and sipped it.

He rested his hands on either side of his plate, gauging her reaction. "I've seen this kind of reaction before," he told her quietly.

"What do you mean?"

With a one-shoulder shrug, Dakota said, "When my platoon was Down Range in Afghanistan, we were always out in bad-guy country. Sometimes things would go wrong. The squad I was with had two of their shooters wounded in a helluva gun battle with an HVT, a Taliban opium drug warlord." He held her dark gaze. "SEALs are more than a team, Shel. They're family. You train, live, eat, breathe with these guys for years. They're my brothers. My family."

She could feel the intensity of his words, the passion behind them. "I'm glad you're letting me into your other life, your world. It had to rock you when those guys were wounded."

"It did. It shook every one of us. We're trained to be combat medics, and believe me, our skills saved their lives." He hesitated, choosing his words carefully. "When we got a medevac in there to take out our wounded, we then were lifted out later. Our team was in shock. Our men being wounded was like being wounded ourselves. We didn't know if they'd live or die at that point. We were caught up in so many conflicting emotions." Dakota pushed the empty plate aside and folded his hands, holding her gaze. "There is no manual, no training on earth, Shel, that teaches you how to react, how to handle your emotions for these moments. When we got back to our base, our officer in charge took us out of combat for a week to decompress."

"Why?"

"Because we were too emotionally rattled to be a hundred percent focused out in the field. He recognized the symptoms. And no matter how hard we tried to sit on our emotions, our anxiety, grief and rage, it didn't work. We're human. In the end, our AOIC, Jake Ramsey, had us stand down and it was the right call." Dakota reached out and slid his fingers across her bruised right hand. "Shel, you're in the same position I was over there. You don't recognize how compromised you are after a traumatic event. You think you're a hundred percent, that you've got a gun in the fight and you're confident in yourself and your abilities."

His fingers tightened imperceptibly on her hand as he watched moisture collect in her eyes. Shelby was fighting back a lot of emotions, trying to control them. It wouldn't work and Dakota knew it. "I wish…I wish I'd had someone like you to just hold me, talk me down, listen to me over there when it happened."

The heat of his hand permeated her cooler one. His words struck her heart and gut. "Okay, so I'm where you were?"

"Something like that."

Closing her eyes, Shelby sat back in the chair, a rush of emotions starting to erupt within her. The terror clawed at her chest, struggling to leap into her throat and fly out her mouth. "Okay," she whispered, her voice unsteady. "I hear you. I get it."

"I know you don't like staying here at the cabin and you want to get back to work, but it's not the right time, Shel. I know you're bored out of your skull. So were we. We had to take our guns out of the fight. We wanted back at that Taliban warlord and take his ass permanently out of the fight. Our OIC knew we weren't ready to climb back into the saddle."

Shelby wiped her eyes with trembling fingers. "I feel so damned helpless, Dakota." She'd spoken the words softly, the pain sandwiched in between the words. His hand moved gently across her forearm, soothing her. His eyes were so old-looking with far too much combat experience beyond them. He saw what was going on with her even though she didn't. More tears rolled down her cheeks. Shelby pulled her hand from his, reached into her pocket and found a tissue.

"So what do I need to do? I have to recover, Dakota. Welton is still out there hunting me. Damn, I feel like a raw target of opportunity." Her voice grew angry. "I want that son of a bitch! I want him so bad I can taste it. He's out there prowling around. I'm so afraid he's going to capture some unsuspecting woman and—" Her voice cracked. "Your sister paid a horrible price. I don't want any other woman to go through what she did."

"That makes two of us," Dakota agreed. With his finger he eased the damp strands of hair behind her delicate ear. "Listen to me, Shel. Decompress for a week. I'm out there, I'm hunting that bastard for both of us. I have a score to settle with him and I'm going to find him."

The words were spoken with controlled hatred. There was such raw rage he held inside himself. And just as quickly, the look of a committed warrior to his sworn enemy disappeared. Her ear tingled where he'd grazed it with his finger. "I believe you. I just worry for you," she said.

"Don't worry about me. I've had years to handle my feelings toward Welton where Ellie was concerned. I'm not coming off a hot firefight having two of my friends wounded. I'm very focused and calm about hunting Welton down. My emotions aren't going to get in the way of me finding and eliminating him. They're going to help me find him."

Shelby knew without a doubt that if Dakota found Welton, the convict was dead. Maybe Cade Garner and the rest of the sheriff's department didn't realize it, but she did. She felt that steel coldness within him, knew it was lethal and knew Welton's last look at the world would be this warrior's face.

"So you want me to just hang around the cabin? I can't even go on another lost child request?"

He shook his head. "I think it would be best if you just rested for a while, Shel. You've had two near-death brushes in two weeks."

"I feel like I've got a black cloud above my head," she griped.

He smiled sourly. "It seems that way. Third time's the charm and, frankly, I don't want you testing that one out to see if it works or not. Okay?"

Nodding, she stuffed the tissue back into her pocket. As she held his gaze, she felt her heart swell with such love for him. There was no question she was falling in love with him. Reaching out, she slid her hand over his.

"There's just something about you that touches my soul, Dakota. I have trouble even putting it into words. I like it. I want it and I want you."

He gently turned her hand over, brushing her

soft palm with his work-worn fingers. "You own my soul, Shel, whether you know it or not." His voice dropped to a rasp. "You're an incredibly strong, good woman. I don't know how I got so damned lucky in finding you, but I'm grateful." He picked up her palm and pressed a kiss to the center of it.

Absorbing his lips upon her flesh, the wild tingles racing up her arm, touching her pounding heart and making her feel safe, she managed a trembling smile. "I don't want to lose you, Dakota."

A silent joy filled his chest. He closed his hand around hers and leaned close. "You won't lose me. If I can survive three deployments in Afghanistan, I'll survive anything the civilian world wants to throw at me." Dakota's brows moved down and in an urgent tone, he added, "But I can't protect you as much as I wish I could, Shel. That's why you have to work with me, stay here and stay safe."

"Nowhere is really safe, Dakota. You and I both know that."

"You're right. But plenty of cowhands here on the Garner Ranch are watching out for you when they can. Just stay here for another week. Let me go find Welton."

Her stomach went queasy on her. Though she was beginning to understand how capable Dakota was as a warrior and a hunter of men, she still worried about him. Welton wasn't as stupid as Hartley had been. He was still around, still waiting, tracking her and timing when he'd reappear in her life. It was a gut knowing. Not one she wanted to share with Dakota. He was fiercely attuned to finding Welton. But who would find her first?

CHAPTER TWENTY-TWO

"HERE'S YOUR GUN and badge back, Shelby."

"Thank God," she said, taking them. When she shot Hartley, it was mandatory the deputy go on paid administrative leave until an investigation surrounding the death was completed. She slid the gun in the holster at her side and pinned her badge on her uniform. "This is good luck," she told Cade. "My weeks of incarceration are up, too."

Cade nodded and smiled a little. "You've had one hell of a month so far, Shelby. I think Dakota was right in asking you to stand down for two weeks. Did it hurt you?"

She grinned sourly. "Not really. He was right." Turning, she said, "Where is he?" He had left her bed early last night, continuing to track and trying to find Welton.

"He's more SEAL than ex-SEAL," Cade warned her. "Night is their specialty, so he's out walking a grid pattern in hopes of finding Welton."

She sighed. "He has reasons to do it."

"I know. If I were in his shoes, I'd be out there hunting Welton, too."

"Well, we have other fish to fry," he told her. Picking up a report on his desk, he said, "Thirty minutes ago, a call came in from the Tetons headquarters. We have a missing two-year-old girl named Susie, who wandered away from the Colter Bay tent camping area."

Shelby scowled. "That's not good. That whole area is heavy with grizzlies."

"No need to tell me." He looked up and said, "Why don't you switch back into your civilian clothes? I need a tracker and Dakota isn't here. Are you willing to do it?"

"Sure. Just take me off the duty roster." She grinned. "I'd much rather track than cruise around looking to hand out a speeding ticket."

Cade smiled. "I thought so. Okay, here's the contact info. You're going to have to talk with the parents first. I got a deputy already on scene, Ken Hutchinson. You can talk to him, too. I'm also arranging a larger volunteer group, but that's going to take a couple of hours. Getting you there right now is going to help us find that lost baby."

"Right you are." She started toward the door. "Oh, when Dakota comes back in, tell him where I am? He's probably going to be exhausted and go to bed like he usually does, but he should know where I am. He's a worrywart."

Cade nodded. "I will." He glanced at his watch. "He should show up any time now. You might even meet him on the way out."

Shelby lifted her hand. "I'm off. I'll be in contact once I'm out at the campsite and have interviewed the parents."

SHELBY GLANCED AT the position of the sun. It was 8:00 a.m., the morning very cool as it always was at this time of year. The sky was cloudless, a light blue. The parents were distraught and that was understandable. The other deputy, Ken Hutchinson, remained with them as she followed the child's tiny tracks from the campfire area to the asphalt parking lot nearby. He'd picked up small prints on the other side of the road. There was a sign that said Day Trail, and that's where the child's print was, he thought. The water from Jackson Lake could be seen from the camping area.

Shelby quickly went to the black sand and searched for Susie's footprint. To her relief, she found none. If she had, it could be an indication the child had walked into the water and drowned. Then her body would be found by dredging. It wasn't something Shelby wanted to do.

Pulling the rifle over her shoulder, Shelby went to the day track trail sign, knelt down and saw the print. The area was thickly wooded with trees and brush, the trail damp and narrow. The child had wandered off in the direction of the boat ramp, about a thousand feet on the other side of this thicket of woods. Colter Bay was a major area for boaters, both with engines or kayaks and canoes. There was a huge launch area and Shelby wondered if the girl had made it to the other side. If she had, she could be in real danger of falling off the unsteady movable wharfs.

Slowly rising, Shelby keyed her hearing, all senses online. Susie had disappeared at 7:00 a.m. when the mother was making breakfast over the campfire. She had been busy and distracted. The father was down at the Jackson Lake boat area, getting their fishing boat ready to take out for the day. It was easy to have a young child wander off in such a situation, Shelby knew. But the child had only an hour's lead and she felt confident she could find Susie shortly.

The other worry for Shelby was the high grizzly bear population around Jackson Lake. Right now there was a mother grizzly with three cubs known to frequent this area near the boat launch ramp. It was the bear's turf. That wasn't good for anyone who was lost. Particularly a small child. If the child started to cry or call out for her parents, the bear, if close enough, would hear it and come running. A young human's voice sounded like the mewing of a baby elk calf calling for its mother.

A shiver ran through Shelby as her thoughts went in that direction.

The woods closed in, the muddy track a thin brown ribbon. Mouth tightening, Shelby followed the toddler's fresh, muddy tracks. Soon, the forest grew quiet and silence thickened around her. She was starting to sweat and halted. Once she pulled off her thick jacket, she stuffed it in her knapsack. She rolled up the sleeves on her pink blouse, took a drink of water and then continued toward the wall of brush ahead of her.

Shelby stopped about two feet from the stand. What was she looking at? Kneeling down on one knee, she studied the disrupted soil. She saw the toddler's track, but there was another, much larger boot track on either side of the child's prints. *What the hell?* She pressed her hand into the soil and leaned closer. Her mind moved over possibilities. Mostly not good. Measuring the length of the track, as well as the width, she figured it to be male, not female. The boot was simply too large for a woman's foot.

Looking up, Shelby studied the gloomy forest surrounding her. Heart squeezing with fear, she wondered if a man had come upon Susie and taken her. To what end? A sexual predator who just happened upon the child? She swallowed hard. She didn't want to think those thoughts, but she was a law enforcement officer and she couldn't afford to ignore the possibility.

She'd seen Susie's mother's and father's boot prints at camp. And this print did not match their boots. Taking the radio from the side of her pack, she stood and called in to Cade Garner. When he answered, she told him what she'd found. His voice went dark with worry.

"Welton?" he demanded.

"I don't know," Shelby said, continually looking around now, feeling a sense of danger. "We can't leave him out of this scenario."

"Damn. Okay, Dakota is on his way out there right now. Give me your GPS coordinates and I'll send them to him."

Some relief filtered through Shelby as she looked at her GPS guide and gave him the info. "How soon will he be here?"

"Thirty minutes. He just got back and is exhausted. He had a run-in with a grizzly where he was."

Her brows flew up. "Oh no. Is he all right?"

"Yeah, and so is the bear. It was a female and he fired a couple of warning shots up in the air and she decided to leave instead of attacking him."

Sighing, Shelby said, "Close call."

"I know. Look, you want to wait there for him?"

"No, I'll push on. I'm going to track south on the path now because that's where the boot prints are leading. I'm sure he'll be able to track me from here. Out."

Worried for the child, Shelby put the radio back into her pack, turned and continued to follow the prints. Whoever it was was in a hurry, the stride lengthening. When she went back to the original track and compared it to what she was seeing later, it was clear the man had picked up the toddler. The depth of the tread was deeper, indicating he was carrying more weight, perhaps the child in his arms?

Shelby tried to figure out other scenarios as she slowly moved parallel to where the boot prints were leading her. Could a fisherman have happened by? Maybe he was carrying the toddler back to the main forest ranger headquarters of the Tetons? That was equally possible. Still, her nerves were stretched as she followed the track toward the lake area.

A second, curving wall of brush and willows rose in front of her. Shelby saw the tracks turn and follow around them. Suddenly, she heard a cry, a child's whimper.

She stopped near the end of the thicket, surrounded by forest and no other humans in sight. Her heart rate tripled. She hurried around the end of the stand and headed toward the sound. The child continued to cry.

Shelby let out a sigh of relief as she saw Susie

sitting just inside a wall of brush. To the child's right was another large thicket.

"Hey," she crooned, kneeling down in front of the dirty, scratched child, "it's okay, Susie." She gently touched the toddler's black hair and smiled at her. "I'm Shelby. I'm going to get you out of here and home to your mommy and daddy...."

Just as she leaned forward, her hands extended to slide around the toddler's waist, something stirred behind her.

Shelby twisted a look to her right, her eyes widening. Too late! There was Welton's leering face, his smile crooked as he jabbed a hypodermic needle into her upper arm. The bite of the syringe exploded through her.

"Too late, bitch," he breathed, yanking the syringe out of her arm. "You're mine...."

Shelby spun around, her arm smarting with pain. As she started to go for her pistol, Welton's boot flashed out. The boot toe caught her in the shoulder, knocking her off her feet. Landing with a thud, Shelby felt her mind starting to short out. She rolled to the left as Welton came at her, his fists clenched, a snarl on his lips. Her hand fell over the pistol.

"No, you don't!" Welton jerked her hand away and yanked the pistol out of her holster. Standing above her, he grinned, breathing hard. "Just be a good girl and let the drug do its work." He chuckled as he saw the woman's eyes begin to close, her body sinking back onto the forest floor. "The last thing you're going to remember is my face, you bitch. You put me away, you killed Hartley. Now I'm going to make you pay for all of it…."

DAKOTA SCOWLED, LOOKING at the extra boot tracks along with the toddler's. He was breathing hard, having trotted to the GPS coordinates Shelby had given him. Exhaustion pulled at him and he rubbed his reddened eyes. For the past week he'd spent twelve hours, dusk to dawn, searching every cabin up on the slopes of the Tetons, hoping to find that Welton had moved to new digs. He'd found nothing. *Now this*. He pulled the radio from his pack and called Shelby.

No answer.

Fear arced through him. Shelby would answer. She couldn't be that far away. Toddlers don't walk miles. They usually walk in a circle of sorts. He called in to Cade Garner.

"Has Shelby called in?" Dakota demanded, his gaze ranging over the wild territory. Grizzlies were everywhere. They could easily hide in the thickets that ringed Lake Jackson.

"No. Not yet. Are you there?"

"Yeah, just arrived." His mouth turned down. "This isn't good. She should be answering her radio."

"Maybe it's low on batteries?"

"Maybe..." The hair on the back of Dakota's neck stood up. Shelby was in trouble. He could feel it. "Look, I'll follow her track and call later. Out."

Stuffing the radio on his belt, Dakota loped down the slight incline. He followed her tracks, which were fresh and easy to read. It was now 9:00 a.m., the heat of the day beginning. Somewhere beyond him was Jackson Lake. He could smell the scent of water in the air. Where was Shelby? Why wasn't she answering her radio? *Damn!*

Dakota followed the tracks down to a huge wall of willows that grew for about a tenth of a mile. Beyond that was a major tourist hiking trail that went around the lake. He saw her track stop for a minute, noticed a dirt impression where she'd knelt down on one knee as if looking at something more closely. As he lifted his head, Dakota's eyes narrowed. Shelby had stood up. But now her boot track changed. She was running, the toe of her boot deeper than the rest of the print. What was she running toward? He hurried around the edge of the thickets. His SIG Sauer rode low on his right thigh so his hand could just naturally reach out and touch the butt of the German pistol. The restraining strap was off and he had easy access to it, if needed.

Dakota turned and stopped. There in front of him was the toddler! She was crawling around in the dirt, playing with it, her tiny hands and arms dusty. Dakota felt a terrible chill move through him as he walked toward the child. The prints became muddled and choppy in the nearby dirt. Frowning, he studied them intently. And then his heart slammed into his ribs. God, there was Welton's boot track! He recognized it because he'd seen it at the original cast at the forensics lab.

Leaning down, he sucked in a breath, a cry strangling in his throat. There were Shelby's tracks. He quickly followed them. There was a depression in the dirt farther down near the thickets. It was a partial imprint of the side of her body. Turning on his heel, Dakota swallowed hard. He rose and went over to the toddler to make sure she was all right. Susie looked up at him with smiling green eyes, a handful of dirt in her tiny fist. Dakota gave the toddler a cursory inspection, and couldn't find any injury.

Jerking the radio off his belt, he called Cade Garner. His voice was dark and hard-sounding. "I've got Susie. But the bad news is, Welton has got Shelby. Their tracks converge here, Cade. I think Welton stole the kid to sucker Shelby into tracking so he could capture her." His nostrils flared as he looked at the surrounding area. "He's got her. I'll get this kid back to her parents and then I'm going after that son of a bitch because he's going to kill Shelby...."

As he trotted back toward the camp with the

toddler in his arms, Dakota's mind churned at a high rate. He had Shelby's sheriff's jacket on the seat of his truck. Storm was with him. As soon as he'd given Susie back to her relieved parents, he would get to his truck. The wolf was good at tracking, too, but her nose could hold a scent and follow it for a long time. He'd be stuck following tracks, but Storm could speed things up.

His chest hurt until Dakota felt as if he was going into cardiac arrest. As he loped through the woods, his long legs taking him closer and closer to the camp, he wanted to cry out in rage and frustration. Shelby had walked right into a trap set by that bastard! Terrible photos of Ellie taken after she was found rose in front of him. *Oh, God, don't let that happen to Shelby. I'll do anything for you. Just don't let Welton torture her. Oh, God, please...*

He ran on powerful legs, his boots digging in hard, dry surface. As a SEAL, he could run thirteen miles with ease, even with a sixty-five-pound pack on his back. His mind went forward. He carried his M-4 rifle in the truck, his major hiking pack filled with medical first-aid items, water and food. Approximating the time as he ran, the thickets swatting at his lower body, Dakota moved into complete military mind-set.

It would take every bit of his ten years as a SEAL to find Shelby before it was too late. He'd keep his cell phone on so Cade Garner could continuously track his whereabouts. A helicopter was out of the question because it couldn't see through the thick forest. Nor could it land if the pilots could locate Shelby and Welton. He wasn't sure if Shelby was conscious or not. He'd find out soon enough, going back to track them just as soon as Susie arrived safely in her parents' awaiting arms.

His whole world anchored on Shelby. She'd gone through so damn much already. And he felt helpless, unable to find Welton before the bastard lured her in and captured her. Angry with himself, angry with the convict, he sprinted the last quarter mile, the camp now in sight.

The only thing between Shelby and Welton was him. The steel resolve coming up through him was a familiar one. He always got that sense of hunting when he and his team were about to infiltrate and connect with the enemy. This time was no different. The only thing on Dakota's side of this terrible situation was that he was a damned good tracker, fast and best of all, he had a wolf that could follow Shelby's scent. He had to bring all his deadly skills together in order to find and rescue her. And kill that son of a bitch in the process. By the time this day was done, Welton was a dead man. The convict just didn't know it yet.

CHAPTER TWENTY-THREE

HEART POUNDING, DAKOTA headed out from the campsite once the toddler was given to the happy parents. He wasted no time in telling Deputy Hutchinson, who was with them, what had happened. Moving back into the forest, retracing his steps, his eyes on the ground, Dakota kept his M-4 rifle in his hand. He'd given Storm a smell of Shelby's coat. The wolf bounded ahead of him, following the exact trail he'd just retraced.

As he ran, the breath tearing out of his mouth, stomach-churning photos he'd seen during the trial of Hartley and Welton ran through his mind. He'd tried to put those photos of Ellie so damn deep down inside him they'd never see the light of day again. But now they hung like specters of the past coming back to taunt him all over again.

The first thing the sexual predators had done to Ellie was use a sharp knife and they'd made six cuts on the bottom of each of her feet. That way, it would be impossible for her to escape them. He cried for what his sister must have felt as they cut her soles to red, bleeding ribbons.

Dakota halted at the site of thickets where the struggle had taken place. All his SEAL training went online. The hatred for Welton and the fear he had for Shelby's life mixed like a toxic shake in his gut. As he was paralleling her footprints, he could tell Welton had done something to Shelby because he was carrying her. The footprints were much deeper and somewhat off balance. Shelby was a tall woman and she had weight to go with her height.

Dakota was intimately familiar with this area, a major tourist trail. That was to his advantage. His mind whirled with questions as to where Welton was going. He knew there was a parking lot nearby. Could he get to it in time? Was that where Welton was headed? Uncertain, he saw Storm stop and lift her nose to the air. Skidding to a halt, Dakota looked around. Where were Welton's tracks? Storm bounded down the incline between the thick stands of trees, heading toward the water. Turning on his heel, he followed the wolf, desperately trying to find tracks.

There! Dakota picked up Welton's boot prints again. He was trying to hide his tracks by remaining in islands of grass here and there. As he trotted behind his wolf, the prints fresh and obvious, Dakota fought photos from the past. He remembered sitting in the courtroom with his parents. When the prosecutors put up slides of Ellie's mouth, he had felt nauseated. The second thing Welton and Hartley did was take a pair of pliers and pull out four of her lower molars in her mouth. The prosecutors theorized that Ellie had fought them, screaming, and they wanted to silence her while they raped her. Wiping his mouth, his eyes watering for a moment, Dakota felt nausea crawling up his throat. Would Welton do the same thing to Shelby? *Oh, God, no. No, please let me find them. Let me find them...*.

They rushed to the edge of Jackson Lake. This part of the lake had much less tourist traffic than farther north. Dakota looked across the rippling lake. No one was in sight. Usually, there were canoes and fishing boats. The lake was lapping at the small pebbled beach where he stood. Breathing hard, his M-4 in his right hand, he watched Storm pace back and forth along the beach, trying to pick up a scent.

The terror swelled inside him as he postulated that Welton had some kind of boat or canoe waiting here. Perspiration dotted his face and he wiped his brow with the back of his sleeve. His mind cartwheeled with possibilities. Where did Welton go? Where could he go from here?

"Storm," he called to the wolf. "Come!" He dug the toes of his boots into the sand and pebbles, leaping up the bank and running parallel to the edge of the lake. Dakota knew there was a small boat ramp on the end of the lake. And a parking lot. It was possible Welton had a vehicle stashed there. It was a huge risk to take, but the only logical choice for Welton. He ran hard and fast, the branches and leaves of brush swatting at his lower body. There were no tourists around, no hikers. It seemed as if the world were holding its breath as he tried to locate Shelby.

The past fueled his determination, his fear for Shelby. Those photos. The slides of Ellie, her hands and ankles tied to the posters of the bed, naked, unconscious, slammed into him. His mother had cried out when the photos had been flashed to the jury. Dakota had pressed his palms against his eyes, crying softly for his dead sister.

The forensics people testified that Ellie had been repeatedly, brutally raped. They couldn't say how many times, but there was no doubt that Hartley and Welton had both raped her. Dakota's heart had torn into small pieces as the forensics expert droned on in robot fashion about the rapes, the many rips and tears and blood found in her vagina. He sat there in shock. His father and mother sobbed, holding each other. He sat there alone, feeling horror and a murderous rage toward the two convicts.

Dakota called on the radio as he approached the wharf and parking area. Cade was mounting a search team as swiftly as possible, but Dakota knew he had the lead and he was Shelby's only hope under the circumstances.

Seeing a fisherman standing on the wood wharf, Dakota signed off, put the radio on his belt and approached the older man with a fishing hat on his silver hair.

"Excuse me," he called, breathing raggedly. "Have you seen anyone with a woman around here in the past half hour?"

The man frowned, fishing rod in hand. "Yes, yes, I did. Strangest thing."

Dakota wanted to scream as the older man halted to think.

"There," he said, pointing up toward the parking lot. "A guy with a woman who was unconscious went up to a green Chevy pickup. He put her in the passenger side and then burned rubber getting out of here."

"A green Chevy pickup?" Dakota's hopes rose.

The elder nodded, a worried look on his face. "I asked him if the woman was all right. She was passed out cold. He was dragging her out of the boat over there and having a tough time doing it. I went over to ask if she was okay. He told me she'd drunk too much liquor and had passed out. He was taking her home."

Stomach turning, Dakota tried to steady himself. "How long ago?"

"Maybe five minutes at the most," he said, studying the watch on his wrist.

"Did you get anything else on the truck? A license plate number?" He hoped against hope that the elder did, knowing in all probability, he hadn't.

"Well," he said, smiling a little as he pulled out a piece of paper from his pocket, "I did. I called the Forest Service headquarters and told them about it. Something didn't feel quite right about it. The truck turned south on the road out there, heading back, I think, toward the entrance to the Tetons Park. Are you law enforcement, by any chance?"

"The woman you saw, what color was her hair?"

"Blond. Real pretty, but she was very pale. I got worried. Are you with the forest service?" He looked at the military rifle in Dakota's hand.

"Yes," he lied, taking the paper. Relief poured through him as he saw the wobbly handwriting and the license plate number the fisherman had jotted down. Quickly, he called Cade on his radio, giving him the intel.

"Is the woman in trouble?"

Nodding, Dakota rasped, "She's been kidnapped." He pulled a photo from his pocket. "Was this the guy who had her?" It was a photo of Welton.

"Why…goodness. Yes, it was." He frowned. "She's not drunk, then?"

"No," Dakota said, his voice low with worry. "She's a kidnapping victim and he probably drugged her."

The fisherman took off his hat and scratched his head. "Listen, you need to get after her, then.

He left here only five minutes ago." He fumbled round in a pocket of his fishing vest, pulling out a set of keys. "My name is Harold Porter. That red Jeep over there is mine. Here's the keys. I'm too old to drive high speed, but my Jeep might get you to her in time."

Grateful, Dakota said, "Thanks. You staying at the Jackson Lake Lodge?"

"I am. When you can, return my Jeep to me?"

"I will," Dakota promised. "Thanks."

"I hope you get to her in time," he called.

As Dakota raced up the hill toward the Jeep, Storm was on his heels. *Hurry! Hurry!*

They both leaped into the open-air Jeep. Dakota jammed his foot down on the accelerator and roared out of the parking lot. He got on the radio again with Cade Garner and filled him in. Dakota's mind leaped with possibilities. Would Welton try driving out of the park? If he did, there was a blockade of deputies and cars waiting for him at the entrance. But there were so many dirt roads he could take instead and head up into the high country and disappear. If he did that, Dakota knew he could lose him.

The Jeep screamed at a hundred miles an hour, the wind tearing at Dakota as he drove intently on the only road in the park. He'd risked passing several slower-moving vehicles. The speed limit was forty miles an hour. It couldn't be helped. There was a long curve up ahead and two roads that turned right and moved up into the slopes of the Tetons.

Just as he made the curve, he saw an SUV parked on the berm near one of the roads. It wasn't the green Chevy pickup. He called Cade and demanded to know if the deputies had spotted Welton at the entrance. They had not. Braking hard, he pulled up behind the SUV. Leaping out, Dakota ran up to the man who was standing at the front of the vehicle, looking under the hood.

"Hey, have you seen a green Chevy pickup pass this way in the past few minutes?"

The man, in his forties, looked up. "Yeah, I did. What's wrong?"

"Which way did it go?" Dakota demanded.

Shrugging, the man said, "He turned up one of those roads."

"Which one?"

"I don't know. I was looking at my carburetor when he came roaring around in front of me. I thought he was going to hit me. He scared the hell out of me."

Frustrated, Dakota nodded. "Okay, thanks." He turned and trotted back to the Jeep, giving Garner the new intel.

Dakota headed for the first dirt road. The roads were a tenth of a mile apart on the same side of the highway. Which one had Welton taken? He braked and got out. Storm remained in the Jeep as he rap-

idly studied the dirt road. It was almost impossible
to tell if Welton had turned into this road. There
were so many sets of tire tracks and he didn't know
which set might belong to the Chevy truck. Loping
down the berm to the second road, Dakota halted
and studied the entrance area. The dirt looked more
disturbed, as if a vehicle had turned at higher speed
than normal and skidded sideways.

Hesitating, his gut still churning, Dakota considered both roads. This second road, a forest service one, looked like the best possibility. He called
Garner as he ran back to the Jeep and gave him
the GPS coordinates. Dakota slammed down on
the accelerator, the vehicle fishtailing as he moved
off the berm around the stalled SUV and made for
the second road.

Dakota headed up into the woods, speeding and
kicking up a rooster tail of thick yellow dust in the
wake of the vehicle. Both hands on the wheel, the
Jeep bounced and skidded on the soft dirt. If he
hadn't had his SEAL training with desert patrol
vehicles, he'd have crashed this civilian Jeep. The
road twisted and turned. They were leaving six
thousand feet and moving up to nearly nine thousand feet. He relentlessly pushed the vehicle, his
mind moving over all the cabins up in this area.

Welton had a plan. Dakota knew there were six
cabins in the area. Which one was he going to?
Each cabin was more than half a mile to a mile off

this forest service road. Each would take time to stop and check out. Shelby didn't have that kind of time. Mouth tightening, his knuckles white on the steering wheel, he tried to figure out a way to tell which driveway Welton would take.

SHELBY SLOWLY BECAME CONSCIOUS. She was aware of being bounced and tossed around in the backseat, the car roaring and skidding around. Opening her eyes, her senses muddied, she tried to understand where she was. Her arm hurt and she lifted her hand. Blood met her fingertips. What had happened? She was slammed against the door, hitting her head. *Oh God!* Her eyes flew open as she tried to fight the powerful effects of the drug. *Welton!*

Jerking a glance to her right, she saw the convict's profile. He was driving like a madman, hands gripping the wheel, the truck shrieking as it flew over the rutted dirt road.

Her mind didn't want to work. She was in trouble. Adrenaline kicked in and erased some of the drugged sensations she fought. Welton had set her up. He'd captured the child to lure her in. Mouth dry, Shelby lifted her badly shaking hand. *Escape!* She had to escape!

Welton had not bound her, so she was able to raise her head just enough to look between the seats. She saw no pistol. Her own holster was empty. He had removed the weapon. Shelby's only priority was to escape. The truck was lurching and jumping around on the bumpy road. Shelby tried to estimate how fast they were going. Did she even have a chance to escape?

Ellie Carson hadn't had a chance. Shelby remembered the woman's trauma at Welton's hands. Her mouth tightened. The choice between staying and leaving was clear. She might break her neck or kill herself opening the door and rolling out. But it was a risk worth taking. Shelby slowly stretched her hand upward, so as not to distract Welton, who was driving erratically. The door clicked open when she pressed a button.

As she slowly turned on her side, her trembling hand moving to the door handle, Shelby thought of Dakota, how much she loved him. He was a wounded vet, but he had a magnificent heart and soul. Saying a quick prayer, Shelby took a deep breath and shoved the door open.

Welton saw something out of the corner of his eye. *What the hell!* The rear right door flew open. Too late!

The woman launched out the door, headfirst. *The crazy bitch!*

Shocked, Welton instantly slammed on the brakes. The truck fishtailed at high speed. It lurched slowly sideways, out of control. Welton snarled a curse as he felt the truck become airborne. Dammit, anyway! He clung to the wheel, the truck sailing off the road, across a gully and nose-diving toward a stand of trees.

Shelby hit the road hard. She tucked and rolled, trying to absorb the slamming pressure of hitting the earth. A cry tore from her as pain reared up her right shoulder. The truck engine suddenly raced, the sound like a roar. Rolling to a stop, she watched the green truck sail through the air, headed for a stand of fir trees.

Without waiting to see what would happen, Shelby dove off the road into the area where head-high thickets stood. The burning sensation in her right shoulder made her think she'd torn something. Breathing hard, wobbling on shaky knees because the drug was still in her system, she pushed off with the toes of her boots and lunged into the forest. The faster she could get away, the less Welton was likely to find her.

She'd gone a few feet when she heard a crunching, crashing noise. The truck had hit a tree! Had it killed Welton? Shelby wasn't going back to find out. He had weapons and she knew he'd come hunting her. Turning, she moved in weaving motions, stumbling, tripping and catching herself. The terror of what Welton could do to her spurred her on at full speed, regardless of her shaky equilibrium.

Steam erupted from the destroyed radiator, a noise she quickly left behind. The deeper Shelby ran down the slight incline, the less she heard.

Good. Because she had to put distance between them or Welton would kill her. Mind churning, Shelby looked around, trying to get her bearings, but it was impossible. Douglas fir surrounded her, thick and silent. The soft pine needles hid her boots somewhat as she thunked along. Breathing raggedly, her breath tearing out of her mouth, Shelby pushed onward. The hill sloped downward. Somewhere below, she had to hit flatland or a trail. There were hundreds of hiking trails throughout the slopes of these mountains. If only she could find a trail, Shelby knew it would eventually lead to help. *Oh, God, let me survive this!*

CHAPTER TWENTY-FOUR

WELTON SNARLED A CURSE as he leaped out of the overturned Chevy. He grabbed the deputy's pistol and hightailed it into the forest. She couldn't have gone far! As he made a diagonal run, Welton's anger soared. How could he have been so damned stupid not to tie the bitch up? He'd been so sure he gave her enough of the drug to keep her unconscious until he reached the cabin. He ran hard and fast, weapon in his hand.

Shelby wove drunkenly through the Douglas fir. She kept seeing black dots dancing threateningly in front of her eyes. No! She couldn't lose consciousness! She just couldn't! Pumping her legs, wobbling and off balance, she stumbled on a hidden root and went flying down the incline. She landed on her belly, let out a groan and rolled. Miraculously, as she pushed up to her hands and feet, she realized she was on a major horse trail. Shelby spotted hoof prints. The trail curved just above where she'd fallen. Hope flared in her.

Her knees were weak. She tried to get fully upright, but her knees buckled beneath her. Fear shot through her as she tried again. The drug was powerful and no matter what Shelby did, she couldn't force her exhausted body to overcome its paralyzing effects.

Suddenly, a horse and rider came trotting around the curve. Shelby's eyes widened. It was Curt Downing! Her mind kept blipping out, but she remembered he was an endurance rider and rode nearly every day to keep his Arabian black stallion in shape for the coming endurance race in September.

Curt yanked back hard on the reins, his stallion grunting and dropping his hindquarters, skidding to a stop, almost running over the woman in the middle of the trail. He gawked, unsure of what he was seeing.

"Shelby?" he called, sitting up in the saddle, disbelief in his voice. She was kneeling on the trail, her hands scratched and bloodied. Her blond hair was disheveled around her taut face. "What's going on?" he called, trying to get his horse to stand still.

"H-help me, Curt," she called, stretching her hand out toward him.

Welton came bounding down the incline. "Don't touch her!" he yelled at Downing.

Curt jerked around toward the sound and scowled as he saw the convict scramble down the slope to the trail, pistol in hand. "What the hell is going on here?" he yelled.

With a gasp, Shelby tried to get up, but she fell to her side on the trail just as Welton reached out for her. His fingers tangled in her hair and he jerked her upright. Pain radiated through her scalp and she cried out.

"Stop!" Downing roared, going for the pistol he always wore at his side. No way was he going to stand back and let Welton harm her. He knew the convict's past, and no woman, not even a woman deputy, deserved to be tortured by the bastard.

Welton snarled. "Like hell I will…" He lifted the pistol and shot twice.

With a cry, Shelby saw both bullets strike the rider. Downing was thrown backward by the power of the bullets slamming into him. He tumbled off the back of his frightened horse. The stallion's eyes rolled. It leaped to the side of the trail, frightened by the booming sounds.

Welton cursed as the careening animal struck him in the shoulder. His hand was jerked off the woman's hair, flying through the air, the pistol knocked out of his hand.

Shelby collapsed on the trail. Her vision blurred. She scrambled to her hands and knees as she saw her pistol flying out of Welton's hand. The horse had run into him, frightened by his rider falling off. Downing lay on the trail, groaning, his arms flopping weakly, blood pumping out of his chest.

With her last ounce of strength, she lurched to

her feet. Shelby had to get to the pistol that had landed no more than ten feet away from her.

Welton snarled and cursed, rolling down the trail. He flew to a stop, his head striking a fir. For a moment he grunted as if stunned. Then he caught sight of the deputy weaving unsteadily on her feet, heading for the pistol. He jumped up.

"Leave it alone, bitch!" he screamed. Welton hurled himself toward her.

DAKOTA HEARD THE two shots. He skidded to a halt, M-4 in hand. Storm surged ahead, speeding toward the noise. His heart plummeted as he breathed raggedly, orienting and trying to locate the direction of the sound. Had Welton found Shelby? He hurled himself down the hill, on the heels of his gray wolf, who ran with her ears pinned against her skull.

The slippery, loose pine needles made him skid as he moved down the steep incline. Between the trees, Dakota spotted a wide horse trail. The noise had come from that direction. As he flipped the safety off on his M-4, he kept running with his focus on finding Shelby. Who had fired that pistol?

Dakota wove around a large thicket near the trail, his heart rate tripling. There, on the trail, was Welton and he had Shelby on the ground. Dakota's gaze jerked to the left. Another man lay lifeless on the trail a hundred feet away. He turned back to Shelby. She was kneeling on the trail, her hands tied in front of her, her neck stretched back against Welton's thigh as he held the pistol to her temple.

"Welton!" he roared, skidding to a halt, the M-4 jammed to his shoulder, the stock tight against his cheek. He had the convict's snarling face in his scope, the crosshairs painted against his sweaty, angry face.

Welton jerked his head upward toward the bellowing sound. His mouth dropped open for only a second. Shelby was drugged and it was easy to get some rope he'd carried with him tied around her hands. She struggled feebly, but his tight grasp on her hair forced her to remain where she was. "Back off!" he screamed at the man with the rifle two hundred feet above them. Who was this bastard? Whoever he was, Welton knew he was military by the way he stood frozen with that rifle. He pressed the pistol into Shelby's temple.

"Drop your weapon or I blow her head off!"

Dakota's entire focus was through the Nightforce scope. "Drop your pistol or I'm putting a round through your head, Welton." His heart pounded wildly in his chest. He tried to compensate for his ragged breathing as he kept the crosshairs steadied on Welton.

"Like hell I will," Welton snarled. His finger curved against the trigger.

Suddenly, out of nowhere, a gray wolf flashed toward Welton.

Dakota saw Storm crash out of the brush to the left of the convict. She charged Welton, mouth open, lips curled, revealing long white canines, aimed directly at him.

It was just the diversion Shelby needed. As Storm burst out of the bushes, she jerked up her left elbow and struck Welton in the crotch.

Welton cried out as her elbow connected with his genitals. The pistol jerked away from her temple. He doubled over, his hand releasing her hair as he aimed the pistol at the charging wolf. Shelby cried out, collapsing on the trail, the last of her energy dissolving.

Dakota took the shot. One to the head. The M-4 bucked savagely against his shoulder. The booming sound echoed loudly. The shot hit Welton and flung him backward a good three feet. By the time Storm leaped upon him, Welton was dead, half his skull blown away.

Dakota sprinted down the hill. Shelby was rolling over, trying to get up, still fighting to survive. He skidded down the hill and onto the trail.

"Shelby, lie still!" he ordered harshly. He just wanted to make sure the bastard was dead, and he was. Storm panted nearby. Dakota ran to check on the other man on the trail. He turned him over and was stunned. What was Curt Downing doing in this mess? He pressed two fingers to the man's exposed throat and found no pulse.

Dakota jerked the radio from his belt and reported it all to Cade. He went toward where Shelby was sitting up, giving the GPS coordinates. They were in deep forest and there was no way a helicopter would get into the area. Signing off, he jammed the radio into his belt and knelt down in front of her. He laid the M-4 aside. Dakota quickly untied the ropes binding her wrists and threw them aside.

His hands came to rest on her shoulders. She was trembling. "Shel, it's all right. You're safe now. Are you hurt?" Of course she was and Dakota examined her from head to toe. He saw no gunshot wounds, no massive bleeding anywhere else on her body. Relief coursed through him. Her eyes were wild, her pupils abnormally dilated. She'd definitely been drugged.

"Come here," he rasped, dragging her into the safety of his arms. "You're going to be okay, Shel. God, I love you." He held her tightly against him. Her breath came out in choking sobs. Her face was dirty, scratches across her cheek and her hands were bloodied. As she quivered uncontrollably, he had new worries. He kissed her tangled hair. "He drugged you, didn't he?"

Shelby felt herself falling off the edge of an invisible cliff, her consciousness beginning to disintegrate. "Y-yes," she forced out, the rest of the words hung up in her mind, not accessible to her mouth. She felt the strength and power of Dakota's arms around her. The shock of it all made her shake uncontrollably. Welton had been about to kill her. She heard Dakota's heart racing against her ear as he shifted. He slid one arm beneath her legs and the other around her shoulders.

"Hang on," he growled, standing and pulling her into his arms. "I'll get you help. Just hold on, Shel…."

They were the last words she heard as he crushed her against himself and turned on the trail. *Help*. She was going to get help. The rough weave of the damp shirt beneath her cheek gave her solace. She was safe….

"SHE'S COMING AROUND," Jordana told Dakota quietly, who anxiously waited nearby. She adjusted the IV drip into Shelby's arm. "Just be with her. She's going to need some orientation."

Dakota nodded. He'd not left her side since getting Shelby down to a major trailhead where the sheriff's deputy cruiser was waiting for them. A U.S. Forest Service helicopter was nearby, rotors already turning, to take Shelby and him to the Jackson Hole Hospital.

The door softly shut and the light blue private room became silent once more. Moving forward, Dakota slid his hand over Shelby's shoulder. In the past hour since they'd arrived, Jordana McPherson had overseen her care. Shelby had been given a cocktail of drugs to combat the drug Welton had given her. All Dakota could do was wait while the doctor and nurses cared for her.

Cade Garner had already stopped by. The two bodies had been recovered at the trail and were now in the city morgue, waiting to be examined by the medical examiner.

Dakota watched as Shelby's long blond lashes began to flutter, a sign of consciousness. He hadn't had time to clean up. He was filthy, dusty and sweaty, but he didn't care. He wasn't ever going to leave Shelby's side until she was awake and he was convinced she was going to be all right. She had gone into convulsions on the helicopter flight to the hospital. The paramedic on board had stabilized her, but it showed the power of the drug Welton had given her. Jordana told him later that she would have died from an overdose and Dakota had found her just in time.

Dakota noticed her lips parted and he saw her swallow. Leaning down, he pressed a kiss to her wrinkling brow.

"It's okay, Shel. You're here in the Jackson Hole Hospital. You're going to be all right."

Dakota gently squeezed her shoulder as he watched her. Jordana had warned him that coming off the drug would cause her to be cold, weak and shaky. Antidrugs given to her earlier would annul the virulent effects of the drug Welton had given her. She would survive, but the withdrawal would be brutal, too.

Shelby could hear Dakota's low, deep voice near her ear. She'd felt the warmth of his lips on her sweaty forehead, his moist breath soothing her. Fighting for consciousness, Shelby oriented her focus to his large hand on her shoulder. It was warm. Some of her fear began to dissolve. It took every bit of strength for her to lift her lashes. As she did, everything was blurry.

"Don't fight so hard," Dakota rasped, touching her cheek. "You're coming out of a drug overdose, Shel. You're okay. You're safe." This seemed to appease her and she ceased her struggles. Even now she was trying to fight. Fight to survive. He cupped her jaw and brushed her dry, cracked lips with his mouth. He wanted to breathe his life into her, erase the death that still held her in its grip. He kissed her tenderly. His heart mushroomed with such love for Shelby that he had to force himself to ease away from her mouth. As he did so, her cloudy blue eyes opened for the first time. He smiled. Her pupils were no longer so dilated.

"Shel?" he called softly, his face inches from hers. Their breaths mingled. "You're doing fine. You're coming out of it…" He threaded his fingers gently through her hair.

A lump stuck in Shelby's throat as she drowned in the glittering gold-brown of Dakota's eyes. They burned with love for her, the raw emotions in them, the care so apparent in his expression. The hardened SEAL mask disappeared. In its place, a man deeply shaken by many conflicting emotions. Closing her eyes, she forced her lips to work. "I love you...."

Her whispered words shattered him. Dakota pulled back a little more, his large hand cupping her pale cheek. "I know you do. And I love you, too, Shel. I'm here and I'm not leaving your side."

It took another hour before Shelby was truly conscious. Her vision cleared, the blurriness dissolving and everything in sharp, clear detail. Dakota was sitting in a chair at the side of her bed, facing her, his hand wrapped firmly around her cool, chilly one. Blips of her experience began to tease her spotty memory. Horror and terror riffled through Shelby like pulverizing ocean waves. She clung to Dakota's warm, strong hand because it fed her strength and helped ground her back in the present. Here. With him. She took a deep breath, her voice raspy.

"Welton?"

Dakota eased out of the chair. He saw clarity in her shadowed blue eyes. "Dead. I shot him."

The finality, the tightly held rage he held in check, pummeled her. Now the SEAL mask was back in place, the implacable warrior who had saved her life. She swallowed hard. "Thank you…" She frowned. "The other man…Curt…?"

"Welton must have shot him. He was dead when I arrived."

Nodding, her mouth dry, she whispered, "Yes, Curt rides his horse on the trails. He was in the wrong palce at the wrong time. He tried to stop Welton." She then uttered, "He shot Curt." Dakota nodded and said nothing. Shelby felt a bit more strength flow into her limbs. "Can you help me sit up? I need some water. I'm dying of thirst."

In moments, Dakota had the bed levered upward so that she was sitting up at a comfortable angle, pillows behind her back. He poured water from the blue plastic pitcher into a glass. He slid his arm behind her shoulders, holding her as he gently pressed the rim of the cup to her lower lip. She drank all of it.

"More?"

"No…thanks…" Shelby sighed as he eased her back against the pillows. She closed her eyes for a moment, her emotions crashing through her like the huge up-and-down drafts of a thunderstorm. Tears leaked from beneath her lashes.

It was heartbreaking for Dakota to see the silvery paths of tears down her taut, pale face. He moved closer to her bedside and gently smoothed them away. He still didn't know what had happened between her and Welton. He was afraid to ask. Jordana had inspected her closely and found nothing but bruises and scratches. He pushed away strands of blond hair from her face, just as she opened her eyes once more. They were dark and filled with emotions he couldn't decipher.

"God, I feel awful. What the hell did he shoot me up with?"

"A drug to knock you out." Dakota wouldn't tell her she'd been given a lethal dose. She didn't need to hear that right now. Maybe much later.

"It did that." Shelby felt more aware, more in her body. She held Dakota's worried stare. "I'm remembering things now...." She reached out, sliding her hand into his. As his fingers wrapped around hers, she sighed. "After he jumped me at the bushes, where the child was, I blacked out."

"The little toddler is safe and sound," he reassured her, seeing the question in her eyes. "Back with her parents."

"Thank God. Welton stole the baby to lure me into his trap."

"Yeah, I finally put that part together, too," Dakota muttered.

"Took me a while to figure it," she said with distaste.

"Hey," he called softly, touching her chin, "don't be hard on yourself, Shel. No one could have seen this coming."

"Maybe not." She shrugged, which caused sharp

pain in her shoulder. She reached up, sliding her fingers across it and remembering more. "I woke up in a truck. I was lying on the backseat. I was coming out of the drug haze and seeing Welton driving like a demon."

"A fisherman at the wharf where he tied up the boat saw him drag you out of it and into a green Chevy pickup truck. Do you remember any of that?"

Shaking her head, she licked her dry lips. "No... nothing."

"That fisherman not only had the license plate of Welton's truck, but he gave me the keys to his Jeep so I could pursue him."

"That was so kind of him," she murmured, touched. "As evil as Welton was, we have people like that fisherman who tipped the scales in the opposite direction."

Dakota breathed a sigh of relief. Shelby seemed almost completely present, her voice stronger, her mind working. He continued to hold her hand. "Welton had chosen one of two dirt roads that were close together. I stopped and talked to a driver of an SUV who had engine problems, and he saw the truck race by, but didn't see which road Welton took. I parked and ran over to both of them to try to figure it out. There were a lot of fresh skid marks on one, and that's the one I took. It was the right road."

"I knew I had to get out of the truck. I knew once he stopped, I was dead. I unlatched the rear door and somehow dived out it." Shelby shook her head. "I felt like a rag doll. My legs wouldn't work right. I was weaving around. I couldn't run a straight line if I tried."

"I don't know how soon after I got to where he crashed the truck." Dakota felt some satisfaction as he added, "Storm already had your scent and when I turned her loose, she headed back down the road where you had apparently fallen out of the truck. She led me directly to you."

Rubbing her brow, a headache coming on, Shelby whispered, "Bless Storm. She made the difference. Curt Downing surprised me. He was riding his horse around the corner at a trot. He damned near ran over me. I couldn't even move to get out of his way. I was helpless. By that time, Welton had caught up to where I was." She shook her head. "Curt Downing tried to help me, but Welton shot him off his horse." She looked up at Dakota's grim expression. "That horse went ballistic and crashed into Welton, knocking him away from me."

"And that's when I arrived on the scene."

"I saw you put the rifle to your shoulder. He had a hold of my hair and I couldn't do anything. The drug was taking me under. I had no fight left in me."

"You had enough left in you to jam your elbow

into the bastard's crotch. You gave me a clear shot, Shel." Dakota reached over and looked deeply into her marred eyes. "You fought with everything you had. You never backed off even with the drug in your system." His voice lowered, unsteady. "You're the bravest woman I've ever seen. You were magnificent. I don't think anyone else would ever have done what you did. You saved yourself from Welton."

CHAPTER TWENTY-FIVE

"I WANT TO go home." Shelby looked up at Jordana and then Dakota, who stood nearby. The doctor frowned as she checked her vitals and the IV.

"Shelby, you nearly died from a drug over-dose." She took out a penlight and held Shelby's jaw lightly. "Look into my eyes," Jordana said, moving the light slowly from one eye to the other.

Dakota said nothing, just watched Shelby's eyes dilate properly and then move back to their normal size. It had been four hours since she'd regained consciousness.

"Okay," Jordana said, concern in her tone. She looked across the bed at Dakota. "I know you were a trained combat medic."

"That's right."

Jordana turned back to Shelby. "You're not out of the woods yet. But what I can do is let Dakota take you home and stay with you. He knows the signs of drug overdose, of convulsions. I'll give him some medicine in case you need it."

Shelby swallowed hard. She was so grateful. "Thanks. I owe you one...."

"I'M SO GLAD TO BE home," Shelby whispered as she was led to her bedroom with Dakota's hand beneath her elbow. Her knees were still unsteady and he was afraid she'd fall.

"You have a beautiful house," he said, looking around. Entering the bedroom, he noticed a pink, flowery spread across the queen-size bed. The drapes were open, allowing in light.

"I feel safe here," Shelby said. She'd called her parents earlier and let them know she was all right. They were going to travel back to Jackson Hole tomorrow to see her and take up residence once more in their home.

Dakota helped her sit down on the edge of her bed. "God, I feel weak. How long is this drug going to make me feel like this?" she asked. His expression was readable, his eyes filled with vigilance. He hadn't cleaned up yet. His beard darkened his face, making him look more the warrior she knew he was and always would be.

"Probably in another twelve hours you should be past most of these symptoms. Would you like a bath? A shower?"

Shelby shook her head. "I'm just tired." She moved her palm across the well-worn spread. It was soft and comforting to her. "I need two things," she told him huskily, meeting and holding his dark gaze. "I need sleep and I need you holding me tonight." The sky was bright with afternoon sunlight.

She lifted her chin and waited for his answer. She saw a glint come to his eyes.

"Anything you want, Shel," he said in a low voice. Reaching out, Dakota grazed her hair. "Do you want help undressing? Do you want to wear your nightgown?"

She caught Dakota's hand and pressed a kiss to the back of it. She drew his hand to her cheek. "I'll get myself to bed. You come when you want."

"I'll get a shower and shave first. I stink," he said.

A slight smile pulled at the corner of her mouth. Shelby released his hand and he felt softened tingles moving heatedly across his skin. How badly he wanted to love Shelby. He wanted to make things right. Make the fear he saw banked in her eyes go away forever. He knew he could do it. "I'll be back in a little while," he promised.

NEARLY TWO HOURS LATER, Dakota slid into bed beside Shelby. She was sleeping soundly on her side, one hand tucked beneath her cheek. There was now a faint blush across her cheeks. It hurt him to see the deep scratch across her temple where she'd run through brush to escape Welton. As he pulled the drapes closed, the sun hanging lower on the western horizon, the room grew shadowed.

Dakota moved slowly to Shelby's side so as not to awaken her. She was as naked as he was. He smiled and gently eased one arm behind her neck and the pillow. He curved his body against hers and placed his other arm across her waist, holding her close. Holding Shelby safe.

Dakota didn't know how long he lay awake. It didn't matter. Beneath his arm, he could feel the slow rise and fall of her breasts as she slept. After he started to hold her, Shelby seemed to breathe more evenly and sink into a deeper slumber. It told him she felt safe in his arms. *Protected.*

He thought about Ellie. The court trial. The horrifying pictures flashed for the jury to realize what had been done to his sister. As Shelby slept soundly in his arms, cocooned by his body, he felt profound relief and the soul-eating guilt over Ellie's death was released. He'd only been seventeen years old at the time, unable to help Ellie at all. Now it was as if he'd been given a second chance to avenge her death. Only this time, he was a SEAL, trained to use controlled violence when demanded. As he inhaled the sweet scent of nutmeg through the silky strands of Shelby's hair that tickled his jaw, he reveled in the fact that he had been able to save Shelby. It didn't minimize Ellie's death. But it helped Dakota to put it all into perspective.

SEAL training gave him the tools, the dangerous edge he needed to find Shelby when no one else could have. Storm had done her part, too. She'd sped up the process of finding her. The wolf had made all the difference.

Dakota closed his eyes. The woman now in his arms, resting safe against him, was the one he wanted in his life until he took his last breath. He knew Shelby loved him as fiercely as he loved her. And he silently promised her that he would show her every day just how much she meant to him and his badly injured heart. Shelby was healing him, whether she knew it or not.

Rising on his elbow, Dakota could see her profile in the gray light. Tears still fell down her cheeks. She was deep in sleep, probably reliving the nightmare of yesterday. Leaning down, Dakota placed his lips over the swollen cut on her temple. Whispering her name, he told her she was safe. He rested his chin against her hair. Almost instantly, the tears stopped and once more, the tension left her body. Humbled that he had a healing effect on Shelby, he slowly resumed his sleep position once more.

Dakota had never thought it possible that a human could heal another. Yet that was what he'd just experienced. Love was deeply healing. He loved Shelby.

And then his old fears came back to haunt him at a moment when he was completely vulnerable. He was far too damaged to be with Shelby. Was it fair to her to burden her with someone like him? Dakota was always afraid of his PTSD. He'd broken a nurse's arm when she'd touched him while he'd been asleep. He lived in silent terror of doing something like that to Shelby. Shutting his eyes tightly, Dakota tried to get a handle on those damn demons of his. He'd never had anyone challenge them until Shelby walked boldly into his life. His love and his darkness were at war. He wasn't sure which side would win.

Dakota wished with all his heart he could remove the pain and trauma Shelby suffered. The body, the emotions, remembered those times, as he knew too well himself. And he was sure that in the coming days, weeks and months, Shelby would experience all of them in their jagged, cutting intensity.

He had suffered similar effects from war. Trauma was trauma. At least he'd be at her side to guide her through. He'd never had support, but she would. The love Dakota felt for her swelled his chest, filled him until he thought he might die of joy. He'd never experienced this before.

Somewhere in the coming night, Dakota heard an owl calling near the window. Exhaustion washed over him as he, too, relaxed and gave in to the tiredness of his body and his wounded soul. Dakota slept with the woman he loved, grateful she was safe, in his arms.

SHELBY AWOKE WITH A start. Her entire body spasmodically jerked. And just as swiftly, she felt Dakota's reaction, his arms automatically holding her a little more tightly, a little more surely, as if to tell her she was safe. *Safe.* Weak morning light filtered in around the drapes. The room was muted with gloom, but she relaxed, an anguished breath escaping her. Her heart was pounding. She felt his long, callused fingers splayed out across her torso, holding her against his warm, strong body.

"All right?" Dakota asked, his voice thick with sleep.

Automatically, Shelby slid her hand over his forearm. "Just images…" she managed, her voice hoarse, emotions still riffling through her. The terror was still with her. But she had Dakota and he needed her, too. It was a frightening thought and she was too vulnerable, too much in shock to absorb it. Was she the woman he needed? Would he always come if she needed him? He'd been there for her without fail. Dark, questioning emotions warred with her heart. The trauma forced her to question everything.

Dakota instantly came awake; it was a natural SEAL reaction. From exhausted sleep to total alertness, as if an enemy were nearby. He pushed up on his elbow and he eased Shelby onto her back so he could look directly into her eyes.

Inwardly, Dakota winced as he saw tear tracks down her drawn cheeks. It hurt him to see her like this. He could stand anything but a woman or child crying. His chest felt as if it were being twisted in two by a vise. Reaching out, Dakota coaxed strands of blond hair away from her cheek. "Bad dream?"

Holding his alert golden gaze, her pulse still pounding, she nodded. "I—I'm a little emotional right now...."

"You're coming off that drug, that's why. It makes you feel crazy and you question everything," he quietly reassured her, holding her shattered blue gaze. Her pupils were okay, but Dakota not only felt but saw the savage emotions working through her. Shelby was struggling to contain them, to combat and suppress them. *Not this time.* "Come here," he rasped, pulling her tightly against him as he rolled over onto his back. "You need to get it out of your system, Shel. I'll hold you. Go ahead..."

The gruff tenderness in his voice comforted her. She turned and curved her body against his, head nestled in the crook of his shoulder. "I—I have this terror in me. I feel like it's eating me alive, making me question everything." Shelby slid her hand across his massive, darkly haired chest. She shut her eyes, fighting back the lump in her throat.

"Shel, I've been where you are. It's a kind of demon that wants to control you. It isn't about drugs, it's about trauma. The key is—" he pressed a kiss to her brow "—to fight it."

As much as Shelby struggled to suppress the sob, it tore out of her throat. The sound that came out sounded like that of a wounded animal. Her entire body convulsed against his. Dakota pulled her as tight as he could, as if to shelter her from the storm within her.

Dakota closed his eyes, jaw resting against her hair. Shelby's arms tightened around him as she sobbed her pain. He did not let her go. Her fingers dug frantically into his flesh, opening and closing almost spasmodically. Dakota understood the depth of her uncontrolled fear. Shelby was familiar with Ellie's trial. She'd been a witness for the prosecution, seen the horrific pictures. She understood what Hartley and Welton would have been capable of doing to her. Dakota buried his face in the strands of her soft hair, her sweet scent mingled with the animal-like sounds tearing out of her. He simply held her, absorbing as much of her pain as he could.

Shelby lost track of time, of place. She felt out of her body, as if her soul were fragmenting, tearing slowly apart into jigsaw pieces. Only Dakota's arms, his quiet strength held her together. Her tears tangled and soaked into the dark hair across his chest. Shelby couldn't stop weeping, controlled by her emotions, the drugs in her system, the overwhelming desire to live.

She felt like a leaf torn off a tree during the most savage storm she'd ever experienced. It was Dakota's low, vibrating voice near her ear, his moist breath flowing across her cheek, that allowed her to hold on, to ride out this violence swirling within her. She fought her own demons now. But he was here, supporting her, feeding her with his strength. His hand ranged slowly up and down her spine, soothing her, taming the violence she felt moving out of her. Each touch of his scarred fingers trailing across her spine, brought her a little more peace and a little less agony with each stroke.

Finally, Shelby lay utterly exhausted in his arms, but he didn't stop stroking her shoulders and spine. He knew she needed this contact with reality, this grounding, to finally loosen the grip of the horror of the past two weeks. And then she slept. Really slept in his arms, his body a barrier against the terror in her life, a protection and promise of better times ahead.

The next time Shelby awakened, she was fully aware of resting on Dakota's shoulder. His chest hair tickled her chin and nose. Unconsciously, Shelby moved her hand languidly across his powerful expanse, fingers tangling in the soft, silky hair of his chest. She felt his flesh tense and a ragged sound escape his lips. His hand moved across hers.

"Shel?" His voice was drowsy, filled with concern.

"It's okay," she whispered, pressing a small kiss to his chest wall. Again, she felt him tense, as if controlling himself. "I want you. All of you," she whispered, pulling her head back just enough to meet his narrowing eyes.

"Are you sure?" he asked, his arm moving across her shoulder. Dakota had no idea of time, only that the room was bathed in eastern sunlight. His mind was groggy, desperately needing more sleep. But right now he was hotly aware of Shelby's body against his, the amazing and stunning clarity in her blue eyes. He could see real life in them for the first time since the incident. His Shel was home. There was no doubt that she was fully present. Dakota felt himself harden, wanting her so damn bad. Yet he knew when people were traumatized, they did things they were sorry for later. Trauma was a chameleon and he had no wish to make love with her if she really wasn't fully aware of what she was asking for. Sex could wait. He was far more concerned about healing her fragile emotional and mental state.

"Do I not look sure?" Shelby arched her brows and gave him a reckless smile. She lifted her hand, her fingertips tingling as she cupped his cheek. "I need you, Dakota. All of you. I know what I'm doing. I know what I need—*you*." She saw his hesitation, maybe his concerns stirring? *To hell with it*.

Leaning up, she pushed him back on the bed, moving her body over his, their hips meeting and branding each other. She planted her elbows on either side of his head, looked deeply into his eyes.

Her fingers moved gently across his scalp, his hair soft as she tangled and engaged the short, clean strands. Their noses almost touched.

"I love you. You saved my life. You held me when I was hurting. Now," Shelby whispered before she placed her lips lightly upon the hard line of his mouth, "I want to celebrate life. I want to love you, Dakota. I'm bruised, not broken. And yes, I'm a little stiff in the shoulder but nothing that won't go away in a few days." Shelby sighed against his mouth. She felt him tremble, as if giving himself permission to return her slow, teasing wet kiss.

His hands roved from her shoulders, down the length of her long, strong spine to her flared hips. Curving his hands down to where her thighs melted into her hips, Dakota heard her moan. His callused fingers enflamed her flesh and slowly, deliberately caressed her. Her mouth deepened against his as he moved his fingers closer to her center of moistness and warmth. His body hardened beneath her cajoling hips, scalding his erection as their mouths clung hotly to each other.

Lost in the strength and tenderness of his mouth, Shelby eased onto her back with Dakota on top of her. The sheets were cool against her heated flesh. His body hard and tense, his flesh hot against her own, sent her arching hips to meet his.

As powerful as Dakota was, Shelby could feel him monitoring the amount of weight he placed against her body, monitoring the amount of pressure against her hungry lips. She ached to feel more of him. Frustrated, she dug her fingers into his flesh, letting him know she wasn't any china doll that would break. She thrust her hips solidly against his erection and instantly felt him tense, a low animal growl vibrating through his chest. She loved the sound rumbling through him, resonating within her body. She placed her lips against his mouth.

"My turn," she whispered against him, and she eased herself across his hips, moving on top of Dakota. She settled her thighs against him. The smoldering look in his eyes scorched her body and her entire lower body spasmed. There were so many small and longer scars across his torso, chest and shoulders. Dakota had suffered so much and she purposely ran her fingers across each one, memorizing each one, licking his flesh, kissing it and wanting to remove the memory forever. He quivered each time her lips lightly grazed each one, heightening her hunger of him. Even though he was a man with demons, he'd risen above his own tortured existence and had held her while she hurt and cried out her pain. Now Shelby was going to help dissolve the memory of each of those battle scars he'd gotten over the years.

Dakota's lips lifted away from his gritted teeth as she moved her wet core slowly up and down him. Automatically, he captured her sweet hips, staring

up into her glinting blue eyes that reminded him
of a hunter stalking her prey. He was no prey, and
lifted her just enough to sheathe deeply into her.
In that instant, Shelby froze, her back arching, a
moan of pleasure tearing out from between her
parted lips. Her eyes closed, head tipped back, a
vulnerable smile across her lips as she welcomed
him into her silky, wet confines. Dakota lifted his
hands and slid them around the soft globes of her
breasts. He leaned up as she sank downward. His
lips met the first hardened nipple, suckling strongly
on it, and then the other. She trembled violently beneath his touch. Hunter had turned into prey with
soft, malleable flesh between his large hands. He
thrust deeply into her, and her eyes closed. She absorbed his male strength into her yielding body, a
flush spreading rapidly across her cheeks.

Shelby was strong, pliant and hungry. He brought
her into a frantic, plunging rhythm with himself.
Breasts teasing him against his chest, Dakota hotly
took her mouth, thrusting his tongue deeply into
her. He felt her stiffen, felt more than heard a cry
of raw satisfaction originate from very deep within
her body. Her spine grew taut as the heat exploded
between them, deluging them with feverish outward ripples of intense primal pleasure.

He was grateful for the fire that rolled through
him. Shelby clung to him, her fingers still digging
frantically into his thick shoulders. He prolonged

her orgasm, moving his hands to her hips, thrusting deep and keeping the pressure against her core. She cried out suddenly and he removed that steel control over himself. She languished in continuing orgasms beneath his onslaught. Drawing in air between his clenched teeth, Dakota gripped her tightly against him, his face pressed against her slender neck, lost in the fusion of scalding oneness. His release went deep into her writhing body. Her breath sharpened against his as she sought and found his mouth. Her lips curved across his, taking him to places he had never known existed before this moment.

CHAPTER TWENTY-SIX

"WELCOME BACK, SHELBY."

"Thanks, Cade. Good to be back." Shelby gave her boss a smile as she picked up her weapon. For the past two weeks she'd been on medical leave. It felt great to be working again.

"How's Dakota doing?"

She slid the gun into the holster on her right hip. "Moving down here to my home." Wrinkling her nose, she added, "Not that he has that much to move. The guy was living off the land. Some clothes, but that's all."

Cade leaned back in his chair and studied her. "You're happy?"

Shelby's smile grew. "You're the first to know, Cade." She held up her left hand to show him a small diamond engagement ring.

"I already noticed that when you walked in," he said drily, his grin widening. "Couldn't happen to two better people. Congratulations. Have you set a date?"

"Thanks. We're looking at an October wedding.

We want everyone to attend. My mother is helping me with the invitations as we speak."

"We'll look forward to being there to see you two married off."

She sighed and said in a quieter tone, "He's an incredible person, Cade. I guess it took this incident with Hartley and Welton for me to really see him.

"He's a SEAL whether he's still in the navy or not. And everything he'd ever been taught was put into play to save my life."

"He was worried about his PTSD and living with you," Cade said.

Nodding, Shelby sobered and sat down in the chair in front of the desk. The morning sun was strong in the east office. "Dr. Jordana McPherson has him on an adaptogen to lower his cortisol levels. That's part of what causes PTSD. She's had success with other people who have had PTSD symptoms. I'm crossing my fingers it will help him."

Cade became grave. "Then Dakota can come and live among the rest of us and feel part of us, not alone any longer."

Shelby gave her boss a soft smile. "No one can live alone like he did. The first time I met him in at E.R., my heart just tore in two for him. Seeing the look in his eyes…"

"You pulled him out of that darkness, Shelby.

Maybe neither of you realized it for some time, but I saw it."

She nodded. "He'd talk to me about his demons from war. And I tried to understand and I couldn't, no matter how hard I tried." She took in a deep breath and admitted, "Until I got my own demons from Welton. Then I understood."

Cade's face grew sympathetic.

"Trauma is highly underrated, but we know that, as law enforcement. Firefighters see it, too, and so do paramedics. With the right woman in his life, Dakota will make the transition from being a loner to part of a group that respects and admires him. And I know he'll help you, too, Shelby. Sometimes two wounded people can be healers for each other."

Shelby folded her hands in her lap. Her voice trembled when she said, "Love heals us, Cade. But you know that from your own experience." He'd lost his wife and child in an accident years earlier. And later, he met a woman and they fell deeply in love. Cade hadn't believed he could love twice in his life, but he was proven wrong. Shelby saw his eyes warm.

"Love can heal the deepest of wounds," he agreed. "Changing topics, what's Dakota going to do with his female wolf? I know Fish and Game isn't going to like a gray wolf prowling around in the city limits of Jackson Hole."

"It got resolved by nature," she told him wryly,

smiling. "Three days ago when we were up at Dakota's cabin, a beautiful black wolf, a male, was standing just inside the tree line. Dakota and I watched Storm trot over, tail wagging, to meet him. They took off and disappeared. Yesterday, when I was helping him pack his clothes, we saw Storm and her new boyfriend again. It's as if she came back to tell us she was in love, too. Then they took off. Dakota thinks this young black wolf will start his own pack. Storm will be his alpha female."

"Two packs in the valley," Cade murmured. "Well, why not? It's a big valley. And we've wanted the wolf population to grow around here."

"Dakota talked to the guys over at Fish and Game yesterday and told them what had happened. They're deliriously happy about it. The head guy, Frank, thinks they'll mate. Storm is fully matured and Dakota's hoping at some point to see her pups. Another happy ending."

Sitting up in his chair, he chuckled. "Good, because I was having nightmare visions of people calling the sheriff's department, reporting a gray wolf trotting through their yard."

"It's taken care of," Shelby promised wryly, understanding his position.

"I like happy endings."

"So do I. Did you know that one of Dakota's SEAL buddies is going to visit today? This is an officer he worked with in his platoon. I haven't seen Dakota this excited about anything."

"Except you," Cade intoned with a grin.

She felt heat sweep up her throat and into her face. "Well…" she said, avoiding his humored look, "yes, except me." Dakota made her feel as if she were the only woman in the world. He loved her deeply and opened up like a book to her, sharing everything. Her heart swelled with a fierce love for the military veteran. Dakota had seen too much and survived when others did not. She became serious and held Cade's gaze. "He's had so much taken away from him. His sister…his family dying four years later. He had no one, Cade. His grandparents are gone, too. I think, in some ways, the SEALs are a brotherhood, another type of tight-knit family group that gave him the support and love he needed to survive all those other losses."

Grimly, Cade nodded. "I wouldn't disagree. So, his friend? Who is he?"

"Captain Jake Ramsey. He was AOIC, assistant officer in charge of Dakota's squad. After I agreed to marry Dakota, he called Jake and told him. So Jake is coming here to check me out." She grinned.

"Oh?"

"Yeah, I guess from what Dakota told me, in the SEAL community if a guy thinks he's fallen in love and wants to get married, someone from the platoon has to come and make sure."

"Make sure of what?"

Shelby chuckled. "Well, you have to hear the rest of this story. In the community they have a saying. If you haven't dirt-dived the woman, then you shouldn't be marrying her."

His brows rose. "Dirt-dived? What the hell does that mean?"

"That's what I asked Dakota because the slang brought up all kinds of weird pictures for me," Shelby said, her smile increasing. "In SEAL training, you get sandy, wet and dirty. It means you've dived down, done the training, absorbed the learning and experience to know it inside out. Dirt-diving means knowing everything about your subject, or," she said as she laughed, "in that case, Dakota learned the width, breadth and depth about me. He knows me as well as he knows himself, so that by getting married, there are no surprises, no hidden agendas. He said the SEAL community is very protective of their wives and children. Jake is coming to make sure Dakota has done his homework." She continued, "And really, I think Jake is coming because he and Dakota are like brothers. They've never been out of contact since Dakota left the SEALs. And from what Dakota has said, Jake lost his wife and baby to a drunk driver a number of years earlier. I guess Jake wants to see Dakota happy because he once had a family himself."

"That's a sad story," Cade said, no doubt feeling a kinship since his wife and child had been torn from him. "Where's he staying and how long is Jake visiting?"

"We have a guest bedroom at my—our house. Jake has three days before he has to fly to Washington, D.C., to the Pentagon for a top secret assignment."

"I'm sure he and Dakota are going to have a good time sharing and catching up."

Shelby rose and grinned. "Yes, I'm sure they will. Me? I'll just make Jake home-cooked meals while he's here and he'll be fat, dumb and happy about it."

Chuckling, Cade raised his hand. "Be safe out there, Shelby. You're back on the roster and back on duty."

She opened the door. "It feels good, Cade. Maybe my life will settle down now."

Grinning, Cade said wryly, "I don't know. Now you're going to be dirt-dived by this SEAL friend of his."

"Oh," she said and laughed, "all Jake is going to do is meet me and find out how much I love Dakota. I think they'll spend some quality time together at the house while I'm out in my cruiser giving speeding tickets and handling calls of bears or moose in backyards."

Shaking his head, Cade matched her laugh. "I'm

keeping you on day rotation for a month. I think you and Dakota can use that time wisely."

Would they ever! But Shelby said nothing and waved goodbye to her boss. Shutting the door to his office, she felt so happy she didn't even feel her boots touching the floor. She glided out the rear of the building to get her cruiser. Pushing open the rear door, Shelby looked up. The summer sky was a light blue with long, graceful strands of high cirrus clouds moving across it. She knew how excited Dakota was to see his teammate. By the time she got off duty and drove home, she'd get to meet this man whom Dakota felt so close to.

She chose a black Tahoe cruiser with *Sheriff* written in gold on both doors, opened it up and began to arrange the gear before she climbed in. Dakota would have all day alone with Jake Ramsey. She was sure they'd have plenty to talk about. She'd already put in a huge beef roast into a Crock-Pot, replete with carrots, potatoes and celery. When she got home at five tonight, she'd have dinner ready, except for making the gravy. Dakota assured her Jake would die and go to heaven with that kind of delicious, home-cooked meal.

Shelby smiled as she turned on the various radios situated below the dashboard. The familiarity of her job made her even happier. The worst was over. Her questioning whether she was the right woman for Dakota had been laid to rest. They'd had a long and deep emotional talk about their individual demons. And Dakota had finally realized that he could live with her, despite his PTSD. He was aggressively pursuing help from Dr. McPherson, which gave her relief. Plus, Shelby knew in her heart of hearts, their love for each other would build an unbreakable bridge between them. Love trumped all. She knew that. She was living it every day with Dakota.

As she pulled out into traffic to begin her shift, Shelby sighed, happy. Being Dakota's wife was an unexpected dream come true. She loved him with a fierceness that defied description. He loved her with an equal fierceness, her body still glowing after their lovemaking this morning. Yes, life was good. It didn't get any better than this.

WHEN SHE ARRIVED HOME, Shelby heard the laughter of two men out back on the patio of the house. Dakota's laughter was easy to recognize and she automatically smiled, dropping her keys in a bowl on the desk in the foyer. She knew Dakota would hear her come in to greet her. He was so damned alert and missed nothing.

She was right. He met her in the kitchen, his gaze growing warm as she walked into his arms. His mouth touched hers lightly and he kept his hand around her waist.

"How was your first day back at work?" he

asked, grazing her blond hair that she'd released from its ponytail.

"Great. It felt so good." She grinned. "Jake arrived?"

"Yeah, come on. I want to introduce you to my AOIC when I was a SEAL."

Shelby was more than a little curious about meeting this man who had been Dakota's officer in charge. As she moved out the opened door, she saw a deeply tanned man with military-short black hair and piercing gray eyes that reminded her of an eagle watching his prey. He wore a collegiate type of short-sleeved light blue shirt and pressed tan chinos. Jake Ramsey had the same kind of explosive, tightly held energy she'd encountered around Dakota. He was ruggedly handsome with a square face and as he stood, he appeared to be at least six feet tall. He wasn't muscle-bound, but clearly in top shape, not an ounce of fat anywhere on his body. Shelby saw a number of white scars on his leanly muscled arms.

"Jake, meet Shelby," Dakota said, releasing her waist so she could walk over and shake his hand.

"Ma'am," Ramsey said, nodding deferentially as he offered his hand to her. "It's nice to meet my best friend's lady."

Shelby looked down at his hand, feeling the thick calluses across his palm, many nicks and small white and more recent pink scars across his long, well-shaped fingers. Sliding her hand into his, she said, "Just call me Shelby. Welcome, Captain Ramsey. I'm glad you could visit Dakota. He really misses his SEAL family."

The man seemed to monitor the amount of strength in his grip and then released her hand. There was an aura of command around Ramsey, his shoulders thrown back, chin held level, his gaze moving across her face, as if memorizing it. If Shelby didn't know Dakota, didn't know that SEAL operators' lives depended upon their alert intelligence, she'd have been unsettled by his swift, intense inspection.

"Yes, ma'am, and we miss him equally as much." Ramsey smiled a little, his gaze moving to Dakota, who stood behind her. "He'll never tell you this, but he was our best operator in our platoon. As LPO, lead petty officer, he took care of the other seven shooters, as well as me and our OIC."

Part of his military lingo was lost on her. Shelby smiled and decided she'd ask Dakota for a translation later, when they were alone. She didn't wish to embarrass Ramsey for his military-speak. "I believe it." She turned and gazed warmly up at Dakota, who stood near her left shoulder. "I hope he told you he saved my sorry ass a couple of weeks ago?"

A reluctant, thin smile crossed the officer's serious features. "Yes, ma'am, he did. I'm not surprised. He saved all of us at one time or another Down Range."

Dakota snorted. "Hey, let's get off the topic of me, okay?" He placed his hands across Shelby's shoulders. She was still in uniform. "Want to get into civilian clothes and join us for some beer and chips before dinner?"

"Sounds like a great way to end my day. I'll see you two in a few," she said.

Dakota watched her leave, the sway of her hips making him want Shelby all over again. They had made love every night for the past two weeks, unable to get enough of each other. He turned and saw his AOIC staring at her with a frown.

"Problem?" Dakota asked, sitting down at the table and spreading his legs out in front of him.

Ramsey sat down. "I just find it hard to believe she's an effective law enforcement officer."

"Oh, here we go again," Dakota griped good-naturedly. He pulled the bag of opened potato chips over and poured more into a nearly empty bowl. "This is your women-are-weak bullshit rearing its ugly head again, Ramsey."

"You had to save her life. Isn't that the point?"

Dakota drilled a hard look into the SEAL officer's eyes. "Don't go there," he growled. "You don't know the full story. Shelby took out Hartley, who attacked her from behind, all by herself. You don't give women enough credit, Jake. Don't throw your bad experience with your sick mother on her. She's a damn good sheriff's deputy and she can have my back any day."

Jake chewed thoughtfully on the potato chip, hearing his LPO's passionate warning. "Thank God women aren't allowed in the SEALs. I'd have a real problem, then," he muttered.

Dakota knew when he said Shelby could have his back, that it was a SEAL operator's highest compliment he could pay to his—or her—comrade in arms. And he could see the emotional reaction in Ramsey's carefully arranged face. Normally, Jake was damned hard to read. He gave little away, if ever. As an operator, he was cool, calm and collected. The men were loyal to him and they trusted him out on an op. The only chink in his armor was women, one way or another. Ramsey had had a lousy childhood, a caretaker for a chronically ill mother. His father, a SEAL of great reputation in the ranks, was never home to care for her. Jake got saddled with caregiver duties for eighteen years of his life. He grew up fast and he matured quickly. Maybe, Dakota thought as he sat there in silence with his friend, that was the wound through which he saw all women.

"She's pretty."

"Yeah, I made the mistake of calling her a Barbie doll when I first met her. She shut me up real fast on that one." Dakota grinned fondly in remembrance of their first meeting. Then he allowed emotion into his voice. "She's got a good heart, is scary smart and has SEAL alertness," he told Ramsey in a quiet tone.

SHELBY SNUGGLED AGAINST Dakota's warm, strong body. It was nearly midnight, the house quiet once more. Moonlight filtered around the drapes, giving her just enough light to see his rugged profile. He lay on his back, his arm wrapped around her shoulders, bringing her solidly against his frame. "You're worried?"

Cutting a glance down at her, he pursed his lips. "I'm worried for Jake. He's like a brother to me, Shel. Something's eating away at him. It has been for years. It's taking him down in a way I can't reach, touch or change."

"You said he lost his wife and baby in an accident years ago?"

He nodded. "Yeah." His nostrils flared and he pushed his fingers through his short hair in frustration. "He's never gotten into a relationship since his wife died. He avoids women like the plague." And then Dakota scowled. "I should amend that. He had a woman in his past, Captain Morgan Boland. They had a red-hot love affair the last two years they were at Annapolis together. She accidentally got pregnant, miscarried his child and he ran from her."

"Ouch. Not the right thing to do," Shelby murmured, moving her hand across his chest, slowly sifting the thick, silky hairs through her fingers.

"Yeah, it was bad. And that's not like Jake. He's as steady and solid an officer any SEAL could ask for. He never runs from a fight."

"Because he took care of his mother for eighteen years? He saw this as a similar trap, maybe?"

Turning on his side, he studied Shelby's shadowed green eyes. "They met again in Afghanistan two years ago. I was there. I saw it. They've always had this fatal attraction for each other since they were twenty. They're twenty-nine now. And out of bed they fight like cats and dogs. It was Christmas and they spent it together. I was happy for Jake. I know Morgan has always held his heart, but I don't think he'll ever admit it or realize it." Scowling, he said, "They had one hell of a fight the third morning when we were saddling up to leave. You could hear them screaming at each other clear across the village. Morgan can't be tamed. She's a strong, intelligent and resourceful woman like you. I just don't think Jake can handle it or her. Not that you 'handle' a woman."

"Morgan sounds like my kind of gal. They're out there, Dakota. I'm one of them. Is he blind?"

"He's got to be. Whatever is stuck in his craw about women being weak is his Achilles' heel.

Maybe that's why he's had no one in his life since that Christmas two years ago."

"What woman worth her salt would want to stay with a guy like that? There's got to be respect between the two or it's not going to work."

"You're smart as a whip. You know that?" Dakota threaded his fingers through her hair, watching the pleasure dance across her face.

"Don't give me too much credit. In law enforcement, you learn a lot of psychology on the job regarding people's actions, reactions and motives. You have to take them into consideration in order to work positively with them."

"You're still a very intelligent woman, Shel." He caressed her lower lip with his thumb. "I'm a lucky man."

"Tell me something," she said, catching his hand and kissing it. "Why was Jake looking at me like I was some kind of alien from another planet? I tried to be nice to him. Not screw up and embarrass you. Did I say or do something wrong to earn that kind of look from him?"

Chuckling, Dakota pulled her against him, her head coming to rest on his chest, her hair a gold coverlet across it. "Don't let him bother you, Shel. He's got problems with any woman in combat."

"What?"

"Yeah, he thinks no woman can handle combat of any kind. Doesn't matter whether it's a woman in the military or outside in a civilian agency, like being a law enforcement officer or firefighter, for example."

Shelby absorbed the slow thud of Dakota's heart beneath her ear. He loved her and she had never felt so happy. "That's such a crock of bull."

"You and I know it. He doesn't."

"So I'm like some kind of bug under his prejudicial microscope of life?" Jake had agreed to be his best man at their wedding in early September.

"That pretty much sums it up."

"You know what I wish for him?" Shelby eased up on her elbow to meet his glittering eyes that burned with desire for her. "I wish with all my heart he someday meets his match. Only it's a woman who sits his ass in place this time around."

As he caressed her reddening cheek, Dakota felt her anger. "Calm down, Shel. I'm a believer. Women handle combat of all types, all the time. It might not be a war overseas, but there are plenty of wars on the streets of towns and cities. Women in the military are in ground combat in the Middle East right now." He lightly touched her nose and added, "You're in combat as a law enforcement officer every day."

Some of her frustration dissolved as he traced her brow with his thumb and his fingers trailed tantalizingly across her jaw and neck. His touch was electric. Provocative. And it made her hungry for him. "Okay, white flag. I'm in bed with you, not him, thank God."

Grinning, Dakota chuckled and hauled her over on top of him, their legs tangling among one another. "You should feel sorry for him, not angry." He slid his hands across her mussed hair and slowly moved his fingers down across her shoulders, tracing the outline of her long torso to her flared hips.

"Do you think he'll be home in time from this op to be your best man at our wedding?"

"I don't know, Shel. He's been pulled in on a top secret assignment. And once he knows what it is, he can't tell me. We'll just have to wait and see if we hear from him. I'm sure he's going Down Range. Back into combat. Jake has my email address. He knows where I live and I know he'll stay in touch with me."

Lying against his hard body, feeling the muscles shift and tense as she suggestively moved her hips against his, Shelby shook her head in frustration. "I hope for your sake he can, Dakota. I know he's like a brother to you."

Dakota needed all the cosmic family he could get. No one went through life alone. Soon, though, this fall, he would be absorbed into her loving family. Her father respected Dakota, and they got along like father and son. Her mother doted on him. She'd been baking him his favorite chocolate chip cookies once a week. No, Dakota would easily become part of her family. He deserved that kind of good dharma. He deserved her.

Leaning down, she grazed the hard line of his mouth, feeling him begin to relax, to focus on them…on her. Shelby saw the unspoken worry in his eyes for Jake. They had two more days together and she knew that time with his friend meant the world to Dakota. She silently promised not to make an issue of Jake any longer. Time was too short and she wanted the man beneath her to enjoy it with Jake. He deserved to be happy.

"I love you, Shel," he growled, capturing her face, tilting her chin to just the right angle to kiss.

A soften whisper slipped from her lips as she allowed Dakota to guide her mouth down upon his. "You are my life, my love, forever…."

* * * * *

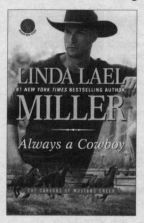

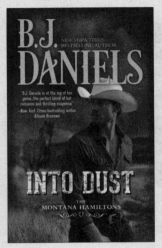

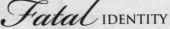

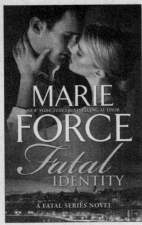